PROMISES MADE AT MIDNIGHT

The Knights of Berwyck, A Quest Through Time (Book Six)

SHERRY EWING

KINGSBURG PRESS

Kingsburg Pres
P.O. Box 475146
San Francisco, CA 94147
www.kingsburgpress.com

Promises Made At Midnight is a work of fiction. Names, characters, places, and incidents are a product of the author's imagination. Locales and public names are sometimes used for atmospheric purposes.

Editor: Jude Knight
Front Cover Design: SelfPubBookCovers.com / Shardel
Back Cover and Fonts: Sherry Ewing

Promises Made At Midnight / Sherry Ewing -- 1st ed.
ISBN eBook: 978-1-946177-50-6
ISBN ePub: 978-1-946177-63-6
ISBN Expanded Distribution Print: 978-1-946177-65-0
ISBN Amazon Print: 978-1-946177-64-3

Library of Congress Control Number: 2022902906

OTHER BOOKS BY SHERRY EWING

Medieval & Time Travel Series

To Love A Scottish Laird: De Wolfe Pack
Connected World

To Love An English Knight: De Wolfe Pack
Connected World

If My Heart Could See You: The MacLarens (Book One)

For All of Ever: The Knights of Berwyck,
A Quest Through Time (Book One)

Only For You: The Knights of Berwyck,
A Quest Through Time (Book Two)

Hearts Across Time: The Knights of Berwyck,
A Quest Through Time (Books One & Two)
A special box set of For All of Ever & Only For You

A Knight To Call My Own: The MacLarens (Book Two)

To Follow My Heart: The Knights of Berwyck,
A Quest Through Time (Book Three)

The Piper's Lady: The MacLarens (Book Three)

Love Will Find You: The Knights of Berwyck,
A Quest Through Time (Book Four)

One Last Kiss: The Knights of Berwyck,
A Quest Through Time (Book Five)

Promises Made At Midnight: The Knights of Berwyck,

A Quest Through Time (Book Six)

Regency

A Kiss for Charity: *A de Courtenay Novella (Book One)*

The Earl Takes A Wife: *A de Courtenay Novella (Book Two)*

Before I Found You: A de Courtenay Novella (Book Three)

Nothing But Time, A Family of Worth: Book One

One Moment In Time: *A Family of Worth, Book Two*

Under the Mistletoe

A Second Chance At Love

A Countess to Remember in *Desperate Daughters: A Bluestocking Belles with Friends Collection*

Learn more about Sherry's books on her website at www. SherryEwing.com/books

Join Sherry's newsletter at http://bit.ly/2vGrqQM

PROMISES MADE AT MIDNIGHT

CHAPTER 1

Berwyck Castle ~ Early Spring
The Year of Our Lord's Grace 1183

Sir Ulrick de Mohan, lately of Berwyck, swung his blade in a downward plunge whilst his adversary lifted his shield to protect himself. The sound of blades shearing against blades rang out in the lists. Grunts of pain resounded in the air from those who attempted to be worthy of becoming a guardsman of the Devil's Dragon. Many had already failed in their attempts for fame and glory—numerous knights were packing up their gear with curses of disappointment.

A raucous laugh escaped Ulrick. Here was another lad unable to hold his own against a noble adversary. Brown eyes glared furiously through the slits of his foe's helmet, and his shield swung in Ulrick's direction. Ulrick jumped back to miss being hit. Their blades made contact again and another laugh escaped him. Mayhap the lad held some promise after all!

Let us see what he is made of, Ulrick thought. His sword once more swung with a speed most would not be able to counter. Surprisingly, the lad did a passable job, until his blade was wrenched from his gauntlet. It sailed through the air end over end, narrowly missing the head of another nearby who fought just as aggressively.

Ulrick expected the young knight to yield the day, but apparently the boy had other plans. He tore off his helmet, flinging it into the dirt beneath his boots before swinging his fist in Ulrick's direction. *Foolish lad.*

"Come on, then, if you think you are man enough to knock me off my feet," Ulrick taunted with a smirk, causing a growl of outrage to erupt from the knight, who lunged forward. Ulrick easily side-stepped and watched in satisfaction when his opponent face planted onto the ground. "Your anger gets the best of you, boy," he warned with a chuckle. "'Twill be your downfall on the field of battle lest you make some attempt to control it."

The knight spat out a mouthful of soil, wiped his lips with the back of his sleeve, and slowly picked himself up off the field. "I am no boy," the youth sneered, showing a fair amount of bravado considering he had just been bested.

Ulrick adjusted his leather jerkin and then folded his arms over his chest. "You will have to do a better job of proving such to me, then. You will not proceed to the next test unless you do so. 'Twas a pitiful display you just gave and will not keep you here at Berwyck, if that is your aim," he mocked, widening his stance.

A squire came bearing the knight's sword, which he sheathed into the scabbard with a fair amount of force. "I am an ample match for you and all of Berwyck's garrison."

A chortle erupted from Ulrick's lips. "You have cheek, I will give you that, but you have much to learn and a long way to go before you will measure up to the Devil's Dragon and his high standards."

"I am more than ready now to take you all on, one by one," the knight said placing his hand on the hilt of his sword."

Ulrick held up his hand to halt any further protests from the youth. "I think not. What is your name and from whence do you hail?"

The knight gave a short bow before standing tall to proclaim his right to remain at Berwyck. "I am Godfrey Hawkins of Stonebrook. My sire—"

"I care not who your sire is, only that his son is worthy to continue training here," Ulrick said. He assessed the youth before him, who appeared as if he might hold promise. Although young in appearance, Godfrey showed evidence of a fair amount of time spent training. Dark brown hair cut close to his nape, solidly built, and just a touch of arrogance that would most likely get his foot past the barbican gate for a least another day. 'Twas that face, though, that made Ulrick wonder at the boy's age for 'twas far too young looking. "You appear as if you are no more than ten and five. Surely, you must be older."

Godfrey puffed himself up much like a rooster fluffing his feathers for the hens to take notice of him. "I will have you know, I am a score of years," he fumed.

Ulrick's brow lifted in amusement. "That old... I would not have thought it. Surely, you jest."

Godfrey pulled his sword forward once more. "Defend yourself and I will prove to you I do not make light of being insulted by you or any other!"

"Ulrick!" His name echoed above the noise on the lists.

He knew its owner and there was no need to turn to know

who spoke. "Aye, my Lord Dristan," Ulrick called over his shoulder, still pondering whether the knight before him would one day be capable enough to join the guardsmen in defending the castle and its inhabitants.

A heavy hand clamped down on his shoulder and Ulrick looked over to see the steel grey eyes of Dristan of Berwyck evaluating Godfrey with a critical shrewdness. A silence descended upon the lists at his commanding presence, and all turned to watch the scene unfolding before them.

"Has he earned his place to sup with us?" Dristan asked, as he also widened his stance to peer at Godfrey.

Ulrick had to give the boy credit, for he did not flinch even the slightest under the close scrutiny of Ulrick's liege lord. There were not many of his acquaintance who would not do so, given his lord's reputation. Godfrey's chin rose a notch as if in a silent challenge to continue the conversation that had been interrupted but moments before. At least he held his tongue and did not snap some insult that would see him flung from Berwyck posthaste.

"Aye, my Lord Dristan. He has earned the privilege," Ulrick at last answered, watching Godfrey let out his breath as if he had been holding it. It took everything in Ulrick's power not to laugh at the look of relief on Godfrey's face when he found he would stay yet another day.

"'Tis good news that we at least found one more person amongst this rabble who appears as if he may be up to the challenge we put before them," Dristan proclaimed, and peered down at Godfrey. "You will continue your training on the morrow with Sir Ulrick."

"My thanks, Lord Dristan," Godfrey answered with a bow of respect.

Dristan laughed. "Do not thank me as yet, as you do not know what is in store for you. Most do not make it past a se'n-night before they give up."

"I will not fail you," Godfrey said as though already pledging his fealty to the man before him.

Dristan smirked. "We shall see. In the meantime, get you to the Great Hall and eat your fill. The morn will be here before you know it."

Ulrick and Dristan stood side by side as they watched the young knight scamper off to fill his belly. Only two others joined him.

"Only three out of more than two dozen," Dristan declared. "'Tis not much of a showing but 'twill have to do. Godfrey did well?"

Ulrick nodded. "Fair enough and he does hold promise, although I would not declare such in front of him and add to the conceit already filling his head. He is full of himself and arrogant."

"A trait I myself and all of my personal guard have, so he may fit right in," Dristan concluded with a laugh. "Keep challenging him on the morrow just to the breaking point. We shall see how he does with the next test."

"Aye, my lord," Ulrick answered as they made their way to the keep. Entering the Great Hall, Ulrick called for mead to quench his thirst, already looking forward to a new challenge and what rewards he may face with the new day.

CHAPTER 2

Detroit, Michigan
Present Day

Bridgette Harris tossed her ball cap into the back seat, opened her car door, and thought about the lit restaurant they passed before heading into the parking garage. It was like a beacon calling to her. It was late but she didn't care. Her best friend, Megan, closed the passenger door and strode to her side.

"Lafayette or American?" Megan asked, hiding her yawn as they made their way from the structure.

Bridgette grabbed her arm, all but dragging her across the street. "I don't know why you ask me that every time. You know if you're going to have a Coney dog, it's got to be Lafayette. They're the best. Besides, we had American the last trip here because they're your favorite. It's my turn now."

"We just had a hot dog and beer at the ballpark. Why do you

want another, especially at this ungodly hour?" her friend asked.

With her hand on the door to the restaurant, Bridgette looked over her shoulder at her obviously tired friend but smiled brightly. "It's tradition."

Megan's sigh of resignation signaled their usual argument was over. Bridgette led the way into the already over-flowing restaurant filled with baseball fans who had the same idea as them. They passed several tables, where people raised their arms, cheering the new arrivals and clearly still ready to party and celebrate their team's win. Bridgette saw a couple who were leaving and quickly squeezed her way through the crowd to grab the table before it was taken by others who were cramming in the door behind her.

With a grin, and still feeling elated to have been able to enjoy the ballgame, she sat and raised her hand to grab the waiter's attention. He wasted no time taking their order, as if he wasn't busy waiting on other tables full to capacity. This place ran like a well-oiled machine even though some might consider it a dive. Sometimes those were the best places to eat.

She watched her friend, who slumped in her chair with exhaustion. Megan had been her best friend since they were very young and had attended Catholic school together. Considering how close they had been for most of their lives, Megan was Bridgette's opposite. Where her friend was blonde, Bridgette's hair was jet black. Megan's eyes were a soft brown, Bridgette's a vivid green. Her friend was an introvert at heart, whereas Bridgette was outgoing and thrived being in a crowd. She couldn't count the number of times Megan had complained that she always felt like she was on the outside looking in at all the cool kids, where she never fit in.

Bridgette's drink arrived and she took a sip of her pop as the liquid fizzled, tickling her nose. She looked over the rim of her glass at Megan who looked... well... wilted. "What's the matter?" she asked, although she knew where this was going, given how late it was.

Megan rolled her eyes, nodded her thanks as her hotdog was put before, and grabbed a napkin placing it on her lap. She picked up the dog and pointed it in Bridgette's direction. "You realize, of course, that we're going to have to get up at the butt crack of dawn just to make it in time before the fair starts, don't you?"

Swallowing the food in her mouth, she swore they must put crack in the chili since it tasted so incredible and was surely addicting. No wonder she kept coming back after every single ballgame she attended at the nearby park. "Might as well start tonight and sleep in the car. Costumes are already in the trunk, along with the rest of our gear," she murmured. Taking another bite, she continued trying to talk and chew at the same time. "Told... you... I'd... drive. You can sleep."

"I don't know where you get the energy. I know the tickets were freebies from work, but couldn't you have passed them up this one time so we could get a decent night's rest? You know how long we've planned for the fair," Megan complained bitterly.

"Are you kidding me? I wasn't going to give up seats behind home plate. Besides... we'll be fine once we get there. You know how it is. You complain about the drive and the fact you're out in nature. I cheer you up and remind you how much you end up enjoying stepping back in time," Bridgette replied with a grin.

A short laugh, followed by a snort, escaped Megan. "There *is* something exciting about being in a re-enactment guild and being treated like a lady at court," she said. "Do you think Brad will be there?"

Bridgette shrugged and tried not to cringe. "Who cares? It's a big enough event that it's hardly likely we'll run into each other."

"Right..." Megan replied snidely. "There isn't a doubt in my mind that he'll be drawn to you like a moth to a flame. Trust me... you'll see him, He's not going to waste anytime hunting you down."

"You make it sound like it's some kind of a conquest."

It was Megan's turn to shrug. "To him it is. I knew he'd be trouble the minute he introduced himself to us last year. You're always too polite. Allowing him to hang out with us all weekend was a mistake. There was just something about him that had me guessing he thought himself a gift to women. A man with looks like that is used to getting his way with the ladies."

"Are you never going to let me live that one down?" Bridgette huffed. "I got rid of him... eventually."

"It wasn't soon enough if you ask me... not that you did. He's apparently one of those men who doesn't take rejection well and clearly he's still in love with you."

"He doesn't know the meaning of being in love," Bridgette frowned. "All he wanted in the end was sex, and surely nothing romantic crossed his mind other than getting laid. If you recall, I was easily replaced with another before I could even blink."

Megan laughed. "Well, he wouldn't be the first man we became acquainted with who only had one thing on his mind."

Bridgette momentarily got lost in the memory of a gorgeous man who had dressed as a knight. His mannerisms while at the fair last year had been exemplary. It would make any woman sigh, which would explain why several women had been following him the entire weekend. But he had given her his undivided attention, when he had not been competing in the sword play. Brad had been tall and muscular, with light brown hair you just wanted to run your fingers through, green twinkling eyes that drew you in, and a personality she had thought at the time matched her own. "You have to admit he made one handsome knight. What a shame he wasn't the same person once the costume came off."

"You mean too bad he didn't have a chivalrous bone in his body," Megan commented, as she drew out a few bills from her wallet to pay for their late meal.

"That, too."

"Really, Bridgette, he turned out to be such a creep. Stay away from him and his kind, will you? You can do so much better than the likes of him."

They began making their way back to the car, careful of their surroundings, especially since this wasn't the best part of town. She clicked the key and the horn sounded while the car unlocked and the headlamps went on to light their way. "Well, he's got to be out there somewhere, doesn't he?" Bridgette asked with a hint of longing in her voice.

Megan got in the car and a frown marred her brow before the interior lights went off, casting them into shadows. "Who? Not Brad, I hope?" she mumbled.

"No, not Brad, but my soul mate. That one guy who will turn my world upside down. I'm pretty damn sure wherever he is, that we're hiding in the same place," Bridgette answered, starting the car and putting it into drive.

"You're looking too hard, sis. He'll show up when you least expect him, and hopefully he'll have a friend for me."

"I suppose you're right," Bridgette said, with a short laugh.

"I still don't know why Zoe didn't want to wait and drive up north with us," Megan replied, before quickly fastening her seat belt.

Bridgette thought of the other friend she had known for years. Zoe was, in many ways, an odd sort, not that Bridgette ever held that against her. She still remembered last Christmas when she and Megan went to Zoe's apartment and they were introduced to another woman named Jade.

"You know Zoe... she wanted to be sure her booth was all set up. She's never one to miss an opportunity to tell someone their future," Bridgette answered as she pulled out of the garage.

Megan pulled a pillow from the back seat and got comfortable. "I suppose... whatever happened to that gal Jade? Considering how much Zoe wanted the two of you to meet, I would have thought the two of you would be BFFs until the end of time."

"No clue. I'm sure we'll meet again someday."

Megan made herself comfortable. "And by the way... first dibs on the purple court gown. I call it fair play for you dragging me to the game instead of sleeping in a comfy bed tonight. You can be the serving wench for the first day."

Bridgette huffed. "Fine... whatever."

"It's Karma getting back at you, dear," Megan replied with a smirk, and leaned her head back onto the seat. "Be sure to wake me if you want me to take over driving, otherwise let me know when we get there."

"Night, Megan," Bridgette replied as she lowered the music on the radio.

Pulling onto the highway, she headed north, knowing the weekend ahead would be so much fun. *Who knows what the days ahead would bring?* she thought. Maybe, just maybe, Karma would do her a favor for a change and send her the knight she had always wanted to call her very own. There was still a small amount of hope deep within her heart that somewhere he existed. She just needed to find him.

CHAPTER 3

L ightning lit the interior of the Great Hall from the windows set high above in the stone walls of the keep. 'Twas not unusual for the rain to fall in huge sheets of water that pelted the earth, leaving puddles that quickly turned to something resembling a fast-running stream.

The only thing out of place was the bit of grumbling from the three new knights, who had been told that they would train come rain or shine. Mayhap the rain would wash away their sour disposition. If not, Ulrick would take great pleasure in booting them from Berwyck with a swift kick to their sorry arses. Their unmanly behavior would not be tolerated by Dristan, nor the guards who had been by his side for more years that most could remember.

Ulrick's vigilant gaze swept the chamber whilst he shook his head, wondering where the past eight years had gone. Had it really been that long since he took part in the siege of Berwyck Castle here in northern England? Looking about the room, 'twas not hard to notice the absence of some of the original people who had resided within the keep's walls.

One, in particular, hovered near to the lady of the keep in a ghostly display that only a few would be able to see. The image of Sir Rolf glistened in the light of the torches whilst his hand hovered near the lady's shoulder. She must have felt his presence since she smiled over her shoulder. Rolf looked up, feeling Ulrick's stare, nodded his head and disappeared.

Several had wed, including his liege who married the eldest daughter of Berwyck, Amiria. They had sired two children with another on the way. Amiria's youngest sister Lynet and her husband Ian now made their home in the northern realms of Scotland. Amiria's twin Aiden had left the estate to make a name for himself whilst traveling abroad for King Henry II. Even now, his sister fretted over his whereabouts. One of Amiria's guardsmen, Thomas, had but recently wed and left with Lady Jade, a woman who had mysteriously showed up at Berwyck's gates one day over the winter.

Even his comrades in arms, Riorden and Fletcher, were now enjoying wedded bliss, their brides also finding their way to Berwyck by mysterious methods. But the loss of Dristan's closest guardsmen had pushed his desire to replenish his dwindling knights to guard his back. There was another brother and sister of the MacLaren clan. Patrick, who was now ten and seven, continued his service as Riorden's squire. Sabina, aged a score and six, had moved to Habersham Abbey after the siege of Berwyck, but had yet to take her vows as a nun.

At times, he envied those who had found someone to love and share their lives. He knew that, if he were to one day lay claim to his birthright, he would be wise to wed a lady with lands of her own along with monies to fill his coffers. The women who attended the Lady Amiria held no appeal to him in any romantic fashion and left his options in that direction to nothing. They flirted with any of Dristan's guardsmen, hoping to catch a husband, and Ulrick wanted more from a potential wife than one whose gaze often drifted.

More! Aye, he wanted more than just some mild infatuation with a pretty face that might fade with time. He wanted to find deep and abiding love with a good woman whom he could love for the rest of his lifetime. Dristan, Riorden, and Fletcher had found such a miracle, although there were rumors about the odd way in which Riorden and Fletcher had come upon their fair ladies. But that was of no matter and 'twas only of import that they had found what he himself wanted. He would not besmirch the name of Lady Katherine, her lady friends, nor Lady Jenna by spreading possible falsehoods of time travel. Aye, he had seen such wonders presented before his very eyes, but he refused to imagine that they were true. Who would believe such a thing anyway? 'Twas unimaginable.

He was nudged and turned his attention to Bertram, who now claimed the title of Captain of the Guard. There was no living near the man now he boasted such a high position of importance.

"What?" Ulrick muttered, pondering what part of a possible conversation he had missed.

Bertram pushed a bowl of porridge in his direction. "You were far away. You should eat, lest it grows cold and your belly goes empty until the noon meal."

"I am not hungry."

"Why not? We have a full day of training and it looks like 'twill be a wet one."

"Why does it matter if I wish to eat or not?" Ulrick grumbled. 'Twas clear his recent musing left a sour taste in his mouth along with a bitter disposition.

Bertram shrugged. "It makes no difference to me, only that you are prepared for the day. That includes eating a hearty meal. Dristan wishes to take us both on first thing to show the new men what will one day be expected of them."

"I will perform my duty as I always do, Bertram. Leave me be lest I take out my foul mood into the lists. Though 'twill surely end once I best you," Ulrick snidely retorted.

"I would expect no less, nor would our liege lord."

Any further conversations were interrupted as the door of the keep blew open and Taegan, one of the guardsmen who had been visiting Fletcher's estate, swept through the portal, shaking off the rain from his cloak. His brother Turquine called out to him and moved over on the bench to make room for him at the table. He came and sat across from Ulrick with a look of longing at the untouched bowl.

"Are you not going to eat that?" Taegan asked eagerly.

Ulrick pushed the full bowl across the table. "Help yourself."

Taegan accepted it with a nod. "My thanks. I am most famished. I could eat my horse, I am so hungry."

Turquine pounded his brother's back. A lesser man may have felt the force of the blow but not Taegan. The two brothers were used to a bit of rough play between them. "I am sure your horse is appreciative of the fact that he still is in the land of the living," Turquine guffawed.

"What brings you back to Berwyck so soon? We did not expect you for at least another fortnight," Ulrick asked.

Taegan finished the porridge and wiped his mouth with his sleeve. Was it Ulrick's imagination or did the man before him look... disturbed? There was not much in life that could faze one of Dristan's guards enough to cause them to actually show emotion so visibly on their faces.

"I had a spat. Felt I should remove myself from Lancashire for a while," Taegan replied, before reaching toward the middle of the table and stuffing his mouth with a piece of cheese.

"With Fletcher?" Bertram inquired.

"Nay... with his... guest," Taegan said looking very uncomfortable. The men at the table all looked to him to continue and Taegan's gaze swept those nearby before leaning in to mute the conversation to those whom he could trust. "Her name is Amy and she is a friend of the Lady Jenna, Fletcher's wife. You may not believe it, but she is from that place that Riorden's wife, Lady Katherine, has also come from... Sanfran... Cisco... and the future."

"Not another one?" groaned Bertram.

"Aye, I am afraid so," Taegan declared, looking ill at ease.

Drake, another personal guard pondered his response. "She was here briefly when Fletcher married, was she not? I believe that is the lady that Dristan kept in Lady Amiria's solar for most of her visit."

"Aye, she was. She is a feisty one, that Amy is, and a more headstrong woman I have never met."

Ulrick was unsure how to respond to yet another woman traveling by some unnatural means to arrive back in time. "We seem to be besieged with women who do not belong here amongst us. Will she... go back... to her own place in time, do you suppose?"

Taegan shrugged. "Who knows?"

"What did you fight about that caused you to return then? She is just a woman and there are plenty to choose from on good

English soil," Bertram asked, looking just as uncomfortable at the nature of the conversation.

Taegan's brows drew together in a frown. "One minute she is kissing me, and the next she is telling me that she wants to wed. Since I am not the marrying kind, I left out of favor, naturally, with the lady."

Turquine began laughing and almost fell backwards off the bench. "Another lass you will soon forget as you move on to the next."

Taegan turned to look over at his brother and his face said everything that he would not dare say aloud. "I am not so sure, brother," he answered seriously.

The mood at their table was a somber one, whilst each knight pondered the mysteries of life and the women who evaded them.

Any further thoughts on the conversation were left unsaid as Dristan rose from his place at the raised dais, calling to his knights. Everyone began to rush to join him in the lists. Perchance 'twas best Ulrick's thoughts turned to the more pressing matter at hand, and that was to continue Godfrey's training. *Time travel,* he mused, *was just a bunch of nonsense. Or was it?*

CHAPTER 4

Bridgette strolled across the grass holding a pitcher of ice water. It was one of those hot, humid Michigan summer days that one never gets used to, especially wearing a lot of heavy costuming. Her long serviceable brown dress was nothing compared to what the men wore. She couldn't imagine how she'd feel roasting from the heat in armor, chainmail, or heavy leather while performing for the crowd. There was no sense in complaining about the heat. She didn't have to do this and could just be one of the tourists in shorts and tank tops instead, but what fun would that be?

She really did love every aspect of this weekend with the exception of one. Brad... Megan had been right when she said he would seek her out. Everywhere she turned, he showed up. Didn't he have better things to do than follow her every move? There were plenty of other women just vying for his attention. But time and time again, she would look up, from whichever cup she was filling, to find him staring at her. It was becoming a bit unnerving and annoying… the damn stalker!

Eager hands reached for the pewter cups attached to their belts and thrust them in her direction. She filled them with a welcoming smile, knowing she was able to offer them a brief bit of relief from the heat.

"My thanks," one gentleman said with a nod of gratitude.

"You are most welcome, milord," Bridgette responded, staying in character and giving a brief curtsey.

As she made her way back to the tent of the St. Christopher's guild, she saw Megan picnicking on a blanket under the shade of a tall oak tree. It was one of those picture-perfect moments of several ladies taking their ease that would have been seen in days of old during the renaissance era. Megan gave her a small smile and one of those annoying smug looks. *No worries*, she thought, *tomorrow it's my turn and Megan can be the servant!*

Setting the pitcher on a nearby table and seeing that everyone was relaxing, Bridgette decided now was as good a time as any to take a much-needed bathroom break. Leaving the tent, she rounded the corner and found herself captured in a tight embrace. The man's armor dug into her sides while she squirmed to free herself.

"Get your hands off me, Brad," Bridgette warned, giving his chest a push. She didn't even have to look up into his face to know who held her. She was at a disadvantage, although there were enough people nearby who would come to her aid if she called out for help.

He let her go, reluctantly, but still kept a hold of her elbow. "Hello, my lady," Brad said in that seductive tone that, at one point in their brief relationship, would have sent her heart flipping end over end. Luckily, the spell he had momentarily wrapped around her heart had long since disappeared.

"If you would care to look at my dress, you would know that I am a mere servant today," she retorted hotly.

"No matter. You are here with me now," he leaned forward to whisper for her hearing alone, "and I don't give a rat's ass how you're dressed for now, only that you get undressed."

"You disgust me," she huffed, yanking her arm and stepping back from him.

He smoothed a lock his hair away from his brow. He smiled, before performing a courtly bow when a woman passing by whistled at him and he followed her with his eyes. His gaze appeared hungry, as though he was stripping the woman's clothing from her body but, when she left his view, he turned his attention to Bridgette. Rocking on his heels, he gave her a smug look that told her he was satisfied that at least someone appreciated his good looks. "You didn't always think so," he finally replied, to carry on their conversation as if he hadn't just ogled another woman right in front of her.

"Lucky for me, I realized fairly quickly that, beneath the armor, there's nothing chivalrous about you, let alone anything else that would convince me to continue having a relationship with you," she answered smugly.

"Always the romantic, aren't you, Bridgette," he replied, looking her up and down once more. "Besides... we don't have to be in a relationship for what I have in mind. There's nothing wrong with the two of us being friends with benefits."

Bridgette threw up her hands. "And *that's* exactly why I don't want anything to do with you, Brad. You really don't know me at all if you think I'd agree to something like that. I want a gentleman who will be faithful and love me for the rest of his life, not some meaningless fling. Go find someone else who will fall into your charms. I'm done with you. Now leave me alone."

She left him there sputtering and cursing her name. She could care less, considering she had a more pressing need to fulfill. She began heading in the direction of the bathrooms when an elderly lady fell into step with her. White hair, wrinkles around her sparkling blue eyes, and a kindly face reminded her of her own dear grandmother, who had passed away many years ago.

"Good day tae ye, my dear," the woman whispered.

Her voice, when she spoke, had a far-off kind of melody to it. The strange sing-song quality was surprising to Bridgette, since the woman was standing right next to her. Even the tone was more Scottish than medieval English. "And the same to you, milady," Bridgette answered politely.

The woman came to stand next to Bridgette when she took her place in line. She was further startled when the woman placed her hand on Bridgette's forearm.

"Ye have been verra busy this morn," she said and there was no mistaking her Scottish accent.

Bridgette leaned over. "This is the renaissance fair, madam. The Highland games are in another two weeks," she said, whispering in the woman's ear to politely correct the woman's dialect.

The lady gave a cheerful laugh. "Oh, aye, I am well aware of the times in which we are, dearie. Dinnae fash yerself, Bridgette.

Bridgette wracked her brain, trying to remember where she had met the woman next to her, but for the life of her she hadn't a clue. "Have we met before? I'm afraid I don't remember your name."

The woman's brow rose. "Ye be breaking character, dear girl."

Damn, she thought, *I broke the cardinal rule of the part I play. Never, ever, break character even if you're standing in line for the john.* She was about to apologize when the woman starting patting her arm as if she understood.

"'Tis alright. Do ye not kin why ye are here?" she asked, with a bright smile.

Bridgette looked at the line in front of her. Her reason for standing in her current location was the same as every other woman in front and behind her. Nature called and she refused to use the men's room where there wasn't a line with no one waiting to enter. She had gone twenty-five years without resorting to such drastic measures. She wasn't about to lower her standards just so she could take care of her personal business.

Realizing the woman was still waiting for her answer, she leaned forward again. "Of course, I know why I'm here. It's the same reason we're all standing here," she replied kindly.

"Oh, I do not think so, my dear. I am here fer a particular purpose but 'tis not for the motive ye may think. Needless tae say, ye, too, shall know that everything has its time and place. Yer wishes have been heard, dearest Bridgette," she said, convincingly. The woman's answer again sounded as if it was carried on the wind.

"What wish?" Bridgette asked, moving forward in line. She turned to wait for the woman's reply, but she had disappeared. Bridgette twirled around in a circle trying to find out where the lady had gone but she was nowhere to be seen. How odd was that? She looked behind her again, only to see another woman point to her that the line was moving forward.

With no further thoughts on the grandmotherly woman, Bridgette entered the restroom, took care of her business and exited into the bright sunlight. She frowned. Good God...he even followed her to the friggin' bathroom! She scowled, causing Brad's smile to widen. It was going to be a long ass day!

CHAPTER 5

U lrick gazed out to the distant horizon whilst the sun rose, painting a stunning display of bright red and orange pigments across the sky. It was a peaceful time of the morn and he took solace in the time to himself here on the parapet of the battlement wall. His brief respite was short lived when he felt a presence behind him.

He should have known she would eventually join him here, since 'twas her ritual to greet the sun each day and also to watch it set. She came to stand beside him and he noticed she was in a lovely gown instead of her normal garb of boots, tunic and hose.

"No training this day, my lady?" he inquired.

"Nay," she whispered. "I am a mite weary this morn." Her answer was somber as she came to rest her hands on the battlement wall to look over its edge down into the inner bailey. The fear of heights had never been an issue with the fair lady.

"Surely not?" he replied, but could see for himself the dark circles underneath her violet eyes.

She gave him a small smile. "I am afraid so. I fear 'tis the babe who is not agreeing with me."

Amiria began to pat her stomach as if 'twas a common habit to discuss such a delicate matter in front of a man who was not her husband. Ulrick became uncomfortable and began to squirm, for he knew of only one other woman who also acted so boldly.

"You sound much like the Lady Katherine," he said, trying to find his composure.

"I miss her friendship," Amiria confided and she must have noticed how he attempted to change the subject of her pregnancy. "I am sorry, Sir Ulrick. I know most men would prefer women in our condition to be hidden away until our children are born."

Ulrick shrugged. "I suppose I must needs get used to such talk with all these future women landing on your doorstep, although I still am not sure I believe such rot."

A twinkle lit in Lady Amiria's eyes. "And yet you yourself have been to Riorden and Katherine's home. Beyond that, we have Sir Rolf who occasionally lets his presence be known. Surely, if you can believe in a ghost, you can believe that all things of this nature are possible?"

"I miss his friendship," Ulrick repeated his lady's words but moments ago.

"Aye, I understand completely but he is still near and if you have need of him, I am most certain he will hear your call. All you have to do is speak his name with a sincere heart and he will appear before you." She said this so convincingly that Ulrick had no doubt she spoke the truth.

They stood in silence again before Ulrick notice her swaying stance. "My lady, are you ill?"

"Mayhap just a little. May I ask you to escort me down to my bedchamber?"

"But of course, my lady," he declared holding out his arm.

"My thanks, Sir Ulrick." She took hold of his arm and they began slowly making their way from the parapet and down the turret stairs. "I am most likely just weary from trying to keep up with Royce and his antics. Garrick, our piper, helps keep him from too much mischief but my son is almost more than we can handle."

"You could always leave his raising to others," Ulrick suggested. "'Twould allow you more time to see to your own needs."

"Aye, I know, but after Katherine told me how much she would enjoy and cherish every moment of her child's development, I wanted to do the same, even though this is hardly normal for our times."

"I am not sure how all these changes will be good for us. But who am I to gainsay you? I only worry that you are unwell."

"'Tis worth it when I see my children's smiles. My son is much like I was at his age, never stopping to catch his breath before he is on to his next escapade. I am hoping Jocelyn might have a quieter disposition, much like Lynet. With the trouble this one is giving me so early on in my pregnancy, I can only assume this child will have a disposition much like my dragon."

Ulrick ignored her reference to her current condition. "Even the Lady Lynet became more and more like you, my lady, as she grew to womanhood."

"We are a stubborn lot, we MacLarens, which my brother would attest to if he would but return home where he belongs," Amiria said sternly, with a frown.

"I am sure he is just attempting to make a name for himself

and prove to the king he would be worthy of any lands he may be granted," Ulrick answered, reaching for the handle of her door. "Do you wish me to get Lord Dristan?"

"Nay, 'twill not be necessary. I will just rest a while and, if needed, I will send one of my ladies to fetch him posthaste," she declared. "I had so wanted to go the festival in the village but mayhap I will feel up to the excursion after a short nap. Do you plan to attend?"

"Aye, I am sure most of the garrison will attend to prove their worth in the games," Ulrick replied.

"Then I wish you the best of luck, Sir Ulrick, and do not forget our conversation about Sir Rolf," she replied.

Before he could answer, she reached forward, cupping his cheek, and then closed the door without another word. Women with child were indeed strange. Shaking his head, he decided he might as well head down to the Great Hall to see if he could as yet break his fast.

Making his way down the torch-lit passageway, he looked ahead, and a vague wispy bit of smoke took the transparent shape of Sir Rolf. He gave a brief bow that Ulrick returned but, before he could speak the thoughts rushing to his head, Rolf disappeared as if he had not been there at all. Ulrick turned to look behind him to see if his friend had appeared behind him, but he was once more alone in the corridor.

Harrumph! *You would think he could at least stick around for a bit of conversation,* Ulrick mused, as he began descending the turret stairs.

I miss your kinship as well, my friend.

Startled, Ulrick almost missed a step as Rolf's voice came inside his head. "Stop that, Rolf, and show yourself," he demanded, only to hear his friend's laugher once again in his head. "Damn ornery ghost..."

I heard that...

Ulrick shook his fist in the air as if that would prove something, but he knew not what. Seeing that food had not arrived on the tables, since few had risen to break their fast, he noticed Godfrey near the hearth. He made his way to the youth, grabbed him by the scruff of his tunic and began pushing him toward the kitchens.

"Come with me," Ulrick urged, grabbing some bread and cheese and encouraging Godfrey to do the same. "There is time enough to get in some training before the faire begins this day."

"But I do not have my chainmail on as yet," Godfrey complained bitterly.

Ulrick glared at the young man, who snapped his lips shut. "You may not always have the luxury of fighting in full gear, Godfrey. We train light this day."

Opening the door to the brightness of sunlight, they made their way to the lists. With his sword in hand, Ulrick swung the blade in front of him as his confidence returned. He would enjoy his training and wonder what the day would bring later.

CHAPTER 6

The crowd of spectators opened a path for the procession of richly garbed men and women. "My lady," a knight declared when Bridgette passed him by.

She caught his stare and he gave her a bow that was polished to the point of perfection. With the briefest of nods to acknowledge him, Bridgette smiled, continuing her stroll as one of the "Queen's" ladies in waiting. *This was so much better*, she thought. She would have to tell Megan that they needed to purchase another gown so from now on they could both be dressed as she was today.

The purple gown was in her favorite color, with long flowing sleeves and a black under tunic that poked through the various slits to puff up the upper shoulders of the gown. The corset and stays she could do without, but she had to admit she would never have a waist this size without them or fit into the dress. They may inhibit her ability to take a deep full breath or eat a huge meal but it was worth the sacrifice to feel this... well... beautiful.

The heat she could also do without, or at least the humidity. It was still early morning. Already the temperature was rising to the point that it was going to be one of those scorching summer days where Bridgette would normally find herself shopping in an air conditioned mall. *No sense complaining*, she thought, and once more returned her attention to playing her part at the fair.

She opened the pretty lace parasol that had been a recent purchase to shield her eyes from the glaring sun. Perspiration formed on her upper lip and it took everything within her not to wipe the moisture away while she had the eyes of the crowd upon her. Seeing the Queen's tent up ahead, Bridgette followed along, already wishing for a glass of ice water to cool herself down.

They continued forward and she saw Zoe's booth, where a line had formed as the tourists waited their turn to find out what their future held. Bridgette gave a slight nod toward her friend and Zoe gave her a bright smile. She waved... which was odd, considering she had a paying customer in front of her. But Zoe recovered quickly, shuffled her tarot cards and continued on as though she hadn't just broken her cardinal rule of giving her undivided attention to the person in front of her.

Bridgette took a linen from her sleeve and dabbed at her lip, the heat finally getting the best of her. *What's the matter with me?* she wondered, hoping she wasn't catching a cold or something else she might have picked up from all the tourists who attended these events. Normally, the heat never affected her like it seemed to be doing today. Maybe the strings of the corset had been tied too tightly. She was certainly finding it difficult to breath. Whatever the reason, Bridgette needed to either loosen them or drink lots of water before she did the unthinkable and faint.

The Queen seated herself under the awning of her tent and, before Bridgette could get to one of the lower stools or chairs, they quickly filled up, leaving her no other choice but to stand to the side. Megan came, bearing the same ewer of water that she herself had carried yesterday and began filling the pretty jeweled cups that were thrust in her direction. Their eyes met and Megan's brow rose in a silent question, asking if she was okay. Bridgette swayed.

Megan came to her and pulled her behind a sheet that would allow for some privacy for the women who may need to attend to their costuming.

"What's the matter?" Megan asked, concern etched on her face.

"I don't know," Bridgette answered. "Can you check the ties of the corset and dress to see if they're too tight? I can't seem to catch my breath." Megan went behind her and loosened the strings, but Bridgette didn't feel any form of relief.

"They're not that tight. Do you want to take it off and just wear a chemise?" Megan inquired, holding out a cup of water to her friend.

Bridgette took small sips of the cool liquid. "I'll never get the dress on if I'm not wearing them...you know that," she snapped.

"No reason to get angry with me. It's not my fault you're not feeling well."

"Sorry..." Bridgette murmured.

"Do you want to change costumes with me or go back to the hotel?"

PROMISES MADE AT MIDNIGHT

Bridgette shook her head. "No, I'm sure I'll be fine and I'd hate to miss something we've been waiting all year for."

"There'll be other festivals, if you're not feeling well," Megan replied obviously still concerned.

"I'll be okay. I'll take a break from it all for a few minutes to collect myself and return in a few. Will you let everyone know that I'll be back in a bit?" Bridgette asked, once again wiping the sweat from her brow.

"Sure. No problem, but take some more water with you. You really don't look well," Megan replied. She poured more water into Bridgette's cup.

"Thanks. I'll see you later."

With her goblet filled with icy water and parasol in hand, she began making her way across the lawn to find a place that wasn't overrun with event goers. Continuing past the living history portion of the fair, she walked toward the back entrance to see a tall maple tree near the fence line. A fountain stood in the center of the empty area and a white iron bench with bushes behind it welcomed her to sit beneath the shade of the towering tree.

She made her way to the bench and sighed in pleasure that she had the place to herself. That seem unusual, given the number of attendees at the fair. Setting down her parasol, she took a sip of water and gazed at the fountain. Someone had really gone all out with this project, and she was a little surprised to see that she was the only one enjoying what was before her. After all, this setting was so completely... perfect.

The fountain itself was round and nothing out of the ordinary, but it was the centerpiece that captured her attention as water bubbled up from its base with a relaxing quality to calm her frayed nerves. Even though he was etched in granite, the knight holding his sword in one hand and a shield with a cross in the other appeared so lifelike it was alarming. He was looking down as he knelt on one knee, and was incredibly handsome, like no other man she had ever seen before in her entire life.

In many ways, he reminded her of a Roman soldier of old, from the arrogant jut of his classic nose to his sinful lips, just begging to be kissed. His hair flowed almost to his shoulders as if the artist had captured its length to perfection as the wind caught its length. Broad shoulders were covered by a cape that also appeared as if it billowed in the unseen breeze. Instead of chainmail, he appeared covered in a leather jerkin vest with a shorter sleeved shirt. His arms bulged with muscle and his hands... Good heavens... what would it feel like to have those long-sculpted fingers caressing her skin? She was almost envious of the hilt of his sword, grasped by his hand.

He appeared as a true and chivalrous knight if she ever saw one or could conjure one up from her imagination. Wasn't it just her luck she'd find the man of her dreams not as a living breathing specimen but one only carved from stone? He really was drop down gorgeous and she would have just loved to see him in full color. Still, the artist had obviously spent an incredible amount of time to create such a vivid display of male sexuality. She wondered who the model had been and what had been the color of the man's eyes.

"Blue," a faraway voice whispered in the afternoon breeze. The sound caressed her body, wrapping itself around Bridgette like a comfortable blanket. She shivered but it had nothing to do with being cold.

Bridgette turned her head to the right, since she swore that was the direction the words had come from but there was no one there. A hand came to rest on her left arm and she about jumped right out of her skin. Startled, she turned to see the lady from yesterday sitting next to her. Where the hell had she come from?

"Hello again, Bridgette," she said kindly, with a welcoming smile.

"Hi," she replied, wondering how she couldn't see someone coming to sit down next to her.

"Ye were far away, my dear," the woman remarked knowingly, as if she had heard Bridgette's unspoken question. Once again, the woman patted her hand in understanding, much as she did yesterday.

"I guess I was. I didn't even see you come to sit next to me."

"'Tis all right," the lady replied, and turned to gaze up at what had held Bridgette's attention. "His eyes were blue."

"Don't you mean *are* blue?" Bridgette questioned.

"*Were* or *are*, 'tis all the same as far as *Time* is concerned."

Not understanding what the woman meant, Bridgette was too polite to question her further and continued to stare at the handsome figure in front of her. She pointed to the statue. "Where in the world do you think they got such a perfect guy in this day and age to model for this? He's just the ideal personification of what a gorgeous knight should look like."

The woman next to her gave a soft laugh. "Oh, he is not from around these parts, dearie."

"That figures," Bridgette grumbled, but she continued voicing her inner thoughts with a dream-like sigh. "I sure would love for our paths to cross."

"Would ye now?"

"Of course. Just look at him. The man is the embodiment of every romantic notion I've ever had inside my head. Too bad he's not a local. He looks like a guy you could fall in love with."

"Hmm...aye, I suppose he was at that, as long as 'twas with the right woman," the lady replied, "and in the right place in time."

"Do you know him? Maybe you could give him my card," Bridgette said discreetly. Reaching inside her sleeve, she pulled out a business card and tried to hand it to the lady. "I know I'm not supposed to carry these, but I sure would like to meet this guy."

The woman gazed at her from the corner of her eye. Since she didn't reach for the card, Bridgette assumed she had offended the woman. She put the card back, feeling like an idiot for asking such a thing of a complete stranger in the first place.

"Funny thing about *Time*," the woman continued, ignoring Bridgette's lapse of etiquette. "'Tis never predictable and never answers yer wishes when ye want it tae, until ye at last find what ye be looking fer."

Bridgette pointed to the statue in front of her. "Do you mean him?"

"Aye."

Bridgette politely laughed. "Believe me, madam, I've been wishing for someone like him to drop into my life... well... for *all* my life."

"Maybe ye haven't been wishing hard enough."

"I don't know how I could wish any harder. A man like that," Bridgette said, pointing again at the statue, "is the stuff dreams are made of. I've never had the pleasure, I'm sorry to say, or ever even come close to finding true love with someone of his kind. I don't think men of his integrity exist in today's world and chivalry is long since dead, unless you're like me, trying to find it at events like this one."

The woman gazed at her as if mulling over her answer. She

nodded her head as if she had answered her own question... whatever that would be.

"Let us put ye tae the test, shall we, my dear? If ye are truly worthy, yer wishes can and will come true."

Bridgette wasn't sure what the woman had in mind but she figured, what the hell did she have to lose? Her attention continued to focus on the old woman's hands as they went to a pouch that hung from the belt of her dress.

She fumbled inside, her brows drawn together in a frown. "Now where has it gone? It has tae be the right one," she muttered more to herself than for Bridgette's ears. Her smile finally widened. "Ha! Here we are..."

Bridgette squinted as the sun hit the gold object the woman held out for her to take. She obviously meant for Bridgette to toss it into the fountain to make a wish, as she had done as a child on numerous occasions. "Oh, I can't take money from someone I don't know. Besides, I could just run back and get my purse to get a penny to toss."

The woman shook her head, objecting to such a thought. She opened Bridgette's hand to put the gold coin in her palm before closing her fingers around it. "No need, Bridgette. This coin is special and has been with my family fer generations. 'Twill bring ye luck. Now make a wish."

"All the more reason for me not to accept it," Bridgette replied trying to return the coin to the woman. She peered down at it and almost gasped at what she was holding in the palm of her hand. For God's sake, it looked medieval in origin.

"I will not hear of it. Please, take it and make a wish before 'tis too late," the woman advised, nodding toward the fountain.

"Before what's too late?"

"*Time*...she is fickle, so ye best make the most of what ye have been given."

"I haven't a clue what you're talking about."

"Ye will find out once ye make yer wish. Make it a good one and say it out loud. Spoken has a better impact, no matter that people tell ye that ye should keep yer wish unto yerself," the woman urged again.

Bridgette laughed again, hoping she didn't offend the kind lady. "This is crazy," she said and turned to try once more to return the coin but the woman was gone as though she had disappeared into thin air. What the hell? She turned the coin over and over again in her hand before rubbing her thumb across the smooth metal.

Hurry, Bridgette! Time will not wait much longer fer ye tae decide yer fate.

Bridgette almost dropped the coin when the woman's voice came inside her head. Deciding to get rid of the coin as fast as she could and return to the fair, Bridgette took one last look at the coin before arching back her arm.

"I wish to find a truly chivalrous and honorable man just like the knight before me," she said aloud.

Swinging her arm forward, she tossed the golden coin and watched it flip end over end as it sparkled like starlight through the air. Waiting for the sound of the money to hit the water, she became dismayed when, instead, it ricocheted off the knight statue in front of her. She quickly stood to catch the errant coin, afraid she'd lose such a costly gift from the old woman if it happened to land in the bushes behind her.

She jumped up, for it sailed through the air higher than anticipated. It landed in her hand and she grinned, feeling triumphant. But as her feet hit the ground, that elation abruptly halted. A trail of stars began circling her body, moving upward and disappearing over her head. In awe, Bridgette wondered what was happening to her and then she had her answer. Nothing could have prepared her for the unknown force that slammed into her, knocking her to the ground. Her eyes blurred and she swore she saw the statue of the knight come to life to gaze down upon her.

Yer wish be granted, my dearest Bridgette. She heard that same faerie-like voice inside her head an instant before her eyes began to roll back into her head, darkness descended, and she knew no more.

CHAPTER 7

Ulrick watched Godfrey land flat on his arse… again. Bare chested with his body slick from oil, his anger once more got the better of him. He rose and charged like a raging bull at his opponent who reached out his arm and caught the angry young knight unawares. The lad somersaulted in the air, landing this time on his stomach. Raucous laughter rang out through the circle of men and women who had watched the wrestling match. Godfrey smothered an animal-like growl when Drake's foot held the youth down in the middle of his back.

"Yield," Drake demanded pushing harder to get across his point that he would be the victor of this set.

"Nay," Godfrey muttered, trying to rise, and failing despite his best efforts.

"I said yield, lest you wish to be further humiliated and allow the crowd to make you a laughing stock of the entire faire."

Godfrey's fists hit the ground. "Aye!" he bellowed. "I yield."

Drake released his foot and the boy furiously got to his feet, rejecting Drake's hand and offer of assistance. He clearly did not know how to graciously accept defeat. "One must learn humility in order to also enjoy the riches of victory," Drake forewarned. "'Twould be wise to learn such a lesson early or you will never make it into Lord Dristan's personal guard."

"I shall make it," Godfrey retorted, before storming off to clean himself.

Ulrick held out his hand and a coin was pressed into his palm. Chuckling, he put the tenure away in a pouch at his belt. "My thanks for the wager, Bertram."

"Bah! I thought he would at the very least put in a fair showing with Drake. Are you sure he will make it another se'n-night?" Bertram speculated.

"He will if he can but learn to control the anger that continues to consume him."

"And yet you placed a bet that he would lose all the same."

Ulrick shrugged with a raised brow toward his friend. "Well... he is not ready yet now, is he? There must be something in Godfrey's past that haunts him to act out so rashly. I shall work on figuring out what plagues him on the morrow."

With a knowing smirk, he thumped Bertram on the back, and gave a salute to Drake. His friend was in the process of readying himself to take on another local lad who thought he could best one of the Devil's Dragon's men. Ulrick strode off to find what would next hold his interest.

It had been some time since the village of Berwyck had enjoyed such festivities and mayhap the merriment was even greater because of the last fiasco of the tourney that would have landed the victor the Lady Lynet as his bride. But that was long since passed. Ulrick knew Dristan would never allow another mistake as to have one under his lord's protection stolen from beneath his very nose.

Hawkers called out to him to perchance buy a trinket or two to bestow upon a lady of his choosing. He passed them by, for he had no need for such frippery. He saw Dristan, Amiria, and their children at one such stall as Dristan purchased a sweet each for his son and daughter. Several garrison knights headed in the direction of a nearby field where jousting competitions were being held, but Ulrick had no need to prove his worth in that direction. A day of rest was, indeed, a luxury and for once in his life since he joined Dristan's personal guard, he would enjoy the day unto himself.

The sun came out from behind a cloud, and he stopped his stroll to shield his eyes from the brightness overhead. He was surprised when he felt his left elbow being taken and he looked down to find an elderly woman with grey hair staring up at him with a mischievous smile.

"My lady, may I be of assistance?" he asked, wondering how she was able to sneak up on him as she had.

"Oh, aye, laddie, that ye may," she said, with a heavy Scottish brogue.

He waited for her to continue to state how he may be of service, but she only watched him. Her gaze was so intense that Ulrick shuffled on his feet under her close scrutiny. His brow rose in a silent display for her to tell him what aid she needed but again she remained silent, as if she had no perception of what she required of him.

"May I ask, how may I be of service, madam?" he at last inquired.

"'Tis the wrong question ye ask. Mayhap ye should be inquiring what I can do fer ye?"

"Since we have just met, I do not understand what I would need of you... no disrespect intended, of course," he mumbled, inspecting this elderly Scottish woman who held his curiosity.

"Fair enough," the woman replied, patting his arm. "'Tis nice tae see a knight who remembers his manners and continues tae live by a code of honor. Ye are honorable, are ye not?"

Ulrick looked down at this tiny woman whilst she urged him forward. No one in his entire adult life had ever questioned his honor. He was a knight of the realm living by a code of chivalry his entire life. 'Twas engraved into his very soul.

"Aye, madam," he answered truthfully.

"I really had no doubt, but I had to ask ye," she answered with a wink. "'Tis required, ye must know."

Ulrick was confused as to where this conversation was going. "What is required?"

'Twas the lady's turn to look confused, as if he should not be asking her anything. She peered at him once more, before smiling up in satisfaction again. "Why, that ye be worthy, of course."

"Worthy of what?"

"Ye shall see. Will ye escort me tae the well at the edge of the village, dear boy? 'Tis a far bit of distance fer these old legs of mine."

"Of course, my lady," he answered, ignoring her reference that he was a mere boy. No one had called him such for more years than he cared to remember, and he tried not to scowl at the reference.

Despite the woman's reference to her age, she seemed to pick up her pace as though she were suddenly in a hurry to reach the well she spoke of. The crowd began to thin as they left the festivities far behind and Ulrick saw their destination up ahead. She continued to pull him along before she sat to take her ease on a log that served as a bench of sorts.

He looked around, thinking that mayhap she was to meet someone, but there was no one else around. He could in no way leave her here alone so he waited somewhat impatiently, not knowing how else he might be of help to her besides standing guard.

"Ye be a good laddie," she said with another bright smile. "Will ye be so good as tae get me a dipper of water from the well?"

Ulrick gave her a brief nod and went toward the well, taking the rope before dropping the bucket down and hearing it splash in the water far below. He began to pull the rope end over end and gazed over his shoulder. He squinted whilst he gazed upon the old lady for, as the sun hit her body, she appeared surreal. The light perchance was playing tricks with him, for she waved at him as if he should hurry with his task. He turned and, before he knew what had happened, a womanly body was hurled into his arms, slamming into him. They began to stumble backwards to the ground and Ulrick quickly maneuvered so she would not be crushed by his weight.

Merde! Where the devil did she come from? He began to worry for her health when she did not open her eyes. He turned to the elderly woman he left on the log only to see that she was gone. Returning his attention to the young woman beneath him, he saw that she was in need of reviving. Rising briefly to retrieve the full bucket, he set it next to the woman in order to splash the cool water upon her face.

"My lady? My lady, can you hear me?" he asked. Green eyes

began to slowly flutter open like the soft wings of a butterfly in flight.

He could only stare in wonder at the vision in front of him whilst she came to life. He refused to think of who she might be. His eyes widened in surprise when a woman's voice sounded inside his head as clear as the day was fair... *Ye be welcome.*

CHAPTER 8

Confusion wracked her head, making her dizzy. What had happened?

"My lady? My lady, can you hear me?" There was no mistaking the deep baritone voice that was obviously male and full of concern.

Bridgette slowly opened her eyes to reveal a man hovering above her. A halo of sunlight surrounded his head, almost making him appear as if he was one of God's own angels. As she became aware of her surroundings and her vision began to clear, she wondered how on earth she ended up on the ground.

"What happened?" she inquired, while an overwhelming sensation of being completely out of place rushed through her. She sat up, and the man gently took her elbow to assist her to stand upright on wobbly feet. Her eyes swept the immediate area. It was no wonder she was feeling out of sorts. Nothing looked familiar. "Where am I?"

The man's brows furrowed at her question but answered carefully. "At the village faire, my lady, in Berwyck."

Bridgette mulled over his answer, still puzzled. "That must be a new one. I didn't realize they were giving these events an actual location name."

"I know not of what you speak, my lady," the man replied, with a furrowed brow.

She waved him off, trying to get her bearings. She began dusting off her gown, still feeling disoriented. "That's okay. What the hell happened?" she asked again. "God damn, what a day I'm having."

"My lady!" The gentleman's voice was clearly chastising her for her language.

She watched him make the sign of the cross and gave a heavy sigh. Once again, she had screwed up by not staying in character. If she didn't watch herself, she'd go and get herself booted from the acting guild. "My apologies, good sir. I seem to be out of sorts," she replied trying to get back into her role.

"I understand," he murmured, but his voice didn't sound convincing to her ears. "Mayhap you should take your ease over yonder, if you can make it that far."

Bridgette gave a brief nod. He followed her a short distance from where she had fallen and pointed to a log. *Where is that delightful bench I was sitting on?* She rubbed her eyes, trying to get them to focus properly. As they opened again, the world seemed to spin before her vision. Reaching out, she clasped the arm of her rescuer.

The world righted itself again and she at last focused fully on the man... or rather knight... who stood before her, rather impatiently. He looked familiar, as though the statue had come to life.

Had she really stumbled into the guy who had modeled for the sculpture?

Her mouth hung open. She was most likely appearing extremely rude and impolite. But it wasn't her fault she was gawking. The man's handsome ruggedness practically begged her to squeal out *take me now!* He towered over her own small stature. Dark black hair with hints of brown hung to his shoulders, almost asking her to reach out to caress its length. Vivid blue eyes were set in a tanned face with chiseled cheekbones, a firm-looking square jaw, and a nose that now appeared as though it had been broken a time or two. This, naturally, only added to her initial attraction to him. His facial features reminded her of a Roman soldier of old.

She continued her assessment. Broad shoulders were barely hidden beneath a dark red cape that fluttered behind him in the afternoon breeze. A well-made tunic of dark blue closely covered his muscular chest. The slightly curved neckline offered her the briefest glimpse of his chest hair, and she had to ball her fingers into a tight fist to prevent her from doing the unthinkable, like reaching out to actually caress a total stranger.

Her gaze went lower, but that was an absolute mistake, as she saw the rest of him was just as perfectly shaped. His costuming was impeccable and, once her senses returned to normal, she'd have to ask where he had had them made. He must be an athlete because, for the life of her, she couldn't see that there was an ounce of fat on his body. She began to wonder if his flat abdomen would contain a six or eight pack of ripples if he stood before her without his shirt.

She took her time as her gaze traveled back up the length of him because, honestly, what was there not to appreciate with the fine specimen before her? When she at last made her way back up to his face, she encountered a roguish grin. *Good lord...* had she really openly ogled him like that? His twinkling eyes held a mischievous glint, as though he was completely aware of his effect on her and the beginnings of a rosy blush crept its way across her cheeks. She wouldn't think of how the rest of her body became flushed when he now started his own assessment. He chuckled as though he knew where her thoughts had taken her.

"Sorry. I don't know what came over me," she murmured in embarrassment.

"There is no need to apologize, my lady," he answered politely, waving again to the log. "Please, take your ease."

"Thanks." Bridgette sat and waited for him to sit next to her on the vacant space. He remained standing. "I'm Bridgette." She offered her hand by way of a greeting. Considering she had just practically stripped the man naked with her eyes, she felt she should at the very least offer her name to the guy.

He stood there, only staring at her outstretched arm, until she placed her hands in her lap. She almost slapped her forehead. She had once more forgotten where she was. She sure hoped no one from the guild was keeping an eye on her. She'd be sacked for sure!

"Lady Bridgette of..." His voice trailed off as he waited for her to finish her name.

"Oops... sorry." She cleared her throat as she continued. "Bridgette Harris." She stood quickly, gave a quick curtsey, and sat back down.

He performed a courtly bow that would rival anything she had ever seen on a stage. "Sir Ulrick de Mohan, currently of Berwyck, my lady, and at your service."

"A pleasure to meet you, Sir Ulrick," she said, keeping a

smile on her face. Ulrick... *What an unusual name,* she thought. And using *de Mohan?* Must be a stage name, since it sounded very old fashioned.

"And I you, Lady Bridgette." He stood tall again and looked around. "Where are your attendants?" he inquired as he widened his stance and folded his arms across his massive chest.

Bridgette smiled, since it was clear he, too, wanted to continue to play his part at the fair. "I am one of the Queen's ladies in waiting," she answered, with a confidence she was back in her role.

Was it her imagination, or did Ulrick's face lose a bit of color? "Queen Eleanor of Aquitaine is here? *Merde,* I was not aware King Henry had released his queen from prison and would travel this far north at this time of year," he stated, clearly ill at ease.

She gave a merry laugh. "You must be at the wrong fair, good sir. I am with the Tudor Queen."

"Tudor? I know not of such a queen by that name."

Bridgette's brow furrowed. Who performed at a renaissance fair and didn't know who Queen Elizabeth was? "You're joking?" she asked, and saw it was his turn to lift his brow in question. "Jesting?"

"Ah. Nay, I was not jesting with you. You must be from abroad," Ulrick assumed. "Mayhap we should have speech with Lord Dristan to ensure there is no mistaking the King's arrival. I would not want His Majesty to think I offended him and must forfeit what little lands I possess. Dunster Castle is not as large an estate as Berwyck but 'tis mine just the same."

Sir Ulrick offered his arm to her. She stood and hesitantly slid her fingers into the crook of his elbow. She was surprised when her fingertips began to shiver. She could feel the muscles beneath her hand. *How many hours did this guy spend in the gym to get his body in the condition it was in?* She raised her head and for the first time stared directly into his eyes. They were as blue as the clear sky above her and Bridgette almost lost her breath.

"Lead on, Sir Ulrick," she declared brightly. She couldn't wait for Megan to see her being escorted about by this flat-out gorgeous knight. Her friend was going to be pea green with envy.

As they began to make their way from the area, Bridgette's steps faltered when she looked over her shoulder. Ulrick tightened his grip to steady her. She did a double take to peer at the place the granite statue of her knight should be. Instead, she only saw a very rudimentary stone well.

CHAPTER 9

Ulrick escorted the Lady Bridgette back toward the festivities. He tried not to stare but 'twas difficult when the woman next to him was one of the most beautiful women he had ever encountered. High cheekbones with a straight nose framed a face with clear skin and a neck as graceful as a swan. Her dark green eyes rivaled the brilliance of the leaves of a forest after the rain and her face was so beautiful it must make the angels weep in heaven.

He dared not look lower, and yet how could he not when he could see the creamy soft mounds of her breasts pushed up so the fabric of her dress barely covered her nipples. A jeweled necklace, surely costly, hung from her neck with the largest bauble nestled in her cleavage, tempting him even further. Her purple gown must be in the height of fashion somewhere abroad for, although similar to others he had seen women wearing at court, 'twas still... different... Not that he was an expert on what frippery women wore these days. Generally,

Ulrick was more concerned about the treasure that awaited him beneath their gowns than anything else.

They approached the center of the village when Lady Bridgette came to a sudden halt. Her hand trembled whilst her fingertips clutched roughly to the fabric of his tunic.

"I don't remember this part of the fair," she whispered in concern, "and I was paying close attention to the orientation speaker."

"What speaker?" he asked, confused not only by the pattern of her speech but also what she thought was so unusual about what was before her.

She ignored his question but looked up at him with a frown. "It looks so... real."

Ulrick was unsure how to answer her and began to wonder if perchance she sustained a bump to her head that had addled her wits when she fell. Mayhap he should seek out Kenna, Berwyck's healer, and see if she could find out what was ailing the Lady Bridgette.

Before he could mention assisting her to the castle, she began tugging on his arm and pointing in the direction of a cleared field. A raised platform had been constructed for Dristan, Amiria, and those within their party so they might take their ease beneath the shade of an awning. Dristan's standard, depicting a fire-breathing dragon, flew high above upon towering poles.

"Jousting? I don't remember that on the program. Can we go watch?" Bridgette exclaimed, with renewed excitement, "that is, if you'd like to go with me. You may have other plans for the day."

"I cannot in all good conscience leave a woman unattended. I will accompany you, my lady, until you are reunited with those in your party," Ulrick answered, knowing he must needs perform his duty to the woman.

"Awesome!" she exclaimed rather loudly, before covering her mouth. "Damn... sorry about that. I'll try to get myself back into character, I promise."

Ulrick shook his head, more concerned than ever the longer he heard her strange speech. There was surely something wrong with Lady Bridgette. He peered at her an instant before they began to make their way across the field. Her eyes were lit with excitement at the sight of the tourney, clearly proving the woman was of a normal mind. He ignored the small nagging voice in his head and the odd premonition that another one of those future women had landed in his arms but a short while ago.

Lady Bridgette began ushering him to where the crowd had gathered to watch the competition as best as they could, but he would not see a lady of worth standing next to the common people of the village. He began escorting her to the platform where he could see his liege lord and his guards already seated.

"Come this way, my lady," Ulrick urged, taking her elbow and guiding her in the direction of his usual seat.

"But we can't go up there," she whispered. "I can see for myself that it's reserved for a knight of honor, considering his standard flies overhead. Since I don't recognize the flag, I can't in all good conscience barge in on another guild."

"Aye, we can. I am one of the personal guards of Dristan of Berwyck, and I assure you my place, and yours as my guest, is near his side."

"Well... if you're sure."

"I am."

Ulrick held out his hand and he watched her come to her

own decision. As she grasped his outstretch limb, a tingling sensation shivered up his entire arm and down the back of his spine. He knew she felt it too, when her eyes widened to stare up at him with wonder.

"Did you feel that?" she asked, not attempting to hide her shock.

"Aye," Ulrick replied, not capable of giving any further comment as he, too, was just as surprised at the phenomenon that had occurred between them.

"What does it mean?"

"I have no idea, my lady," he replied, as they continued to stare one to the other. Any further conversation was halted when he heard his name called. "My liege lord calls to me. Come with me and I will present you."

They came to stand before Dristan and Amiria. Ulrick bowed and he watched Lady Bridgette perform a curtsey.

"And who is this vision that you bring before us, Sir Ulrick? I do not believe we have had the pleasure," Dristan asked, taking a sip of his wine and peering at him over its rim.

"Good day to you, my Lord Dristan and Lady Amiria. May I present Lady Bridgette Harris of..." Ulrick turned to lean down and whisper in her ear. She shivered. "My apologies, but you never answered from whence you hail."

She smothered a womanly giggle before quietly replying. "Bridgette from Michigan."

Michigan? Where the bloody hell is Michigan, he pondered, before bringing his attention to the matter at hand. "My liege and my lady... I present to you Lady Bridgette Harris of... Michigan."

Dristan almost choked on his wine, and he and his wife exchanged a knowing look.

"Where?" Drake demanded, leaning forward in his chair where he sat behind Amiria. "Did he say Michigan? I have never heard of such a place."

Bertram slapped his forehead. *"God's Wounds...* 'tis another one!"

"Mayhap she is acquainted with the ladies Katherine, Jenna, Amy, and Jade," Taegan proposed, with a grin.

"Does she have a friend?" Cederick called out, before Morgan gave him a shove for being rude.

Dristan held up his hand to halt further conversations running amuck amongst his guardsmen. "Enough," he ordered, quieting his men before smiling kindly. "Lady Bridgette, may I present my wife Amiria. Please be seated next to her. Turquine, make room for our guest, and you as well Taegan, so that Ulrick may be near his lady."

"Oh, I'm not his lady," Bridgette replied warily, looking to those who were staring at her with mixed emotions racing across their visages. "We just met."

Muttering beneath her breath something about how she did it again, she bobbed a short curtsey. "My thanks, my lord," Lady Bridgette answered, smiling brightly before she took her seat and began watching the jousting. She was not aware of the undercurrents of disbelief circling around her as Ulrick's comrades all began to surmise their own opinions.

With a nod from Dristan, who glared at him with a raised brow, he took his place next to *his lady.* 'Twas clear she had no idea everyone near her was observing her every move with a fair mix of curiosity beneath lowered eyes, especially him. Completely absorbed in the competition she was viewing, she clapped and cheered those who won a match and flinched when knights lost, especially when some were unseated from their horses. She had not even been aware of clutching his arm in fright when Kenna was called to see to a knight's injury.

With a halt to the jousting, some of the crowd began to disperse to attend other festivities. Ulrick was about to ask Lady Bridgette if she wished to find her attendants when she stood upright peering into the crowd.

"Oh my God! There's that lady I was talking to before I passed out at the fountain," she exclaimed, pointing into the crowd.

Ulrick looked in the direction and also saw the old woman from the well. He rose, too, knocking over his chair, knowing he must needs have speech with her.

"Excuse me, please," Bridgette began as she started to hurry from the platform. "I've got to talk to her."

"My lady, wait..." Ulrick declared, but before he could follow her, Killian gasped. He was one of Amiria's guardsmen, although he was more of an uncle than just a warrior to protect her.

"Bless my soul! 'Tis yer grandmamma, Amiria," Killian stated, before snapping his mouth shut.

"Where?" Amiria proclaimed. She must have recognized the woman, since she gave a friendly wave with a smile of happiness radiating across her face. "Now isna this a wonderful gift? I canna believe she has appeared before us after all this time."

Since the lady's Scottish brogue became very pronounced, Ulrick assumed Lady Amiria was speaking the truth when she said her dear departed grandmother had appeared as a ghost. Everyone seemed to realize that a specter was amongst them, as some stood in disbelief, whilst others began to make the sign of the cross.

"Go find Bridgette, Ulrick," Amiria warned, "and quickly.

There's no telling what will happen when she discovers she is no longer in her own time."

With a sense of urgency, Ulrick caught a brief glimpse of the purple hue of the lady's gown before taking the steps two at a time in order to pursue her. Only God above knew for sure what he was to do once he caught up with her.

CHAPTER 10

Bridgette gathered up a fistful of her dress to try to catch up with the woman outrunning her—an astounding feat for someone her age. She would catch glimpses of the old lady through the crowd, but she continued to remain out of Bridgette's reach. How did she do that anyway?

Bridgette had a moment of hesitation, knowing she was getting farther and farther away from the jousting field. She should head back to Ulrick, not that he was her keeper or anything. When she realized the woman had disappeared, Bridgette finally took a moment to get a good hard look at her surroundings. She almost fell down right where she was standing, but a smelly pile of manure on the ground warned her of what she might actually plummet into. She closed her eyes and opened them slowly, but there wasn't any kind of a change to what her vision beheld.

Her hand rose to her throat in shock, while she made every attempt to calm her breathing. Several more gulps of air filled her lungs before she shook her head in denial. It just couldn't be possible but there it was… a castle and a very large one at that.

She had to be imagining the sight. Bridgette tried closing her eyes again and rubbing them for good measure. She exhaled a shaky breath and slowly opened them once more. Nope… it was a castle, rising majestically a short distance away and sitting on the edge of a cliff. She inhaled again and almost lost it when the salty scent of an ocean breeze came into her nose. The distant sound of waves crashing into the shoreline reached her ears. Certainly, her ears weren't deceiving her, also. *Where the hell am I?* she wondered trying to keep what sanity she had left in her poor meager little brain. *What happened to the fair in Michigan?*

Her world spun around her… or, rather, a world that was clearly not her own. Thatched-roof cottages were everywhere she looked. Serfs went about on whatever business they were attending when not tilling the fields. A man in a blacksmith shop pounded a large hammer on the anvil in front of him before holding up the sword he was working on and plunging it into a bucket of water. She heard the sizzling sound as the metal began to cool. Hawkers called out to come buy whatever products they were selling.

Bridgette continued her assessment of her situation in disbelief. There wasn't any pavement, or tourists, or any trace of a modern convenience anywhere! No cameras flashing in her face as people came to take her picture, no people chatting on their cellphones, no vendors trying to sell ice cold beverages or junk food, no electricity, and no modern buildings of any kind! Nothing… zip… nada! *Dear God! Where the hell am I?*

Ulrick. His name resounded inside her head, and she knew without any doubt she'd be safe with him if only she could find him. She needed to head back to the jousting field. Quickly turning, she didn't expect someone directly behind her and she ran right smack dab into a man who was encased in metal chain-mail. As she fell backwards, he grabbed at her arm before she ended up in the dirt.

With wavering legs, she was brought up against the knight and began to quickly disentangle herself from his embrace. He, on the other hand, tried his best to keep her near to his side. She gave him a push. "Thank you for saving me from landing on the ground but that's as far as my gratitude is going, I'm afraid," she said, through clenched teeth. Eyes peered at her through the slits of his helmet before he wrenched the iron from his head. He tossed back his hair to look at her fully with an appreciative stare.

"My lady," he said, in an overly friendly tone.

She couldn't believe who she was staring at. Would this man stop at nothing in his attempts to stalk her, no matter where she went? "Brad? What are you doing here?"

His brows furrowed before he looked behind him, perhaps wondering if she had been speaking to someone else. "My apologies if I startled you, my lady. I but offered my assistance so you did not harm yourself."

"Brad?" she asked again.

"Nay. I do not know this Brad of whom you speak. I am Godfrey Hawkins, at your service," he declared, with a short bow.

Her hand went to her forehead in confusion. Of course, it wasn't Brad, but it sure could have been a version of him a few years younger. If it was true what people always said, that everyone had a twin walking the face of the planet, then surely she was looking at Brad's doppelganger. The knight standing there, looking her up and down, was just as handsome as Brad and just as cocky, if the grin he had plastered on his face was any indication of the man's true character. They were physically different but not by much. Godfrey had dark brown hair where Brad's had been lighter, and Godfrey's eyes were brown instead of green.

She was losing it… that's all there was to it. She needed to find Ulrick fast. "I have to go," she murmured, as she began to walk back toward the jousting area.

"You cannot go," Godfrey said falling into step next to her, "not when you have not told me your name, fair lady."

She barely acknowledged the compliment, considering she was obviously not playing a role anymore. And then she saw Ulrick up ahead of her as he pushed his way through the crowd to reach her. Good Lord, he was tall. He reminded her of a huge mountain, towering over everyone near him in his magnificence.

Bridgette picked up her pace to reach the one man she knew would help her. True, she didn't know him, but he must be the reason she found herself in this crazy ass position of… well… whatever position she could call this that she was in!

The closer he came, the faster she began to run toward him, until she hurled herself into his waiting arms. She didn't care that she was practically throwing herself at a complete stranger, but she needed him. He wrapped his arms around her as if he, too, had known they were supposed to be together. Her heart picked up its pace while her breathing quickened. Her whole body didn't feel as though it was her own. Tingling currents raced through her veins, as if Ulrick was pouring his life force into her own. She sighed and his arms tightened around her, until a voice behind her interrupted.

"Sir Ulrick, I was not aware that you were acquainted with

the lady," Godfrey grunted, then began clearing his throat as if that would pull them apart.

Ulrick gazed down upon her before setting her on her feet. "You know Godfrey? Are you his kin?"

"We just met, and no, we're not related," Bridgette replied, and took hold of Ulrick's hand. There was no way she was going to let go of him.

"Are you not jousting in the next meet, Godfrey?" Ulrick asked, bringing her closer to his side.

"Aye, that I am, but then I encountered this enchanting creature and but meant to follow her," he answered, still gazing upon Bridgette like she was his next meal, or so it seemed in her mind. It made her uncomfortable, and she moved a step closer to Ulrick.

"Then you should head that way lest you miss the opportunity to show Lord Dristan you can remain seated on your horse." Ulrick ordered. "Lady Bridgette is in my care."

"Ah... Lady Bridgette... a pleasure, my lady, to at last be privy to your name," Godfrey stated, with another bow, before taking his leave.

As Bridgette continued standing there, she began to uncontrollably shake. She reached out for Ulrick, who took her about the waist. "Oh God... where am I?" she whispered, before the world began its spinning once more. The last thing she remembered was Ulrick's concerned voice calling out her name.

CHAPTER 11

Ulrick crossed the dimly lit passageway floor for the hundredth time. The chamber Bridgette had been taken to remained off limits to him. Yet he persisted on staying near at hand, waiting for word from Kenna or Lady Amiria that Bridgette was well.

Go above to the parapet whispered a voice inside his head, causing Ulrick to make haste up the turret. Opening the tower door, he climbed the stairs to the narrow walkway and waited. He did not stand there long before Rolf began to take shape to hover near him. His ghostly friend smiled and Ulrick returned the gesture.

"You have been busy again," Ulrick surmised, assuming 'twas Rolf's doing that Bridgette had arrived in Berwyck's village by unconventional methods.

"Nay, not this time," Rolf answered, his voice now reaching Ulrick's ears instead of inside his mind. "I had nothing to do with your lady being brought here.

"You did not?"

"Nay. I did not want to meddle in people's lives yet again. The feat took a lot out of me the last time. Almost a full fortnight was necessary for me to completely recover."

"And yet Fletcher is thankful to you, all the same," Ulrick said, knowing how pleased his friend was with his wife from a place not of this time.

"Aye... I suppose he is at that," Rolf declared, with a smirk. "'Twas Amiria's grandmother's doing bringing Bridgette here."

"Why?"

Rolf shrugged. "You met the older woman, you tell me. You must have voiced a desire to have a lady brought into your life."

"I did no such thing," Ulrick voiced, sullenly.

"Well, no matter. She is here now."

"I did not ask for a future woman, and I certainly never spoke such a desire aloud. These women who keep showing up amongst Dristan's knights are trouble with their passing strange ways," Ulrick grumbled, before looking over the battlement wall, trying to distract himself.

"A lady of this time or from the future... what does it matter from whence she hails?"

"It matters to me. I do not need a woman who is bold in her ways or one who continually speaks her mind. I want someone who will obey my commands," Ulrick argued.

Rolf laughed, causing Ulrick to raise a brow. How he had missed his friend. "And you would be completely bored, *mon ami*. I somehow think Amiria's grandmother had your best interest at heart, if she went so far to bring you a woman worthy of you," Rolf said knowingly, pointing a finger in his direction.

"What am I to do with her?"

"Love her," Rolf simply answered, as he began to fade.

"But she does not belong here amongst us," Ulrick yelled.

Rolf gave a broad grin. "Aye, my friend, she does."

Ulrick opened his mouth to give a sharp retort but Rolf gave a salute before disappearing from view. He knew his friend was not completely gone since he could hear his merry chuckle on the breeze blowing in from the ocean.

Ulrick made his way below yet again, wondering—not for the first time this day—why he had been chosen to see to the needs of a woman who was not of this time. He halted on the last step, almost hoping, as he peered into the passageway, that the old woman would answer his question by appearing to him or at the very least answer inside his head. But there was no one there other than a servant who rushed out of Bridgette's chamber carrying some linen.

Ulrick was about to make his way to her room when Dristan motioned to him from down the corridor. He followed his liege lord to his solar, where he closed the door behind him. He waited for he knew not what as Dristan went to pour wine. Ulrick took the goblet Dristan held out and they drank in silence.

"I know not what to say," Dristan began, running his hand through his hair and making his way to the window. Opening the shutter, he took a deep breath almost as if to collect his thoughts.

"My liege?"

Dristan returned his attention to Ulrick. "I have the distinct feeling you will also now be leaving us."

"Have I offended you in some way, my Lord Dristan?" Ulrick asked, in concern that he was being released from his oath of fealty.

Dristan waved him off. "Nay, of course not, and yet it seems to be the way of things when these future women come traipsing to my door. First Riorden, Fletcher, then Thomas and now you. Even Taegan boasts of one of Lady Jenna's friends to whom he has taken a fancy, even though they have had a falling out. With the loss of my retainers, 'tis the reason I am recruiting for men who are capable of taking their places."

"I have no desire to leave your service or Berwyck for that matter."

Dristan's gaze swept over him. "I have been expecting you to take your leave since word came about the passing of your brother."

Ulrick's sigh was heavy. He was still regretting not going home for Lief's burial. "My responsibilities were to Berwyck and the training of new men. My mother can continue to manage Dunster."

A muffled laugh rumbled in his liege lord's chest. "Your mother has managed your estate for far too long if you ask my opinion. You have been given a rare opportunity to have a woman to love and, with such a commitment, you will want to claim your birthright and lands," Dristan surmised.

"I did not ask for such a prospect to present itself," Ulrick groaned.

"One never does, but when the love of a good woman comes your way, 'tis best to not let such a treasure leave your side."

"I barely know the woman, Lord Dristan, and surely cannot profess to love her."

"Be that as it may, she will remain in my care until such a time as you come to a decision about whether to pursue a relationship with her," Dristan declared. "But be warned, I will not take kindly to another of my knights taking advantage of a woman I claim as my ward. Wed her if you so desire, but do not bed her without the union being blessed by a priest, lest you wish to test my wrath."

"I give you my word, my Lord Dristan," Ulrick responded with a short bow of respect.

"Good! We shall see where the winds will take you and the Lady Bridgette."

"May I see her?"

Dristan's gaze practically drilled into him, as though to test his commitment he would leave the lady untouched. 'Twas the last thing he was thinking about. He was only concerned that she was well. Dristan must have realized Ulrick would not harm the woman for he gave a short nod of his head.

"Aye but do not stay long. She has been torn through *Time* and must needs have her rest," Dristan answered dismally, before raking his fingers through his long black hair yet again. "*Merde!* When will these women of her kind cease showing up at my gates?"

Dismissed, Ulrick took his leave and made his way down the passageway. When he knocked upon the door, he heard a call to enter. As Ulrick stepped through the portal, he had the distinct feeling he had just sealed his fate.

CHAPTER 12

Bridgette turned onto her side, pulled the covers up to her chin, and snuggled into its warmth. Not wanting to awaken as yet, she savored the remnants of one of the most fascinating dreams she had ever had in her entire life. Imagine being pulled through time to enjoy living in a medieval castle, let alone the handsome knight who had stolen her heart with just one glimpse into those incredible blue eyes.

Ulrick... just pondering his name caused her to let out a heavenly sigh. Such an odd name for this day and age but who cared. He had been... well... perfect, at least to her way of thinking. Gorgeous. Chivalrous, too. He saw she was taken care of and treated like a woman wanted to be treated instead of just a one-night stand. There was something to be said for being pampered like a lady, no matter that she had been in costume. A person couldn't ask for much more than that. Too bad he wasn't real.

She supposed she should rise, since she and Megan would

need to pack up their gear and head home. She rolled over onto her back, threw off the covers, and began stretching before finally opening her eyes. As they came into focus, she blinked, seeing the fabric of a canopy above her head. Bridgette also became aware that, perhaps what was giving her a feeling of comfort was the low baritone of a man humming a tune that halted abruptly with the blankets being thrown from her body. She wasn't alone.

Startled at being seen, she began to reach for the covers and gasped. She was garbed only in her panties and camisole. Where the hell were her clothes? With trembling hands, she quickly pulled at the blanket to cover herself. Her gaze spun around the room, or perhaps she should call it a chamber, for the walls weren't her hotel room with plaster and painted drywall. No! They were made of stone. Shaking as if her whole world had been turned upside down, and maybe that wasn't too far from the truth after all, her eyes searched the chamber and settled on the man who but a few seconds ago had been just a figment of her imagination. He stood, and he seemed to fill up the empty spaces of the room with his presence. This wasn't a dream at all!

"You have come from afar, fair damsel," Ulrick murmured, holding her stare.

The soothing sound of his voice was like a calming balm to her soul. Suddenly, her body reacted to his presence by becoming exceedingly warm under all the covers. Bridgette knew this had nothing to do with what she was holding up as a shield or the fire blazing in the hearth to heat the room.

"Yes," she answered simply, "although I don't have the vaguest idea how I've come to be here."

"Aye... well... I may have somehow had something to do

with that, although 'twas without my consent or knowledge that I would disrupt someone's life."

"How could it be your fault I find myself here? Not that you really have any idea of where I truly belong?"

"I know."

Such an easy statement. Yet how could he have any sort of a clue that she had actually crossed time. His knowing eyes continued to bore into her as though her thoughts had revealed her true identity. "You do?"

"Aye. You are not the first to arrive at Berwyck's gates from a place that is surely farther than one can travel by horse or boat," he answered, before his hand rubbed the back of his neck. She gulped, watching his long fingers emerge from under all that gorgeous black hair, and she tried not to lick her lips at the image he presented.

She scrunched her eyes closed only to open them again. There was a more pressing matter at hand than that she came from the future. "Where are my clothes? Please tell me you didn't undress me," Bridgette asked, with a warning glare.

Ulrick held up his hands. "Nay, I did not, nor would you ask such a question if you knew me at all. 'Twas Lady Amiria and our healer Kenna who saw to you. They went to see about procuring you another dress that would be more… appropriate for the time."

"What was wrong with the dress? I ensured every detail was proper for the sixteenth century. The guild makes certain of it before we can be a part of their group," Bridgette said, louder than she intended.

Ulrick's eyes widened. "Is that from whence you hail? The sixteenth century?"

"Umm… no. I'm from the twenty-first."

"I see. Then mayhap you know the Lady Katherine or Lady Jenna. They are also from this place called Sanfran Cisco."

"Never been to California. I'm from the North East. In Michigan, like I told you at the fair." Was it her imagination, or was this the craziest conversation she'd ever had? She held up her hand. "Michigan looks like a mitten. She pointed to about the spot where she lived. "I live about here."

A snort left him, while his brow furrowed in confusion. "You live at the North East coast of this Michigan of which you speak?" Ulrick asked, as he began to finger the hilt of a dagger in his belt. He must have realized what he was doing, since he got a sheepish look on his face and folded his arms across his massive chest in an attempt not to finger the knife again.

"The north east of America," Bridgette muttered and held up her hand to halt whatever Ulrick planned on saying next. She began dragging the blanket with her as she started to pace the chamber. She was nervous. Not because of him but because of the situation she found herself in. "Maybe we should start over. I'm clearly *not* in Michigan so where and *when* am I?"

She waited for him to say something, but he only continued to stare off into space as if he was pondering what he would tell her. She pressed the issue further. She *had* to know! "Ulrick... where am I?" she asked with a raised voice.

"England. Near Scotland's border. 'Tis the year of our Lord's Grace 1183."

Her knees buckled and she fell to the floor. "The twelfth century? You've got to be kidding me?" She held her hand up yet again when he made a move to help her from the floor. His arm dropped and instead he went to sit down in a chair set by the hearth, motioning for her to do the same with the vacant seat across from him. Keeping the blanket clutched to her bosom, she did as he asked, and sat with shaking hands.

Once she was settled, he continued. "I would not jest about such a grave matter, my lady. I am most sorry you find yourself in a time not your own, but we will figure out how to return you as soon as we can find Lady Amiria's grandmother. We are certain she is the culprit who instigated your arrival here."

It was Bridgette's turn for her eyes to widen. "Little old lady with a kind face, white hair and twinkling blue eyes?" As Ulrick's nod, Bridgette swore. "I was having a conversation with her by a fountain designed with a statue of a knight in its center... you to be exact."

"'Tis not possible, Lady Bridgette. I assure you I have never been to this future world of yours, nor do I wish to be taken there."

"All the same, the figure was you. She gave me a coin to toss in the fountain to make a wish..." her voice trailed off, not wanting to divulge the nature of her deepest desire.

"And what were you wishing for, Lady Bridgette?" Ulrick inquired, his dark brow arching with his question. He was clearly curious about what wish could have opened up the heavens to allow her to travel back in time.

He waited for her answer somewhat patiently before his hand clenched the arm of his chair, his knuckles turning white. She watched his every feature in mild fascination that he was really sitting here before her. She supposed she could have lied but what was the point? She *had* been wishing for him to be real and... well... now he was. "It was you," she whispered, watching his eyes widen in surprise.

"Me? But you do not know me."

"At the time I just wanted someone who was the personification of the statue I saw in front of me. How was I supposed to know that, when the coin ricocheted off the marble and I caught it, I'd be transported back in time? But there you were hovering over me when I woke up. What are we going to do now?"

He stood and held out his hand to assist her from the chair. The minute their fingers connected, those crazy little currents raced up her arm. She knew he felt it too from his sharp intake of breath. She could understand what he was going through, because the rapid beating of her heart felt as though it would burst from her chest.

"We will think of something. I will send in Amiria's ladies to help you dress for the evening meal after Mass. We can attend together, if you would care to join us. That is, if you are feeling up to it. Otherwise, I will see that someone comes to your chamber to show you to the Great Hall at the appointed hour. Will that be satisfactory?" he inquired politely.

"Yes, and please call me Bridgette," she murmured shyly.

He gave a short nod of his head. "And you must needs call me Ulrick. Under the circumstances, I believe 'tis only fitting. I will see you shortly."

With another formal bow, he left, leaving her to gaze at the closed door, willing him to return. Shaking her head at the crazy situation she now found herself in, Bridgette went to sit on the edge of the bed. She tried to figure out how she was going to get herself out of this predicament, but she didn't have a clue. Time travel… who knew?

Bridgette took a deep breath to steady her nerves and let it out slowly. With a new resolve, she figured she might as well enjoy the opportunity that had presented itself, since she had always been someone to land on her feet during difficult times in her life. If she was going to be stuck in time, at least she had the acting experience of portraying a lady of olden days. How much harder could it be to go back another few hundred years?

When a knock sounded at her door, she took another gulp of air to get herself into character once more and gave the call to enter. However hard this was going to be, she was about to find out. This was going to be one hell of an adventure!

CHAPTER 13

Berwyck's chapel was filled for the evening Mass. Ulrick listened as the priest droned on with his sermon. He was having a difficult time with his prayers, since the woman seated next to him continually fidgeted, either fingering the fabric of her dress or tapping her leg up and down at a brisk pace. The priest cleared his throat, hoping to gain her attention to his words but 'twas no use. Lady Bridgette appeared uncomfortable in the chapel, although why she should feel this way whilst offering her petitions to God was beyond his ken.

He leaned over to whisper in her ear. "My lady, be at ease. No harm shall come to you, and you must needs pay attention to Father Donovan."

Her eyes pleaded with him to understand what was bothering her. She moved closer to him so she could answer him with a hushed tone of reverence. "I don't know Latin, which means I haven't any idea what he's saying," she said quietly, as she reached for his hand.

He was surprised at the gesture. It made him both uncomfortable and elated at the same time. Holding hands to touch someone so familiarly when you had only just met must be common practice in her future world. He squeezed her hand but briefly before letting go, knowing the good Father would not approve of an open display of affection from two people who had not pledged their troth. Was it his imagination, or did she look disappointed?

"Follow my lead," he prompted softly. "He is almost over, and we must pay heed to his words."

She nodded and folded her hands in her lap. They were shaking.

'Twas not much longer before Father Donovan gave the congregation his blessing with a final prayer. When the word *amen* resounded in the chapel from those seeking forgiveness of their sins, everyone began to rise with the exception of Bridgette. He caught Amiria's eye, and she nodded in the lady's direction, so he sat back down on the bench next to her, waiting until they were alone.

"My lady," Ulrick began, looking at tears glistening on the length of her lashes, "What may I do to ease your sorrow and suffering?"

Bridgette attempted a smile but 'twas a poor effort at best. "I'm not sure that you can. I'm feeling very overwhelmed at the moment. I thought I could do this but now I'm not sure I can."

He reached over and took her hand and, as had happened before, goose bumps dashed up his arm when they touched. "I thought mayhap attending Mass would give you some semblance of comfort and would be familiar to you. 'Twas not meant to make you sad."

She gave his hand a squeeze along with a heavy sigh. "I was

raised Catholic but that's the first time I've ever felt inadequate in church," she confessed, with a catch to her words. "I thought it would be so easy to fit in, but maybe I was wrong to assume it would be similar to any other acting job in the guild. I'm generally not one to feel so melancholy. I tend to land on my feet no matter what life throws at me. But my being here... now... in this time and place... how does someone prepare for something of this nature?"

"I do not know how you could be prepared for such an anomaly, my lady. Please know we will be as helpful as possible to ensure your transition into our world until you can be returned to your own, if that is your wish." Ulrick managed to deliver a smile with the declaration, no matter how unnerving this conversation was.

"That's very kind of you. Lord Dristan and Lady Amiria have been thoughtful, too, welcoming a total stranger into their home, although I don't think the lord of the manor is all that pleased that I'm here," she replied whilst worry filled her eyes.

"They are used to their hall filled with guests and, as for my liege lord, he has accepted responsibility for you as his ward. You are under his protection and he will defend you to his last dying breath," Ulrick declared with conviction.

"Well... I hope it won't come to that," she murmured, a short uncomfortable laugh escaping her lips. She raised those incredible green eyes to him as if searching for what only she knew for sure. She continued to wait for him to go on with the conversation. Perhaps she expected him to declare himself, but he could not make such a vow to a woman he barely knew.

"Perchance we should go take our place in the hall for the evening meal," he offered instead, believing a full stomach was the answer to all their problems.

They rose, and he extended his arm to escort her. She tentatively placed her hand in the crook of his elbow. *God's wounds...* there it was again, as though fate was telling him to open his eyes to the gift he had been given if he would but let love into his heart. They walked the short distance to the keep. When they made their way through the portal, 'twas evident that the meal was already in the process of being served.

Roasted venison was piled high on platters that servants were carrying to the tables as eager knights were ready to eat their fill. The faire had been a fun filled day of competition and merry making and Ulrick's mouth began to water when the aroma of food reached his nose. He had not realized until now that he had not partaken of the noon meal due to the distraction of the lady next to his side.

Dristan waved them forward, and they took their place on the raised dais. Ulrick began filling the trencher that was placed between himself and Bridgette. He waited for her to begin until he, too, reached forward to eat his fill. Wine was poured and he offered a chalice to Bridgette who gladly accepted it.

She took a sip and sighed in pleasure. "Oh, that's good and just what I needed." Her smile was so infectious that he gave one of his own.

Conversations filled the room and, for the first time this eve, Bridgette appeared as if she was enjoying herself. Ulrick relaxed and sat back to just watch her face alight with pleasure as she took in every detail going on around her. He could only imagine the thoughts racing through her head as she took in life from the twelfth century. Reaching out for her chalice, she took another sip of her wine and turned those stunning green eyes upon him. The smile she gave him reached her eyes as they sparkled mischievously from the torches in the Great

Hall. He did not have long to wait for what she had in store for him.

※

Any sense of her early downhearted mood had left her the minute they had arrived for the evening meal. Medieval life swarmed around her in every direction, and she was thrilled to actually be living a part of it. No play acting. No trying to figure out if her costuming was accurate. These were real knights, ladies, and a castle to boot. She was in heaven, especially considering who she was dining with. She still couldn't believe she was sharing a trencher... *a trencher for God's sake...* with a knight of old, although there was certainly nothing *old* about Sir Ulrick.

She glanced at Ulrick and had a bazillion questions race across her mind. "So... what do you do for fun?" she asked, before quickly taking another bit of the meat in front of her.

"Uh... fun?" He glanced around to those who sat nearby, as if looking for rescue. He would be out of luck since they were too busy eating.

"Yeah, like, in your spare time."

"I do not have... spare time, my lady."

"Everyone gets free time."

"We are knights in service to Lord Dristan, Lady Bridgette. There is not a lot of time to do anything, as you say, fun, with the exception of the faire today. But we do not have those often here at Berwyck."

She thought for a moment, before continuing her one-sided game of twenty questions. Except, by this time, it was more like fifty questions. Her brain was bursting from her curiosity.

"Sir Ulrick, how does it feel to wear all that chainmail?"

"It does not bother me. I have grown strong donning the gear that keeps me alive."

"Well, obviously. The stuff weighs like a thousand pounds."

He raised an eyebrow. "That is impossible."

"No, I was just guesstimating…"

"Lady Bridgette, you have a strange way of having speech."

"I get that a lot. Most people think I'm from outer space."

Ulrick looked around uncomfortably. He was clearly intrigued by this mystery woman sitting next to him but also seemed incredibly confused, and who could blame the poor guy. She supposed she should be more careful with her speech. She certainly didn't want to scare away the one man or person she felt safe with.

"I do not know this *outer space* you speak of," he quietly grumbled.

"Yes, well, that might be a little too much information for me to explain to go along with a dinner conversation, at least for now. What about the water? Is it really as bad as they say it is in our history books?"

He almost spat his food from his mouth at the reference to the future. "We do not drink it much. Since I have no knowledge of your future world, I cannot vouch for how your tomes may reference what we drink and regarding our way of life."

"They've said it was really bad."

His brow rose. "Is it mayhap your wish to taste it to see if you would agree with your history? 'Tis but a simple matter to have a servant attend to such a request, no matter how odd it may seem." He smirked and she knew he was teasing her.

Bridgette held back a laugh. "Maybe I'd better refrain."

Ulrick's smile broadened. "A wise choice, my lady."

She leaned forward to rest her elbow on the table and put her cheek in the palm of her hand. She watched him intently. "How about family? Do you have any brothers or sisters?"

"You are most inquisitive, Lady Bridgette." He reached for his wine and peered at her over its rim.

She shrugged. "Wouldn't you be, if our situations were reversed?" she asked honestly.

"Aye, I suppose I would at that, although I must admit I may be at a loss at how to deal with such a circumstance if the opportunity presented itself," Ulrick stated. She figured the last thing this medieval knight wanted in life was to be thrown into some future world. "As to your question, I had an older brother who has perished in service to our sovereign King Henry, so I am now head of my family. I also have a younger sister and brother from my mother's second marriage whom I have not seen in many years."

"Where is home? What about your parents?"

"My home is many miles to the south, near the coast of West England. My sire passed many years ago. My mother remarried, although her second husband, too, has passed on. Since she refuses to wed for a third time, this has left her to the raising of my brother and sister alone. I send them what monies I can." He began eating his meal as if he were starving and had not already consumed half of what had been put in front of them.

She remained silent for a few minutes, wondering if perhaps she had pushed him too far. "Okay, I've got it. Mother, brother and sister living in the south, haven't been there in a while and sounds like you have no plans for a visit anytime soon. I assume you've been a vassal to Lord Dristan for a while now. Are you one of his minions? I heard he is called the Devil's Dragon and no human survives who crosses his path?"

"The servants talk too much," he muttered, almost attacking his food and most likely wanting her to change the subject.

She leaned forward so she wasn't overheard. "But are the rumors true?" she whispered with a wink, trying to keep from laughing.

If a look could pierce into her soul, then surely Ulrick's did just that. My God his eyes were so blue with a hint of steel grey coloring they were almost her undoing. She realized he had been answering her question but she didn't have the foggiest idea what he had been saying.

"What?"

"*Merde!*" he swore, wiping his mouth with the back of his sleeve before glaring at her with a frown. "I said, my lady, that since you yourself have crossed Lord Dristan's path several times today and still sit here before me jabbering away with more conversation than I am used to having at the evening meal, then you have obviously survived to tell the tale that such rumors are a falsehood!"

He began sputtering away in a language she couldn't understand. Her eye's widened when she guessed what he was speaking and a laugh escaped her lips. "Oh my God, are you speaking Normal French? That is just so incredibly cool. I never thought I'd ever hear the language aloud. Say something else."

His lips snapped shut so quickly he cut off whatever he had been muttering on about. "Nay, I will not." She gave him a pretty little pout to tease him further into possibly getting her way but he was on to her ploy. "And such a face will not sway me to further your jesting of me."

"I wasn't making fun of you, Ulrick," she remarked, feeling the heat of his stare. "I liked the way you sounded speaking it, that's all."

Bridgette heard a harrumph once more coming from her dinner companion until a sly roughish grin graced that handsome face of his. She took hold of her goblet of wine that was efficiently filled by a passing servant, and decided to leave the rest of her questions for another day. She could get used to this.

CHAPTER 14

Ulrick swung his sword with a broad smile, not that his opponent could see the satisfaction on his face through the plate of his helmet. Godfrey was improving and he had finally achieved the maneuver Ulrick had been trying to engrain into his thick skull for the past two hours. The young knight just might prove himself worthy of becoming one of Dristan's personal guards after all.

It had been a pleasurable morning, with nothing to occupy his mind but his training. No trying to look as if talk of the future did not bother him, no woman's chattering asking questions until his head hurt, and no brilliant green eyes boring into his soul. He supposed her constant speech was not so much undesirable as it was exhausting. The woman had been correct when she had declared she had a thousand questions. During their last night of supping together, he was sure he had answered mayhap half of them.

He had not seen Bridgette for the past several days, as she

had accompanied Amiria and a small contingent of guards to Habersham Abby where Amiria's sister, Sabina, had been living. He was still unclear why the abbess allowed Sabina to stay there without taking her vows, but he would leave such a matter alone. 'Twas no business of his what the young lady did with her life and whether she wished to devote her life to God... or not. This was her choice alone. Perchance she just needed time to heal. Only the good Lord above knew the complete details of what Lady Sabina had to endure after the siege of Berwyck many years ago.

He had learned Amiria and Bridgette had returned early last eve, and yet the women had not attended the evening Mass or meal. Instead, 'twas rumored they had spent the eve in Amiria's solar after seeing to her children. He was unsure how he felt about Lady Amiria taking Bridgette under her care, given the lady of the keep was not like other women he had known. Not that he would ever speak ill of her, or any other woman for that matter.

Was it possible he actually missed Bridgette since he had last seen her? A part of him waited anxiously for when she would attend the next meal. Another part prayed she had not been returned to her own time without him having a chance to bid her Godspeed. 'Twas confusing and he had attempted not to dwell on what the woman did to fill her day, or nights for that matter. He had training to see to with the young knight, who tore off his helmet, assuming they were done for the day.

He removed his own helmet and Ulrick's brow rose to silently question Godfrey's motives for a break. "Think you we are done? We have only just begun."

"Your jest is not amusing, Sir Ulrick," Godfrey proclaimed,

with a grimace. "We have been hacking away at each other since the sun came up."

"And we shall continue to do so until it sets, unless you concede and wish to leave Berwyck posthaste," Ulrick taunted, knowing the young man would never give in so easily. He was starting to admire him for his gumption to see the matter through.

"Nay, I will continue until you deem me worthy to be a part of Berwyck's garrison," Godfrey answered, shoving his helmet back upon his head. Raising his sword, he waited for Ulrick to do the same.

Instead, Ulrick sheathed his blade in the scabbard hanging from his belt. "Mayhap I will give your sword arm a rest and test how you hold up in a wrestling match. Get you to the Garrison Hall and remove your chainmail and hie yourself over to the others who will test the strength of their arms," Ulrick ordered. "I will meet you there.

"Aye, Sir Ulrick, gladly," Godfrey said, with the enthusiasm of a youth ready to prove himself with his elders.

Ulrick called out for mead and a tankard was thrust into his waiting hand. He eagerly quenched his thirst as if he was a man parched for many a day. With feet spread apart, for he would not dare sit and have Dristan chastise him for being weak, he took a moment to rest, whilst his gaze went about his comrades who were busy training.

He had fought beside many of these men and also called them friend for more years than he would care to count. Aye, 'twas true some were no longer here with him now, but that was life and to be expected. Situations and people change. Ulrick was content that his life was a daily routine he could count on to remain the same.

His eyes came to rest on none other than Lady Amiria, who was dressed as usual in her chainmail. He had never in his life met another woman who could yield a sword as she could, and he had remarked several times to Dristan that he had been lucky to find such a rare woman to call wife. His brows drew together as he peered across the lists. 'Twas odd Amiria was not showing her normal aggressive behavior with a sword in hand, despite her being with child. He took another sip of mead before almost choking on the brew knowing what appeared out of place with the scene before his very eyes.

Black hair pulled together with a leather strap swayed back and forth as the small knight twirled in a circle and met Lady Amiria's sword. 'Twas done in slow motion since 'twas apparent that said lady was teaching the other *knight* the finer points of sword play. He could not believe what he was seeing, for he knew without any doubt 'twas Lady Bridgette beneath the helmet.

He was halfway across the lists, narrowly missing several blades coming into contact with his body, before he even realized he was moving. He continued his careless stride toward the two women, only knowing he must needs reach Bridgette before she did the unthinkable and harmed herself. By *Saint Michael's Wings*, what was Lady Amiria thinking, trying to teach a lady from the future the use of a blade?

Ulrick quickened his pace and observed in dismay when Bridgette tripped and landed in an undignified heap on the ground. He ran to her side, offering his hand to assist her. A laugh of unmistakable joy burst from beneath her helmet. She took off the metal, placed it under one of her arms, and stood on her own accord.

"Thanks, Ulrick, but I've got this," she answered merrily.

"Damn, that was a blast, Amiria. Can we do it again tomorrow?"

Ulrick took her by the upper arm and watched as her eyes narrowed. "By the blessed Virgin Mary, you will not be lifting a sword any more today or any other day for that matter, Bridgette," he said with a fierce scowl. "And what is this *blast* thing you speak of?"

"Blast can mean fun... you know... something you obviously don't know anything about, since you're chastising me in front of the whole company," Bridgette replied in a huff. Her confidence was unnerving.

Amiria chuckled, whilst sheathing her own sword at her side. "I will leave you two to settle this between you," she declared, with a mischievous grin. "Bridgette, I will see you later at the evening meal."

"Thanks again, Amiria, for this and the outing. It was nice to meet your sister and also to see some of the countryside," Bridgette happily said.

Ulrick stood there, trying to get his temper in check whilst Bridgette tried to get him to loosen his hold on her. Instead, he gave her a little shake. "What did you think you were doing, lifting a sword? Do you not know you could have been hurt? The lists are no place for a woman," he bellowed, before he leaned down whispering in her ear, "and 'tis not like your *play acting* you spoke of from your world."

"And yet the lady to your own liege lord just left these very same lists," Bridgette answered, pointing in the direction of Amiria. "From what I understand, she held her own plus protected her family during the siege of *this* very castle. I applaud her courage *and* her husband for allowing her to continue to do as she pleases."

"Amiria is not your normal woman for these times," Ulrick shouted, trying to justify his anger to the lady before him.

"And neither am I." Her chin jutted out in her determination for him to see her point. She was going to be the death of him!

Dropping her helmet, she firmly took a hold of his fingers around her arm until he at last released her. He folded his arms over his chest. She then proceeded to copy his manner. Her stance would have been comical, had they not had the attention of every garrison knight attempting to show their amusement at the dispute. He would not admit aloud that her determination was to be admired, considering she barely reached to his chest. He prepared himself for a battle of wills and he was unsure if he would come out the winner.

But 'twas her eyes flashing fire that gave Ulrick the briefest glimpse of the woman's strength lying just beneath the surface. "Let's get a few things straight between us for the sake of both our sanities. First and foremost, I'm used to doing things when and where I want to. I don't need you, or anyone else's, permission if I want to take a stab at hacking away at someone with a sword in my hand," she fumed.

He could no longer remain silent. "You will not—" Ulrick began, only to clamp his lips shut when she raised her hand to stop his words.

"Second. Although I appreciate the gallantry offered with trying to get myself up from the ground, I'm perfectly capable of standing on my own two feet. I'm pretty independent where I come from," Bridgette stated, reaching behind her head to take the strap from her hair. She gave her head a shake, freeing the locks as they danced in the wind before his eyes. God... what a beauty!

"I am a knight of the realm, hence I am honor bound to

ensure you are taken care of," Ulrick replied, trying to think of anything other than wishing to feel the silkiness of her hair between his fingers.

"And I appreciate the gesture, but, again, I'm capable of taking care of myself," she reiterated, and proceeded to once again tame her hair with the leather tie.

Ulrick did everything he could not to sputter his displeasure. "Have you no one that takes care of you in this future world of yours? Surely your sire, at the very least?"

"Yes and no. My parents live clear across the country and I've been on my own for several years now," she answered, with a far off look in her brilliant green eyes. "It does make me wonder, though, how my friend Megan is dealing with my sudden disappearance. I mean… did I just cease to exist, leaving no trace of my former life? Am I on television as a missing person? Do they all think I was abducted? Are they even now looking for my body, believing I'm dead?"

Ulrick wiped at his brow. "You are very inquisitive. You have questions but I can offer you no answers, my lady. It makes my head hurt."

"Welcome to my world. Can you imagine how you would feel if the situation was reversed?"

"Nay! I do not wish to think on being trapped in a world not my own."

"You wouldn't like to be freaked out by modern technology?" Bridgette asked, then burst out into laughter with the face he must have shown her. "Never mind. I'll stop teasing you. How about if we continue on where Amiria left off?"

"Why," he said, aghast at the thought of lifting a blade toward a woman.

"To protect myself, of course," she replied with a grin, as she put on her helmet.

"I can assure you that I will protect you to the best of my ability. There is no need for you to do so yourself," Ulrick huffed.

"Then I'll learn so I can protect *your* back... in case the need ever presents itself," she declared, lifting her sword. "That is... if you're up to the challenge to spar with a mere woman.

He cursed beneath his breath at her outlandish challenge, as though his manhood was at stake if he did not endeavor to amuse her. "Then do not hold the sword thusly," he answered, going to stand behind Bridgette. He wrapped his arms around her to help her position the sword and to show her the correct handling of the blade. 'Twas almost his undoing, being this close to her, despite the metal links between them. He could sense everything about her, even when she took a breath and held it with his nearness.

And that was how Ulrick reluctantly began training with the lady from the future on the proper ways to swing a sword. *Merde...* she was really was going to be the death of him!

CHAPTER 15

Bridgette opened the door to the hut belonging to the castle's healer, Kenna, after hearing the bid to enter. The place was like no other she had seen. She wasn't sure what she expected, but it certainly wasn't the beautiful woman with long black hair busy near her hearth.

"Good day tae ye, Bridgette," Kenna said, without looking up from her task. "I have been expecting ye."

"You have?" Bridgette asked skeptically. Amiria had discreetly made mention that Kenna could *see* events before they occurred or sometimes had other visions. Although some people in her own time would swear up and down they could talk to the dead, Bridgette had always been wary of their ilk. Not necessarily because she didn't believe them, but more because there was always someone out there in the world ready to scam you if you let your guard down. Well… maybe with the exception of Zoe.

"But of course," Kenna answered, finally looking up and

waving her to enter. "Come take a seat by the fire and let me look at yer hands. 'Tis nippy outside this day, and I am certain ye could use the warmth tae take the chill from yer bones."

Bridgette didn't even try to question how Kenna knew she had injured her hands. She went to sit on a stool by the hearth. She held them out, but the woman didn't even take a glance at the blistering fingers, so she put her hands in her lap. She supposed she shouldn't have been so confident that she could just pick up a sword and start swinging it around with any sense of accuracy and not get blisters on her hands. It would take years for calluses to develop before something like that wouldn't affect her. She wasn't sure she had that much time.

The dwelling of the castle's healer wasn't overly large, but it seemed about as perfect a place as anything in Bridgette's imagination could muster up for what a healer's place would look like. She honestly couldn't identify the herbs for various uses hanging upside down from the ceiling. A fire welcomed her in the hearth where a pot had something boiling in it. Pans and utensils sat on a sideboard made of wood. The cottage's smell reminded her of the earth or the oak trees after a rainfall in the forest. It had a very calming effect on her.

"I am sure they must pain ye," Kenna said softly, as she began taking various herbs hanging from the ceiling to place them in a mortar. She picked up a nearby pestle and began grinding them into powder.

"Yes, but please do not tell Ulrick. I would hate for him to think this was his doing and not my own fault for my stupidity in trying to impress him," Bridgette said, trying to remember that she shouldn't be using contractions when she spoke. It might be okay with those close to Ulrick, including Dristan and

Amiria, but she wasn't sure it would be in her best interest for others to learn her origins.

Kenna stopped her task as she peered at her from over the table with raised brows. It was almost as if she read her mind. She then gave her a bright and friendly smile. "'Twill be our secret."

"I appreciate your kindness."

Reaching for a thick cloth, Kenna took hold of the pot hanging over the fire and poured water into the mortar on the table. She returned the heavy kettle back to the hook over the fire before she began mixing whatever the concoction was again until she set it on the edge of the table. Reaching for a stool, Kenna moved it next to Bridgette and began examining her hands with a grimace. "Do not thank me too quickly, Bridgette. I am most sure 'twill not take long for Ulrick tae figure out for himself as tae the extent of yer injuries. He is most astute, much like my own husband, Geoffrey. I cannot hide much from that man, and I am the one with the gift of second sight."

"You really can see things before they happen?"

"Aye, but not all things, although I do not make such information public knowledge. 'Twould be costly, if such information fell into the wrong hands, much like yer own situation, I am afraid."

Kenna stood once more, and Bridgette followed the woman about the room with her eyes while Kenna collected some clean cloths and began tearing them into strips. Once more seated, she took the paste she had made and began smoothing it onto Bridgette's torn skin. The effect was immediate, as the blisters at last felt a bit of relief from the previous stinging.

"You know where I'm from," Bridgette said, as a statement

instead of a question, since it seemed obvious the woman before her knew her deepest secret.

"Aye, that I do. Ye are not the first woman tae come a greater distance than could be traveled on either a ship or horse. Ye will not be the last," Kenna answered as she began to bandage Bridgette's fingers and hands.

"I won't be? How do you know?" Bridgette asked, feeling there was no need to hide the way she normally spoke in front of this woman.

Kenna smiled. "Suffice tae say in the years tae come, Berwyck will lose many a great knight who will venture on tae their place of birth tae take over the titles they have disregarded over the years. They have ventured for fame and glory with the Devil's Dragon for many a year and their departure have been a long time in coming."

"I understand Sir Rolf and Amiria's grandmother have had a hand in introducing a couple of recent visitors, including myself."

"Aye, this is true, and yet another came of her own accord, but I will leave the telling of that story tae those who wish to share it. Amiria's grandmother may show herself tae ye at some point when she is ready. Do not be afraid of her, for she has yer best interest at heart."

"Wow! I really can't believe I'm having this conversation, let alone I'm sitting here in the twelfth century."

"I will assume this *wow* is a form of expression from whence ye hail, but I will have tae agree with ye. 'Tis a most unbelievable tale that could land ye in much trouble. Take heed that ye only share such information with those ye can trust," Kenna cautioned.

"I'll be sure to watch my speech," Bridgette answered,

having figured out she might be burned at the stake or worse if someone with ill intent learned of her origins.

"'Tis good that ye have *performed* in yer previous life, much like the bards who come tae Lord Dristan's hall tae sing their songs or tell their stories tae amuse us. 'Twill be in yer best interests tae continue using our speech except when alone with Ulrick," Kenna said, finishing her task. She stood and began cleaning her hands.

Bridgette flexed her fingers and was amazed how much better they felt. She also stood, getting ready to leave. "I'll remember and thanks again for the aid. My hands feel much better."

"'Ye are most welcome." Kenna reached over to the sideboard again and then handed Bridgette a pair of softly made leather gloves. "Please take these. They may hide yer injuries from Ulrick, but for how long I can only venture tae guess."

"I'm sure he'll figure it out pretty quickly. Nothing seems to pass him by," Bridgette replied, as if she had known the man all her life.

"He is most astute," Kenna repeated but tilted her head while she gave Bridgette an odd look. "I mayhap should not ask this, but I canna help myself. How is Zoe?"

Bridgette swayed before falling back into the chair she had been sitting in. "Zoe?" she asked in a hushed and strained whisper.

"Aye, Zoe," Kenna said with a soft smile. She is my granddaughter… or she will be in yer future time."

"You know of Zoe," Bridgette said in awe. "S-she was f-fine the last time I saw her. D-do y-you see her, too?"

"Only in visions from time tae time. She came tae me right before Lady Jade fell through *Time* this past Christmas." She beamed as if Bridgette should have figured out what had happened to a lady she had only met once.

"Jade! Jade is here at Berwyck, too?" Bridgette couldn't believe someone else she knew was close by. She stood up, ready to head to the door. "I've got to find her!"

Kenna came and took her elbow before she could leave. "Slow down, Bridgette," she said, shaking her head. "I knew I should have kept quiet but I had tae know. And, nay, Jade does not live here at Berwyck. She and Sir Thomas live north in Scotland."

"Oh... that's too bad. It would have been nice to have someone to talk to who experienced something similar to me." Bridgette couldn't hide her disappointment.

"Then ye must needs have speech with Lady Ella. She is married tae Sir Killian who is Lady Amiria's uncle of sorts."

"And Lady Ella is here at Berwyck?" she asked.

"But of course. Where else would the lady live, since she and Killian are now wed?"

"I'll seek her out and see if she'll speak to me," Bridgette replied, feeling a sense of comfort knowing she might have answers to some of her questions.

"Ye have much in common, at least as far as traveling through time is concerned," Kenna said. "And as for the Lady Jade... I am most certain she will make herself known to you at some point. Her husband Thomas was once Lady Amiria's guardsman and called Berwyck home. They are sure to come for a visit to see you."

"Thank you again for all your help," Bridgette turned to leave, but paused at the door. "May I ask you a question?" At Kenna's nod she continued. "Was I brought here to be with Ulrick?"

If a person's face could light up, it was Kenna's. "What do you think, dear?"

Bridgette gave her a nod. There wasn't really any answer to give her. She already knew within her heart her reason for being here. She could only ponder if Ulrick had the same premonition. With a smile, she left Kenna's dwelling and shielded her eyes from the brightness of the sunlight. Looking out into the inner bailey, she shouldn't have been surprised to see Godfrey standing there as if he had been waiting for her. She shivered as though it was really Brad pestering her across eight hundred years of time.

He strode forward and Bridgette could see that he was confident she would find him appealing. She was wary of him, but she didn't want to judge the man based on her past experience with a look-a-like.

"My lady," Godfrey said with a bow.

She curtsied. "Good day to you, Sir Godfrey," she softly murmured.

"You were impressive in the lists this day. Besides the Lady Amiria, I have never come across another woman who had such a desire to learn the art of sword play."

"It may come in handy someday. You never know when I might have the need to defend myself."

"But that is why you have us knights here to protect you. Surely 'twill not be necessary for you to lift a sword, my lady. Such a delicate flower as yourself should leave the fighting to us men," Godfrey urged, taking another step closer.

Bridgette stepped back rolling her eyes. *Delicate flower*, indeed. "I am not like most women, I am afraid. Besides, I am certain Sir Ulrick will come to my aid if the need arises."

Godfrey's brow rose. "I see…" he said, as though there was a bitter taste in his mouth with her confession. "I had no knowledge that you and Sir Ulrick had come to an understanding between you, and that you had pledged your troth to one another."

"We haven't," Bridgette blurted out forgetting her pattern of speech. "I mean, we have not announced this as yet."

"Then there is hope that you might still consider me as a suitor," Godfrey said with a wide grin.

Bridgette shook her head. "I do not think so."

"You know, Ulrick is not as good at sword fighting as I am" he said, with a crooked cocky grin.

Bridgette's laugher bubbled forth, since she had already seen Ulrick's sword techniques, and he was a master at them. "You may not think so, but he is good at other stuff," she retorted hotly. "I gotta go."

"The way you sometimes talk confuses me. Why do you have speech like that?"

She was so stupid for letting her anger get the best of her. "I am from abroad," Bridgette declared, hoping such an answer would stop his assessment of her. With a toss of her head, she cursed herself for quickly falling back into the routine of normal twenty-first century speech. *Idiot!* How could she forget Kenna telling her to be careful but an instant ago? Bridgette really needed to be careful about how she spoke when in public. She was already failing. She went to move passed Godfrey, but he stepped in front of her to block her path.

She widened her stance and was about to give a nasty retort when she saw her knight coming to her rescue. He just didn't realize he was about to do so, and she was more than happy to have Ulrick put Godfrey in his place.

CHAPTER 16

Ulrick rose from the tub whilst a squire poured rinsing water over his head. The lad finished and stepped down from the stool to hand him a drying cloth. Ulrick thanked the boy, dismissing him. The lad gave a curt bow and hastily left the chamber. Rubbing the cloth over his furred chest and the rest of body, he went to his bed and began donning his attire.

He paused momentarily when he reached for the tunic he had chosen to wear this eve. 'Twas one of his finest and he wondered if Bridgette would notice the richness of the blue fabric. He was not one to boast, but he wanted to impress her as much as she had done him this day on the lists.

Aye, impress him she did and who would have thought a woman from the future could wield a sword passably well. *Guard his back indeed*, he mused with a deep chuckle. Well, if someone was going to watch it, he would not mind if 'twas the fair lady herself. She did remarkably well, considering how she attempted to hide the fact her hands must be smarting toward the end of their training.

She had laughed when he asked if she had had enough for this day. He should have listened to the inner voice and let her save face by saying he needed to see to Godfrey's training. Yet, he had also wanted to see just how far she was willing to push her limits. He would not have expected her to last yet another hour.

Ulrick did not miss the fact Bridgette sought out Kenna's hut afterwards nor would he forget to take extra care with her apparent need for adventure. Aye, she was a kindred soul, wanting to enjoy every minute of her fall into the twelfth century. To Ulrick, this was just the life he led daily but, to Bridgette, everything was to be enjoyed to the fullest potential.

Your lady is in need of your assistance, Ulrick. Go to her and quickly.

Rolf's voice came inside his head, and he hastily threw his tunic over his head, reached for his belt holding his sword, and began racing out of his chambers and down the turret stairs. He had no idea of where he should be looking for said lady until a premonition overtook him and he headed out of the keep.

His eyes quickly adjusted to the sunlight, where he espied his lady having speech with none other than Sir Godfrey. As least he could say the young man had good taste, and yet Bridgette did not look pleased with the attention she was receiving.

Ulrick came forward with a short bow. "My lady, all is well since you went to Kenna's hut?" he asked, mildly curious about how she would play out her ploy of seeing the castle's healer.

"Oh, aye, Sir Ulrick. Mistress Kenna and I were just getting acquainted."

His brow raised at her obviously falsehood, not that he

would call the woman out in the presence of another. "If you insist."

"Why else would I need her?" she inquired, although she nervously shuffled from one foot to the other.

An amused grin momentarily lit his face, but he would let the issue go, for the moment, at least. He turned his attention to the young knight, who had obviously been unknowingly annoying the lady. "And what of you, Godfrey? Are you in need of Berwyck's healer?" Ulrick was not pleased that the youth watched Bridgette most intently.

"Nay. I had but hoped Lady Bridgette would favor me with a dance this eve after we sup," Godfrey finally replied. His look of longing was not missed by Ulrick, and he did all in his power not to growl out his frustration. Yet, he did not have an understanding with Bridgette, so there was only one reply he could offer the man.

"I am sure the lady will oblige you but, as you can see, she must needs change so she may join the festivities."

"I look forward to our dance together this eve, my lady," Godfrey beamed, knowing he had gotten what he desired. Time alone with a beautiful woman. He made his bow and then departed.

Ulrick extended his hand toward the lady. It was swiftly grasped until he tucked her hand into the crook of his elbow. Bridgette winced, and Ulrick could only imagine the state of her hands that were hidden from his view by the soft leather gloves she wore. He gazed down upon the fair maiden, who only offered him a small smile. They began to make their way silently into the keep and Ulrick continued escorting her to her chamber on the upper fourth floor.

He opened her door for her and waited for Bridgette to enter.

Instead, she turned, practically staying close within his embrace. She seemed to be struggling with what she wanted to say and, when she raised her face to him, Ulrick swore he lost a bit of his heart.

"Why did you say I would dance with Godfrey this evening?"

Ulrick was uncomfortable since he had no idea why he had given the lad hope when he himself wished to occupy her every moment. "I am sure many a knight will ask such a request of you."

"And what about you?" she whispered, taking a step closer to him.

There was so much hope in her tone that Ulrick smiled. "Most assuredly, I will be amongst them."

Bridgette smiled brightly. "You may normally appear rough around the edges, but I think there is a soft side to you that you don't let too many people see."

"Soft?" Ulrick scoffed. "There is nothing soft about me."

She surprised him by reaching up to gently caress his cheek. "We shall see," she replied softly, before leaving him there alone in the passageway, staring at the closed door.

His hand actually went to knock so they could finish their conversation before he balled his hand into a fist and marched back down the stairs to await the evening meal. He would require a good deal of wine to dull the ache that suddenly found its way around his weary heart.

Bridgette twirled around her chamber, wishing for the hundredth time that she had a full-length mirror so she could get the entire effect of the dress she was wearing. Where it came from, she could only guess. She would like to think Ulrick had some hand in it, since the blue of the fabric would match the tunic he was wearing when he came to her rescue just a short while ago. The sleeves were long with flowing fabric at the elbow that reached the floor. A white under tunic barely concealed the cleavage of her breasts at the scooped neckline. And she could breathe, thank the good Lord above, since she didn't have to wear a corset and stays in order to fit into the garment!

Her hair had been braided. One of the young girls, who had performed such a labor of love to tame her tresses, had woven flowers and matching blue ribbons into it. A golden chain hung low on her hips and at the end of the metal's length a blue stone winked at her from the firelight of the chamber. She felt like a medieval princess waiting for her handsome prince. Surely, she wasn't too far off the mark, knowing one knight in particular was waiting for her downstairs.

Guessing it was about the right hour for dinner, or the evening meal, Bridgette gave her hair one final pat and exited the chamber. Looking both ways into the passageway, she headed toward the turret stairs but halted with a sudden premonition. She turned back in the direction of her room and caught the slightest glimpse of Amiria's grandmother waving her on, as if she approved of Bridgette's attire, before she disappeared once more. If the woman ever fully showed herself to her again, she would have a lot of questions for her.

All in good time, dearie. All in good time. The voice of the lady of her musings popped into her head, causing Bridgette to stumble. She wasn't at all sure she would get used to that happening.

Before she changed her mind and ran like a scared rabbit back to her room, she descended the circular stairs to see none other than Ulrick waiting at the bottom step. His back was to her while he watched those gathering inside the hall. Quietly, she snuck up on him but remained on the second to last stair to give her some height while she covered his eyes from behind.

"Guess who?" she whispered into his ear and felt a rush of excitement when those strange little currents rushed between them. She hadn't meant to get that close to him, knowing ladies didn't just throw themselves at men in this age, but all the same her chest came in contact with his back when he took hold of her arms. There was no mistaking the connection between them, especially when he didn't have his chainmail on. She could feel and sense everything about him when he turned, including the warmth that shot up her body like a fiery shooting star to explode high up in the heavens. Her heart flipped, since the stairs allowed her to remain eye level with her knight. *My God, he is so handsome*, she thought trying to slow down her heart rate. She failed.

His gaze told her he was perplexed by the game she played that he clearly didn't understand. Vivid blue eyes met green, and if this was the last moment she would be standing in the twelfth century, she would remember this very instant for the rest of her life. Nothing prepared her for the emotions sweeping through her like the wildest of hurricanes. Fear of the unknown pleasantly mixed with a measure of certainty that she could search the world a hundred times and more, and still know within her heart that she belonged with this man no matter the time he lived in.

And still they held their silence as they searched and saw

into one another's souls. Surely it was there for all to see that love, if they allowed it into their hearts, would envelop them like a secure cocoon and entwine their fates together. Ulrick was so close, Bridgette wanted to throw herself into his arms and kiss him, although she was sure that would have shocked him clear down to his very medieval boots.

"Glad tidings to you, *mademoiselle*," Ulrick murmured. The deep husky baritone of his voice caused Bridgette's skin to rise up with goose bumps.

"Good evening to you, Ulrick," Bridgette replied, with a hushed whisper. She was almost certain that any longer response might cause her to become tongue tied and she didn't want to appear like a simpleton or some lovestruck schoolgirl. She wasn't sure how she'd ever get through supper with him looking at her in such a heated fashion.

A catcall from someone in the hall broke the spell between them and Ulrick cleared his throat before taking a step back, finally showing his normally gruff exterior. "Shall we sup?" he asked extending his arm for her to take.

"Yes, of course," she answered, with a small smile. She placed her hand upon his, and they began making their way into the hall with the others who were already present and heavy into their conversations and cups.

So, this was how it felt to be a lady and have one of the most handsome men she had ever met give his fullest attention only to her. Bridgette was glowing from the sheer thrill of being on his arm as if she, instead of anyone else, was a woman to be treasured. She witnessed some of Amiria's ladies begin to whisper and she wondered which one of them fancied herself in love with Ulrick. After another brief glance in their direction,

Bridgette came to the conclusion that it was a blonde. If the woman's gaze shot daggers, they'd be aimed straight into her heart... or back. She didn't recall the woman's name, but apparently they wouldn't be friends anytime soon.

They came before the main table that seated Dristan, Amiria, and his personal guardsmen. Bridgette dropped down into a deep curtsey at the same time Ulrick offered them a knightly bow. Dristan waved them to their place at the table, while a rush of conversation suddenly picked up speed as the food began to arrive. After Ulrick helped her with her chair, she once more took in each and every detail of the progression of the meal being served before the hungry knights and ladies dining at the lower tables. It was an impressive sight to see so much food arriving, and, at almost the same time, beginning to be consumed by the men with a gusto not seen in her time. Apparently, the saying *"no one is going to take your food away from you"* didn't apply here. Best to grab what you could before it was gone, although it appeared there was a never-ending supply of game that continued to be brought forth from the kitchens.

Bridgette at last turned her attention to the trencher that was being piled high with an assortment of beef, venison, fish and what could possibly be turnips. It smelled heavenly and maybe she could understand the men's appetites, for she herself had worked up a hunger with her swordplay today. She only worried what Ulrick would say about the gloves she wore. As if sensing her mood and thought, he waited for her to begin eating before he partook of even a morsel.

She reached for a two-prong fork set on the table and stabbed at a piece of turnip, hoping it didn't drop in her lap before it reached her mouth. It wasn't that she wasn't skilled with the utensil, it was just that it was hard for her to hold anything in her hands because of the blisters from her carelessness earlier in the day. She should have quit with her attempts to learn how to swing a sword with Ulrick, but she couldn't resist staying with him as along as he allowed her on the lists.

She managed to take a bite of food but Ulrick continued to intently watch her, and she knew he had to be hungry since she heard his stomach rumble in protest that he wasn't eating.

"Is something wrong?" she asked knowing what was about to come.

"Aye," he said gruffly holding out his hand for her to take. "Let me assess what damage you have done this day."

"What damage?" she asked shyly, afraid of the roar that would surely shake the rafters once he got a good look at her injuries.

She swore a growl of outrage came from his lips. "Do not play games with me, my lady. You know that of which I speak. Now let me see your hands," he answered, brooking no disobedience to his order.

With a heavy sigh, Bridgette began to take off the gloves, but he would have none of it and began to gently peel off the leather. He swore at the bandages before lifting one of the edges to peer beneath. "Have you no sense, woman? You should have stopped our training earlier, before your poor fingers and palms came to such a state."

"Don't be angry with me, Ulrick," she said warily. "I was having fun and didn't want to stop."

"Next time, you will listen to me and concede when I say you have done enough for the day."

"I was trying to impress you," she blurted and could feel the blush rushing to her cheeks. Good Lord, it was like an inferno in this room. Ulrick continued his administrations, gently putting her gloves back over her fingertips.

He smoothed his thumb across the top of her hand before raising it to his lips. Never once breaking eye contact, he at last answered her. "You did..."

And with those two small words, she was lost...

CHAPTER 17

Ulrick sat back in his chair and continued perusing the fair maiden seated next to him whilst the evening meal approached its end. He was surprised how well Bridgette had adjusted to being in his world, considering the centuries between her own and the one she now faced. Over eight hundred years was a vast amount of time, but she acted as if she had been born and raised here.

Her banter was infectious, her wit had him laughing as hard as the rest of those seated near enough to hear her words, which included the lord and lady of Berwyck. Aye, if a friendship was in the making, then Lady Amiria and Lady Bridgette were to become true sisters of the heart.

Ulrick was not sure if such an anomaly was good or bad, not that he would ever gainsay his liege's lady. Amiria was head-strong, sometimes stubborn to a fault, but also one of the kindest women Ulrick had ever met. He had a feeling Bridgette would be of the same ilk… God help him.

Before long, the tables began to be cleared and the castle's minstrels started to tune their instruments. He was about to ask Bridgette if she would like to dance when Godfrey bowed before them extending his hand toward the lady.

"I believe you gave me the honor of this dance, my lady," Godfrey commented dryly, all but taunting Ulrick with the tasty treat that was about to be swept away from his side. Since he himself had foolishly given the young knight permission, he could in no way take back his hastily spoken words... unless Bridgette declined Godfrey's invitation. Her next words had him cursing inside his head at his own stupidity.

"Excuse me," she said rising from the table. Before she left him, she placed her hand upon his shoulder and leaned over to whisper in his ear. "I wish you hadn't given Sir Godfrey permission for a dance."

There was some consolation to his injured pride that her words confirmed the lady would rather stay in his company. "Has he offended you?" Ulrick answered instead, ready to come to the lady's defense if necessary.

"No. It's something else."

"Explain..." His words trailed off as he awaited her answer.

"Later," she replied. Patting his shoulder, she proceeded, none too happily it seemed, considering the grimace she attempted to hide, to join the others who began to form a circle in the middle of the floor. Ulrick's mood soured, wondering what could possibly be troubling the lady where Sir Godfrey was concerned. The man was full of pride but, on the whole, Ulrick did not fear that Hawkins was a threat to Bridgette or the people under Lord Dristan's care.

He carefully watched the pair as the knight of his musings began to show Bridgette the pattern to the dance. Again,

Ulrick observed nothing in the younger man's actions that were anything other than courteous. He never once placed his hand any place other than where it should be, which gave Ulrick no need to demand satisfaction. Nay, Sir Godfrey conducted himself as any knight would when dancing with a lady, especially one who had been taken under his liege lord's wing. But 'twas clear Bridgette was uncomfortable. Ulrick could only ponder what was causing the look upon her lovely visage, as if she were wishing the dance would come quickly to an end.

The music at last faded as the final notes echoed throughout the hall. Before Ulrick could rise to claim Bridgette, he saw Bertram making his way across the stone floor. He gave the man a glaring warning from across the room but, given the smirk of satisfaction on his comrade's face, he undoubtedly had no intention of heeding such a silent command.

Ulrick reached for his goblet of wine and drank deeply, although it had no taste whilst his eyes wandered around the room, watching Bridgette's every move. A laugh erupted from Lady Amiria sitting next to him and he turned his attention toward her. She was watching him intently.

"I fear I remember another similar situation with one of Dristan's knights years ago," she murmured gaily.

"You mean Riorden de Deveraux?"

"Aye. Are you out of sorts with the lady?" she asked, taking a sip of her own wine.

"Nay, I am not."

Setting her chalice down, Amiria turned in her seat to watch him. "I thought mayhap you had a falling out, given the frown upon your brow. I have said this once before to Riorden so I will repeat my words to you... if you do not want others to dance with Lady Bridgette, then you should go and dance with her yourself," she declared calmly.

As another tune came to an end, Drake now came to claim the lady with a flourished bow, bringing a smile to Bridgette's countenance. Now that she was no longer dancing with Godfrey, her whole demeanor had changed as she all but threw herself into the dancing. She learned the steps just as quickly as she had been learning everything else, with an exuberant amount of energy surrounding her.

"There is no need to be jealous, Ulrick," Amiria said, as though she knew the lady's heart.

"I am not jealous," Ulrick replied, taking another sip of wine and watching Bridgette over the rim of the cup.

"Then go to her. I think she would much rather be dancing with you than any other."

Ulrick finally rose, coming to the same conclusion. He bowed. "My thanks for the wise words of wisdom and your counsel, Lady Amiria."

"You are most welcome, Sir Ulrick, although I am sure I said nothing you yourself have not been thinking. Enjoy the eve," Amiria declared, trying to hide her smile behind her chalice.

"My liege, if you will excuse me?" Ulrick asked.

"Aye, of course, Ulrick," Dristan answered with a wave of his hand.

Taking his leave, he made his way around the table even as the last chords to another tune came to an end. He watched in amusement when Godfrey came from the opposite side of the room to attempt another dance with Bridgette. They reached her at the same time, and Ulrick made his bow to her before turning to the younger knight.

"Godfrey, I believe you have already had the honor. This

dance is *mine*," Ulrick declared, all but claiming the woman as his own. Godfrey looked askance at Bridgette, but she only gave the man a small smile before placing her hand within Ulrick's.

"Of course, Sir Ulrick," Godfrey said, before excusing himself to go stand near the hearth, defeated in his quest for the lady's attention.

The music once more began with a soft and pleasing melody. Ulrick began showing Bridgette the steps, but they could have been alone in the hall instead of it being filled with the others with whom they came in contact as the dance progressed. They met in the middle of a circle. Their hands touched whilst strange tingling sensations coursed through his fingertips. They broke apart only to dance one on one before Ulrick took Bridgette about the waist and lifted her high. She slid down the length of him and he swore he felt every glorious inch of her even through the linen of their clothing. She moistened her lips and Ulrick wanted to lean down and taste the sweetness that surely would drive him mad.

What the devil had come over him that a mere woman he had only just met could draw such a reaction from him? 'Twas those damn *Time* fairies meddling in people's lives when a person did not wish for the interruption.

"*'Tis nothing tae do with fairies, ye stubborn, man,*" came a woman's voice inside his head. "*Just enjoy the gift ye have been given or else she may be taken away if ye dinnae accept it!*"

His eyes widened at words that would have torn his heart asunder. Aye, and mayhap that was the reality of the problem he faced. Thoughts of Bridgette leaving him left him in a foul mood, as if his fate with the lady had already been decided whether he willed it or not.

As he glanced away from Bridgette's smiling face, he caught

the briefest glimpse of Amiria's grandmother. She gave him a saucy smile, waved her finger at him as if in warning to heed her words, and then disappeared from view.

"Is everything alright, Ulrick," Bridgette asked as they stood together in each other's arms, the dance all but forgotten.

Her words brought him back from his musings and he could only stare in wonder at the woman before him. Those mesmerizing green eyes of hers were certainly going to be his undoing.

"Aye, I am well. Why do you ask?" he questioned her.

"One moment I swear you were going to kiss me and the next you're frowning. Obviously, something has upset you," she answered. Her eyes were etched in concern that perchance she was the reason for his sudden change in his demeanor.

"'Tis nothing," he grumbled, until he realized she continued to intently watch him. A sudden rush of excitement filled his body with thoughts of kissing the lady who gently rubbed his arm with her thumb, as though to comfort him.

"You don't appear as if it's nothing, Ulrick," she said in a hushed tone before she, too, began to frown. "Have I done something wrong? I don't want people to think I don't fit in here in the twelfth century."

"My lady, you have done nothing to make anyone believe otherwise," he replied confirming his thoughts but a moment ago, "unless 'tis your speech if others are close enough to hear your conversation."

Her eyes widened before she looked around to see if she had been overheard. With no one paying attention, she stepped closer. "That's a relief. So why do you continue to look as if you're ready to hack away at someone with your sword?" she replied lowering her voice.

A snort escaped his lips. "I have no idea what you are talking about, my lady."

A couple bumped into them reminding Ulrick that they had all but forgotten they were standing in the middle of the revelers with no participation on their part to continue the patterns of the dance.

Bridgette tugged on the sleeve of his tunic. "Come with me," she all but demanded.

Ulrick hid his smile at the fierceness of her command. He followed, not knowing her objective. She did not lead them far, only to an alcove near the kitchen entrance. They were certainly in view of anyone who cared to see them but hidden enough that they could have a private word together.

She crossed her arms over her chest as if she mimicked his own stance when he was observing the training of the knights under his care. "Well? Were you going to kiss me or was that all my imagination?"

He was momentarily startled at her question and could barely hide his amusement. "My... you are a bold one, are you not, Lady Bridgette?" he murmured, watching her carefully.

She came to him, stepping so close he swore he could hear her heart beating within her chest. "You didn't answer my question... did you want to kiss me?"

He watched her tongue sweep across the seam of her lips before she bit her lower one. Ulrick almost swept her into his arms to ensure this woman was kissed... thoroughly.

"I cannot kiss you here in the middle of the hall under the watchful eyes of our liege lord, Bridgette. He would have my head sitting on a pike outside his gate for such an atrocity, especially since I am more than aware you are under his care."

Her laugh was bright before she answered him. "I hardly think a kiss is worthy of you being beheaded, Ulrick."

"You have not been here long enough to truly know the Devil's Dragon. 'Tis more than enough reason in his eyes. You are his ward and under his protection," he reminded her, even as she moved closer to him.

"I don't want to be under his protection," she murmured, smoothing the fabric of his tunic. "I want to be under yours."

"Such a confession is going to be my undoing," he growled out, as he felt a part of him stir to life with her confession.

"I suspect it'll be mine as well," she said honestly. Her seductive smile caused his body to heat with a burning desire to make her his in every way. "Since I suppose I cannot fault you on your truly chivalrous nature, which is completely refreshing by the way, meet me up on the parapet at midnight. The dancing will be over by then and we can have a quiet word together, just the two of us."

Before he could comment, she stood on the tips of her toes whilst pulling on the fabric of his tunic, causing him to lean down. Bridgette surprised him when she placed a gentle kiss upon his cheek. She left him standing there, completely dazed, whilst she returned to the dancing. God help him, but that woman was going to drive him insane.

CHAPTER 18

Bridgette pulled the hood of her cape close around her head before opening the turret door. A blast of cold night air met her face, carrying the distinct salty smell of the ocean, invisible in the distance. Taking a deep breath, she made her way toward the battlement wall and up the stairs leading to the narrow parapet.

Disappointment filled her when she didn't see Ulrick already there. Considering his words about her being *bold*, perhaps she shouldn't be surprised. Yes… she knew she was taking her fate into her own hands when she asked if he wanted to kiss her. Yes… she probably knew deep down inside what his answer would be. She hadn't been wrong when he declined in the middle of the hall. But she swore he had wanted to kiss her, and she was more than ready for him to do just that! She was a modern woman used to taking care of herself stuck in medieval England where women had very little say on how their lives would be lived. Surely a kiss wouldn't be too out of line and cause much trouble?

She shook her head. When she had kissed his cheek earlier, her lips had tingled from the contact of his skin. Her heart had soared along with her body, coming alive for the very first time as never before. She wanted to see what was happening between them because of their odd connection. For heaven's sake, she had crossed *Time* for this man! Good or bad, Bridgette had a gut feeling they were bound to one another, as though God had righted a wrong that they had been born in the different centuries. She just knew they were meant to be together. Now, she could only wonder if Ulrick felt the same.

Just thinking his name made her warm all over... and she meant, *all over!* She smiled as memories of their day together on the lists merged with the urgings of her heart. She had never wanted a man as much as she wanted Ulrick, and she supposed she would have some explaining to do at some point in their relationship that she wasn't a virgin. Deep down Bridgette knew he was feeling the same way, which was exactly why she asked him to meet her here. In the dark... with only the moonlight to shine down upon them.

She waited another fifteen minutes with only her own thoughts rambling inside her head. Obviously, since he hadn't joined her, she had made a horrific mistake. She wondered how she would redeem herself in his eyes with the rising of the sun. Maybe she wasn't fitting in as well as she thought she had. Since she had learned that other women had previously made their way to Berwyck from the future, Bridgette had thought Ulrick would be used to them showing up unexpectedly. But she couldn't expect a medieval knight to be completely accustomed to a woman who spoke her own mind and did as she pleased.

Or could she? Lord Dristan certainly didn't seem to mind that his wife was more than just a lady who gave him his offspring.

She turned to leave, ready to find her bed very much alone, when the turret door squeaked open. She smiled when she saw Ulrick making his way toward her. My God... would she ever get over how overwhelming his entire presence was? He was larger than life, in her opinion, with his dark red cape billowing in the breeze along with that long black hair when he approached. She was dying inside to feel its length running through her fingers.

"You came," she whispered in a breathy tone and she at once realized how fast her heart was hammering away inside her chest. She was excited and scared all at the same time while she tilted her head back to see his face. She felt so tiny next to this giant of a man, who must be well over six feet tall.

"Aye."

Bridgette searched his face, waiting for more of a reply but he appeared unsure of himself and that was entirely out of character of the man she had come to know.

"You didn't want to?" she couldn't help herself from asking.

"I am uncertain if this is wise, Lady Bridgette. Lord Dristan—"

She placed her fingertips on his mouth. "Let me worry about Lord Dristan," she replied, stepping closer.

His brow rose at her statement. "You have no idea what you are asking of me when I defy my liege lord by being alone here with you."

"I just wanted some time with just the two of us, Ulrick. Is that too much to ask?" She took hold of his arms, and he placed his hands gently on her waist. "I promise I won't bite... much."

She gave him what she hoped was a wicked wink. A deep

chuckle erupted from him, and his smile brightened her whole mood.

"I hardly know what to reply after such a comment. You are a feisty one, to be sure, Lady Bridgette."

"I just know what I want," she replied with a sincere heart.

"And what is that exactly?" he asked pulling her fully into his body.

"You have to ask?" She moved her palms to rest on his chest. One hand continued upward until she fingers brushed over the back of his head feeling the softness of his hair before settling on his neck. She began a gentle message with small circular motions and heard a soft moan escape him.

"Aye," came a strained reply.

"You are a man of little words sometimes. Do you know that?"

"If I am going to be damned for my actions, then I must needs know your mind. What *do* you want, Bridgette?" He asked, again ignoring her comment, but she could tell that whatever control he was briefly holding onto where she was concerned, it was about to break.

"What do I want? You... I want *you*, Ulrick" She let her answer linger in the space between them, but she didn't have to wait long for his nonverbal reply.

His arms tighten around her waist, lifting her up and bringing them chest to chest. And in that one brief moment, their heartbeats fused as one. As she stared up into those mesmerizing blue-grey eyes, the reflection from the stars above were twinkling in their depths. Her gaze was drawn to the sensual chiseled lines of his mouth. His lips turned up with a slow roguish grin before swooping down to take full possession of her. A gasp of surprise gave him what he wanted when his tongue dipped inside her mouth to dance with her own while their bodies all but melted together as one. She lost all thought of anything else but this man who claimed her. Bridgette had released Ulrick from whatever restraints he had been holding onto and she was delighted he was equally moved to finally share their first kiss.

A hushed moan escaped her when his lips moved from her mouth to place a trail of soft kisses as he went from her cheek to her neck. His teeth nibbled at the lobe of her ear and the warmth of his breath was almost her undoing.

Taking hold of his cheeks, she all but demanded another kiss in her attempts to take back control of their moment together. But who was she kidding? She lost any attempt of self-control the moment Ulrick stepped through the turret portal.

Their kiss continued for several more minutes—an exploration of two missing souls who had finally found one another. It was as binding as if they had already promised themselves an eternity together... at least in Bridgette's mind.

The chink of chainmail with the changing of the battlement guards brought their kisses to an end. Bridgette gulped in air in her attempt to calm her breathing, but she wasn't sure if she would ever be able to breath normally again... at least whenever Ulrick was in her presence.

He held out his hand for her to take... a gesture of understanding between them to continue what they had just started. Or so Bridgette thought. She gladly placed her own hand in his warm one.

"Come with me," he said, and began escorting her off the parapet. They set off down the winding turret stairwell, but Bridgette was surprised when they stopped on the fourth floor where her chamber was, along with those of the Berwyck family.

She thought he would proceed to his room on the third floor, where most of Lord Dristan's personal guard resided instead of the garrison hall. But if he wished to continue in her bedchamber instead of his, Bridgette wouldn't complain.

Ulrick opened her door and as she slipped inside, she turned with a bright smile on her face only for that same smile to fade when she saw he still stood in the passageway. Confused, she quickly crossed the distance and stood in the portal.

"You're not coming in?"

"Nay."

"But why not? I thought you wanted to continue on with—"

"'Tis not that I do not wish to be with you in every way, Lady Bridgette, but—"

"But what?" Her voice was louder than she expected, proving to herself at least how disappointed she was. "I want to be with you. I thought you felt the same."

Ulrick moved slightly into the chamber but still not far enough inside to shut the door. His hand reached out to caress her cheek and she leaned into the warmth of his palm. His hand then skimmed around to her neck, and he gently pulled her forward to place a soft kiss upon her already swollen lips.

"I will not defile you while my liege lord is but several doors down this very corridor, my lady," he said quietly, while his thumb once more caressed her cheek.

"Defile? Could you please rephrase that word? Making love is hardly sullying my reputation, Ulrick. Remember… I'm a modern woman."

"Aye, you are a woman from the future but you best remember that you are no longer in a time and place where your actions do not have consequences," he warned, with narrowed eyes.

She placed her hand upon his chest and gazed up into his determined face. "But I thought you wanted us to be together."

"Aye, I do but at the right time and place. I make you my vow that we will be together."

"You do realize you're making me a promise at midnight, don't you?" she smiled up into his face.

"Does the time of night or day make a difference when you make such a vow?"

"Oh, yes! A promise made at midnight is like sealing your fate to one another. Very unbreakable," she said, stepping closer and running her hand along the fabric of his tunic.

He took her hand and kissed her knuckles before stepping back into the passageway. "Then I gladly make you my promise at midnight that we *shall* be together soon."

Before she could answer him, he gave her a wink and quietly closed her door. Bridgette twirled around her room before taking off her cloak and dress. She finally climbed in between the linen of her bed. Staring up at the wood beams on the ceiling, she wondered how on earth she would ever be able to sleep. Wide awake, she could only think of Ulrick's kiss and what might come next.

CHAPTER 19

Ulrick yanked off his helmet, throwing it to the ground. "Godfrey, you worthless cur, if you do not pay attention, you will lose your head. Do you have any idea how close you just came because you diverted your training to stare at a woman on the lists?

"'Tis hardly my fault, Sir Ulrick," Godfrey complained before also taking off his helmet. "How does Lord Dristan allow his wife and Lady Bridgette such an intrusion that should only be reserved for his knights?"

Ulrick crossed the distance to the young man and took him by his chainmail at the neck giving him a mighty shake. "You would do well to not place your nose in Lord Dristan's business, including the activity of his lady wife and ward."

"But look at them, Sir Ulrick! 'Tis not normal for women to behave thusly. Mayhap they are daft in their heads," Godfrey surmised rolling his eyes upward.

A growl of outrage burst from Ulrick and before the young

knight knew what was happening, Ulrick's fist landed in Godfrey's face. The crunch of his nose as it broke left a trail of blood running from his nostrils and had the young man reeling on the ground in pain.

Ulrick pointed his sword at Godfrey's throat. "You would do well to remember to never, *ever*, besmirch the good name of Lady Amiria and Lady Bridgette. You may be dealing with me at this time, but Lord Dristan would see you flung from Berwyck's gate and never give you a second thought for such an offense."

"You broke my bloody nose!"

"You are lucky you yet live. Now get yourself to Berwyck's healer and remember this lesson well," Ulrick ordered, watching the young knight pick himself off the dirt to depart on wavering legs to the healer's hut.

"Any problems, Sir Ulrick?" Lord Dristan asked from across the field."

"Nay, my liege. Nothing that I have not handled."

Lord Dristan nodded and returned to his own training, leaving Ulrick to make his way to the side of the lists to quench his thirst. With a cup in hand, he took a long gulp of the cool ale before his own eyes wandered to the ladies who had been Godfrey's downfall.

But look at them... Godfrey's words echoed in Ulrick's head. Yet Ulrick had been doing everything in his power to, at the very least in his outward appearance, remain unmoved to one particular lady as much as humanly possible. Aye... he had gone out of his way to never be alone with Bridgette for the past fortnight because he was not certain he would not grab hold of her no matter where she might be and thoroughly kiss her yet again. He did not trust himself, and, may God above help him, she had become a daily distraction since her return to the lists a se'nnight ago. This fact left Ulrick to assume her hands had healed enough that Lady Amiria felt their training together could resume.

"She is glorious, is she not, *mon ami?*" Bertram said with a cocky smirk, whilst a cup was thrust into his hand by a nearby squire.

Ulrick tore his attention from the women to peer at Berwyck's captain of the guard. He was about to respond by saying he did not know what Bertram was sputtering on about, but obviously 'twas of no use. He had been caught staring and there was no use denying what he had been doing.

He drained what remained of his ale. "Aye, they both are," he replied with a heavy sigh before thrusting his arm toward the squire to refill his own cup.

"You have known Lady Amiria for many a year but Lady Bridgette... now *that* woman belongs here no matter her origins."

Ulrick frowned. "How can you make such an assumption? She is only a visitor and could at any moment be whisked away to where she truly belongs."

Bertram clapped a hand upon Ulrick shoulder. "Then you best hurry and make up your mind if you plan to claim the woman."

A short grunt of displeasure escaped Ulrick's lips. "I do not believe the lady would like to be *claimed.*"

"Call it what you will, but how will you feel if you do not take advantage of the gift you have been given for finding what has been missing in your life?"

"How do you know what I am missing in my life?

Bertram scowled nodding to the woman of their musings.

128

"Do not be a fool! That woman crossed *Time* for you and you alone. If you are not careful, you might just lose the one person your soul has been searching for."

"You sound like an old woman spouting tales of romantic nonsense," Ulrick ranted in response. He ran his hand across the back of his neck in irritation even whilst his eyes returned to the woman he had been avoiding. His gaze roamed over her shapely legs covered in hose until he stopped at the opening of her tunic. The roundness of her breast was tempting him to enjoy their bounty, as no woman had ever done before.

A chortle left Bertram before he cleared his throat. "Even a seasoned warrior gets melancholy occasionally. I am but giving you advice on what you yourself have seen with the other women of Lady Bridgette's ilk who have crossed Berwyck's gates. Do not ignore your feelings fer her and let her slip through your grasp. I am most certain you will regret such a decision," Bertram said, before finishing off his drink. Handing the empty cup back to the squire, he returned to his training on the lists.

"He is correct with his words that ye must choose and do so quickly, Sir Ulrick, lest the decision fer her tae remain, or not, be taken away from ye," a woman's words whispered quietly.

He looked down to his right and there stood Lady Amiria's grandmother as though she were a real living and breathing person instead of the ghost he knew her to be. He thought of another specter who roamed Berwyck's halls.

"Will not appearing before me as you are now take a toll on you, my lady?" he asked with a raised brow.

"Aye. 'Twill take days fer me tae recover but I am trying tae make a point on the urgency of choosing whether ye will be a foolish idiot or come tae yer senses."

He frowned at the woman at his side. "I have been told 'tis not seemly to argue with your elders," he replied, before once more turning his attention to the lady of their discussion. His life was now plagued with events that were clearly out of his control. And yet... would it be so horrible to give in to his growing attraction for the lady not of his time?

"Nay... 'twould not be horrible, ye daft man," the lady replied apparently reading his inner thoughts. "What would be horrible is if ye remain a stubborn lout and not take advantage of what I have given ye."

"She must be upset with me for ignoring her this past se'n-night," he surmised whilst ignoring the further insult that he was stubborn, and a lout for that matter. Lady Amiria's grand-mother was very opinionated.

"Aye and ye have no one tae blame but yerself. Ye made her a promise and then made her think ye broke such a vow by letting her believe ye fergot all about her. But Lady Bridgette is a fergiving soul. I am sure there will be much groveling on yer part in order tae return tae the lady's good graces. Ye best get at it!"

Ulrick looked down to reply to the lady and was astonished when he watched her transform into a ghostly apparition before completely vanishing from sight. Knowing he could do nothing about his situation whilst the training continued, he went to where he had thrown his helmet, picked it up from the ground, and resumed his habitual task of putting himself back into what was his normal daily routine. *Normal...* his life would never be normal again!

Bridgette swung her blade over and over again until she felt as though her arm was going to be pulled from its socket. Amiria was relentless in her ambition to see her fully trained but who was she kidding? Amiria had a sword in her hand from when she was a small girl, or so Bridgette had been told. Until Bridgette slipped through *Time*, the closest she ever came to one was when Brad would occasionally humor her and let her attempt to lift his own. It was heavier than she could manage, which always left her ex-boyfriend laughing and she agitated.

But the one she now owned, curtesy of the lord and lady of Berwyck, had been fashioned just for her much like the one Amiria continued to swing with all her might. Given that the woman was pregnant, although barely showing, she fought as though her life depended on her training. After learning about the siege and how eventually the event had gained Amiria her husband, Bridgette supposed that wasn't too far off its mark.

Distracted, when from the corner of her vision Bridgette saw Ulrick's fist land in Godfrey's nose, she barely brought her sword up in time to defend herself from Amiria's unrelenting training.

"You will never learn the mechanics of fighting if you are so easily distracted, Bridgette," Amiria called out, before placing her sword in her scabbard. "'Tis imperative that these moves I am trying to teach you become an automatic response to keep yourself alive."

"I understand and appreciate all you are trying to do for me, my lady, but I highly doubt I am going into battle," Bridgette said keeping her speech correct and not using contractions, knowing others could easily hear their conversation.

"I will not have a woman who is now considered my

husband's ward unable to defend herself. What do you think these lessons are for?"

"Fun?" Bridgette teased. Amiria's brow rose causing Bridgette to gulp.

"There is nothing *fun* about what we are trying to accomplish." Amiria began to leave the field and gave a wave of her hand. "Come with me," she ordered.

Bridgette gave a heavy sigh, knowing some form of reprimand was forthcoming. Thinking Amiria would give up on the training and return to the keep, Bridgette was surprised when they only went as far as a nearby well. Taking the bucket sitting on its ledge, Amiria dropped the pail down into the water with a splash before pulling the rope up. A dipper hung on a bent nail and she filled it with water before drinking. Repeating the gesture, she offered the dipper to Bridgette. She was hesitant at first, remembering her previous conversation with Ulrick but the water was clear and appeared safe enough or else Amiria wouldn't have drunk it. The water was cool on her parched throat, and she drank greedily until she felt refreshed.

A white stone bench was placed up against a wall and Amiria sat, waving her hand for Bridgette to sit next to her. They sat in silence for several minutes watching the knights train, but Bridgette only had eyes for one, even though she was angry that he had been avoiding her. It was hard to figure out what had gone so terribly wrong when the person you're trying to talk to wouldn't give you the time of day.

Amiria readjusted the leather strap of the ponytail of flaming red hair before turning those stunning violet eyes upon Bridgette. *Violet eyes!* She'd never seen such a color on anyone else in her life, but those orbs drilled silently into her own green ones.

"You are troubled," Amiria surmised, before returning her

gaze to the field. "'Tis no doubt the reason behind your inability to learn the move I have been attempting to instill in you for the entire morn."

"It's nothing," Bridgette answered returning to her normal speech pattern since they were alone and Amiria was more than aware of her origins.

A sarcastic chuckle escaped the woman beside her. "You may wish to ignore the situation but 'twill only make matters worse, my friend. Ulrick is as stubborn as most of my husband's personal guardsmen, but that does not mean some gentle pushing on your part could not help your situation."

Bridgette leaned her head back on the wall behind her. "I'd be more than happy to have such a conversation with him. It's extremely difficult if he will not give me a moment or two of his time. He has refused to be alone with me in fear Lord Dristan will have his head on a pike outside his gates... Ulrick's words, not mine," she fumed in frustration.

"You worry about getting Ulrick alone and let me worry about Dristan. You are not the first lady who has gone to unconventional methods to ensure love finds its way into the heart of their knights. I have the feeling you will not be the last."

"He won't like it," Bridgette said, before leaning forward, resting her forearms on her thighs and clasping her hands together."

"They generally do not know what is good for them. A good woman will change all that for the better," Amiria replied, before standing. "Shall we return to your training? I fear Dristan will only allow me a short period to continue upon the lists before he feels this activity might harm our babe if I continue. 'Tis best to take advantage of the time we have. There is still much for me to teach you."

Knowing their short reprieve was over, Bridgette was thankful for the break while she followed Amiria back onto the field. She walked right past Ulrick without giving him even a short glance. His grunted annoyance only caused Bridgette to smile. She was done playing games. He made her a promise and by God he was going to keep it!

CHAPTER 20

U lrick made his way across the inner bailey and observed Godfrey leaving the healer's hut. He motioned for the knight to join him.

"Well?" he inquired, his words lingering in the air between them. He would see if the young man had enough sense to guess what was required of him.

Godfrey shuffled his boots in the dirt beneath his feet. "I apologize for my earlier indiscretion relating to the ladies, Sir Ulrick. 'Twill not happen again."

Satisfied with Godfrey's reply, he was about to speak when Lady Amiria and Lady Bridgette passed by. They laughed with one another whilst they continued on their way. 'Twas not hard to notice Godfrey's hungry gaze following one particular woman until they were near the keep. Amiria's children ran to their mother, who kneeled down to hug them both.

Ulrick folded his arms across his chest, irked that another obviously had feelings for Lady Bridgette. The boy needed to be reminded that the lady was under the protection of their liege lord.

"You continue to ogle Lady Bridgette. Why?" he asked, attempting to hide the annoyance from his voice.

Godfrey heaved a sigh before returning his attention to Ulrick. "I cannot explain it. I know you have an unspoken interest in the lady but, for some reason, I feel drawn to her."

"You would be wise to refrain from any infatuation with the lady. She is spoken for," Ulrick warned.

"I had not realized your relationship had progressed so far."

"'Tis none of your business what my relationship is with the lady. Suffice to say, you have enough to worry about with your training and proving your worth to Lord Dristan, instead of wasting valuable time attempting to dally with a woman," Ulrick said gruffly. "If you do feel inclined to seek a lady's hand, choose another." He began making his way toward the keep. Godfrey decided to walk with him.

"I will heed your advice, Sir Ulrick," Godfrey said, although Ulrick could see for himself 'twas done reluctantly.

Ulrick stopped to stare at the younger man before he nodded. "You may just pass Lord Dristan's inspection after all."

Godfrey beamed, apparently pleased he had earned Ulrick's praise and respect. He had come a long way from the cocky lad but weeks before. As they neared the women, Ulrick slowed his pace, hoping he might have a private word with Bridgette. Her eyes roamed all over his entire visage before falling upon the man at his side. She frowned and Ulrick wondered what bothered her about Godfrey, as he realized she had never told him her reason for being leery of him.

"Sir Ulrick. Sir Godfrey," she murmured quietly, before she once more turned those green eyes in Ulrick's direction. A sensation of utter disbelief fell over him as if the woman held him spellbound. He was unsure he would ever get used to the feeling.

"My lady," they answered in unison, further increasing Ulrick's scowl.

Amiria stood and began ushering her children toward the keep. "I shall see you at the evening meal, Bridgette," she said.

"Thank you for the lessons today, my lady," Bridgette replied, before once more turning toward Ulrick.

"Do you have some place you need to be, Sir Godfrey?" he questioned, with a raised brow.

"Aye, of course," the young knight replied with a bow, before taking his leave and heading toward the Garrison Hall.

Ulrick waited until Godfrey was gone from their side before he gave his own slight bow. "Lady Bridgette... did you enjoy your training with Lady Amiria?"

"Yes." Her reply was short, but he watched in fascination whilst her eyes sparkled like the brightest gem as she gazed upon him.

"You did well today," he replied, attempting to draw some kind of response from her. "I could see for myself how you have improved."

Her smile lit her entire countenance. "Thank you, Ulrick, for noticing."

"Might I ask you a question, my lady?"

"You can ask me anything, Ulrick, and I'll give you an honest answer," she said and waited for him to continue.

"What is Sir Godfrey to you?"

Her eyes narrowed, obviously not prepared for this question amongst so many others he might have asked.

"You haven't spoken or been near me for how long and you

wish to ask me about another man?" she huffed. Her eyes now blazed with unsuppressed anger.

"You had told me you would tell me about him, but we never had the conversation," he replied, as though this would justify his words.

"There are a lot of conversations we have yet to have, but Godfrey is the least thing we should be worrying about."

Her feet braced apart, Ulrick wondered if she realized how she appeared like the fiercest of shield maidens in her stance. "Will you tell me?"

She gave a heavy sigh, looked around to ensure no one would overhear their conversation and began. "If you must know, Godfrey is identical to a man I used to date back in my own time. His hair and eyes are different colors, however. This twelfth century version is younger than the Brad of my time, but a lot of his mannerisms are identical."

"Surely you jest," Ulrick muttered, whilst his attention moved toward the Garrison Hall to watch Godfrey disappear within the now closed portal.

Bridgette shook her head. "Nope. Same annoying guy no matter the year, although his manners have improved of late since we danced that one night."

"'Tis uncanny and hard to image how someone could be the same, centuries apart."

Bridgette laughed, causing a smirk to cross Ulrick's lips. "Well… we call them doppelgangers in my time. Others may call it reincarnation, if you believe such things. I suppose since you and I both know time travel can occur, then why not identical people no matter how many centuries apart they are?"

"You have given me much to think about, Lady Bridgette," Ulrick said, before running his hands through his hair.

She watched him, seemingly enthralled when his tresses fell back into place. She then moved her hand to push back a lock of his hair from his forehead. She hesitated near his cheek before she reluctantly let her hand fall back to her side. "Is this all you wish to speak to me about, or is there something else I can answer to cease any troublesome thoughts running through that gorgeous head of yours?"

A guffaw left him, when he heard she thought him handsome. "We have much to have speech about, but not where everyone can listen in on something that should be done in private."

"I couldn't agree more," she remarked, with another sweet smile. "Perhaps you should figure out soon what you want out of life before you don't have a choice in the matter."

He frowned at her words, as though she was making him come to a decision about his life he was not ready to deal with. "What is this you are talking about?"

She surprised him when she reached out and quickly took his hands in her own. Tingling sensations ran up his arms, as though the blood pumping in his veins suddenly came alive at her touch.

"Do you feel that or don't you?" she asked, gazing at him as if his visage would give her the answers she needed. "When we touch, I come alive with burning like currents racing up my arm. It's as though you've found me or, more importantly, that our souls have found one another. It's a reminder that we're supposed to be together."

A low rumble escaped his lips as though to deny what was happening between them. "I cannot explain this connection between us, my lady."

A tear escaped her eyes before she pulled her hands from his.

"If you continue to deny this sweet confusion that consumes us whenever we are together, then you deny the miracle that has brought us together in the first place. If you persist in this direction, then what is the point of me being here? I might as well attempt to find our ghostly matchmaker and ask her to return me to my own time. I know I'm right here in this place and exactly in this precise time *only* because of you."

"I was not looking for a wife," he growled in frustration.

"And I wasn't looking for a husband in the twelfth century but here we are standing on the brink of something that could be so incredibly magical if you but allow your heart to open up to the possibilities of finding love."

"I know nothing of this emotion called love," he grumbled in denial.

"And I've never experienced the depth of emotion when I am with you. To me... that's love, but if you don't feel the same way then I suppose my time here at Berwyck must come to an end." Tears rushed down her cheeks and he could feel her sadness as though it were his own.

"Bridgette..." he began, before she started backing away from him, her chin jutted out in self-righteous anger. Her eyes, however, never left his face.

"My previous life may not have been all that exciting, but I gave up everything, including my friends and family, to be with you," she sobbed. She shook her head as though to clear her thoughts, then wagged her finger at him before continuing. "And stop being jealous of a man who means nothing to me and figure out what... or who... you want, Ulrick, before it's too late."

The lady gave him no time to respond. Instead, she left him standing alone in the inner bailey. He watched her disappear into the keep. *Jealous?* Him? A snort escaped Ulrick. He had to admit he was bitter about the past connection she had with Godfrey... or this *Brad* person. He finally went into the keep, up to his room and spent the remaining part of the day contemplating his life and exactly what it would mean without Bridgette filling his days and nights.

CHAPTER 21

Bridgette threw another log onto the fire of the hearth in her bedchamber. The day, and evening for that matter, had been long and stressful. Earlier, she had sat next to Ulrick as they shared a trencher during the evening meal. The silence stretching between them had worn on her nerves. She swore she'd soon be running and screaming from the hall if this stubborn medieval man didn't soon realize what he was about to lose.

She held her hands before the flames to warm them, but she had never experienced a cold such as this in her entire life. The sensation consumed her whole body down to the deepest recesses of her heart, much as if a stormy cloud hung over her. She wasn't the type of person to be so melancholy or depressed and she began to wonder if she would ever return to the normal person who used to stare back at her in a modern-day mirror. She hated feeling like this. She vowed she would confront Ulrick with the truth he failed to recognize by the morning. She couldn't continue living like this.

She began singing a sad song from a time that now seemed foreign to her. How long had it been since she'd been swept back in *Time*? How were her parents and Megan faring with her absence? They must be frantic when Bridgette went missing, but perhaps they would consult with Zoe who could surely put their fears to rest. Zoe would know that Bridgette was fine, at least physically. Mentally, she was unsure if she would ever be *fine* again.

Elbows resting on her thighs, her hands went to her tear-soaked cheeks to wipe away the wetness that had unknowingly crept from her eyes. She shook her head as if this alone would put her back in the right frame of mind. Confident... happy... But who was she kidding? There was only one thing, or rather one person, who would truly make her happy.

Ulrick... His name rushed across her soul as though, if she thought his name often enough, then the man himself would appear before her. She smiled for the first time that evening and wondered if she should test that theory. He'd be mad as hell if it worked but she had nothing to lose at this point. Or did she?

Ulrick... Come to me, my love.

Over and over, she whispered these words until they became like a mantra in her mind. She could sense him resisting when he first recognized she was asking him to come for her. But then, a glimmer of trust began to surface through his confusion, giving her hope. A feeling so overwhelmingly strong began to take shape and she knew with every fiber of her being that Ulrick was no longer struggling with the pull of her calling.

When a soft knock came at her door what felt like hours later instead of minutes, she wasn't overly surprised. Bridgette took

her sword in hand to ensure her safety in the miniscule event
that it wasn't Ulrick rapping on her door at this ungodly hour of
the night. She slid the bolt before opening the wooden portal a
crack to peer out into the dimly lit passageway. Ulrick leaned
against the stone wall with one booted foot propped up against
it as though for extra support. His hair was tousled, and he
looked as uncomfortable as any medieval knight would be from
what could only be termed pure magic.

He nodded to the sword she held in her hand before she
leaned the blade against the wall inside her chamber.

"Glad tidings to you this eve, Bridgette. I am glad to see you
are prepared to defend yourself if the need had arisen," he
murmured. The husky tone of his voice caused her to shiver in
delight. She hid her smile, although nothing could have pleased
her more to see Ulrick standing there waiting for her reply.

"Best to have it and not need it than to need it and not have
it," she teased, although this only caused him to frown. The look
on his face would have frightened most people, she supposed,
but she wasn't one of them. She opened her door wider and
waited to see what he would say next. A silent invitation, if he
chose to accept what she willingly offered.

He appeared more perplexed than moments before, so Bridgette stepped out into the passageway. There was a light breeze
rushing down the corridor causing the torches in their scones to
sputter. But the sensation didn't make her chilly, not as she
stepped closer to Ulrick. The heat radiating from his body was
enough to warm her until the end of time itself.

"Do you trust me?" he asked, as though finally coming to a
decision.

She smiled up into his face before she raised her hand to cup
his face. "Always."

"Then come with me." He held out his hand for her to take and hers slipped into his as easily as taking her next breath.

Down the passageway they went like two young lovers stealing away under the cover of darkness until they reached the turret stairs. Again, down they went to the next floor until they came to Ulrick's room. He pushed open the portal, holding the door for her to enter if she dared. Bridgette hesitated only an instant before she went inside his chamber. The door closed behind her, the bolt slid into place to ensure their privacy, and Bridgette held her breath for what was surely to come next.

The room was tidy with furnishings much like her own. A small table sat near a shuttered window that was closed against the night's chilly air, a fire burned brightly in the hearth, but the large bed seemed to dominate the room. Or perhaps it was Bridgette's overly active imagination about what could happen in that very bed that caused her breath to hitch. She went to sit in a chair near the fire while he poured her a chalice of wine. She took the goblet he handed to her, sipped from it, and inspected him as he sat across from her.

"You called to me." There was a strange tone in his voice that was more of a statement instead of the question she was expecting.

"And you answered," she replied, before setting her cup down on the small table between them.

He took a few moments before he spoke, also taking a sip of his wine as if to calm his nerves. "You were singing. I could feel the sadness of your song."

She nodded in acknowledgement of their connection. "And I could feel your confusion about what was happening when I called out to you."

"'Twas a lot to take in and I could no longer deny what has

been happening between us," he murmured, before heaving a sigh. He reached over to take her hands in his and rubbed his thumb over her trembling skin. The calluses on his fingertips were a reminder of the life he led, always ready to fight in battle... to train for battle... to kill in battle, if necessary.

She would not think about him taking his life in his hands through his work. Instead, she focused on the fact he was now acknowledging the magic that surrounded them. "You have no idea how happy it makes me to hear you say that you now believe in our connection."

"I could hardly gainsay you any longer, Bridgette. Not with you filling my head with a *need* I swear I could hear across *Time* itself."

A hint of her conversation with her friend Megan echoed inside Bridgette's memories. God... that seemed like a lifetime ago. She again wondered how Meagan handled her disappearance, but this was not the time to worry about her friend. This moment belonged to her and Ulrick.

"Do you know why soulmates meet?" she asked in a breathy whisper. She watched the firelight reflected in those blue-grey eyes and held her breath.

"Nay, I do not," he murmured before rising and pulling her to stand before him.

She smiled before reaching up to caress his cheek, smoothing the stubble of the five o'clock shadow that had formed there from the day before. "They meet because they are hiding in the same place while waiting to be found by the one other soul who will make them complete."

His hand ran through her hair before he brought her up fully against her chest. It was like leaning against a mountain of hard perfected marble and she relished how her body came alive being in his embrace.

"Aye… you complete me, Bridgette, as no other woman has done before," he said, cupping her face with his hands.

"Then make me yours in every way, Ulrick. From this day forward, I never want to be parted from you again." She offered herself willingly and her heart soared when he leaned down to capture her lips with his own.

His tongue dipped between the seam of her lips that curled around his seeking tongue. He tasted of the wine he had sipped when he deepened their kiss. It was a claiming, a possession in the sweetest sense of the word as he all but devoured any sense that the world hadn't just righted itself with this first act of love.

When he broke off their kiss, his sweet warm breath lingered just above her swollen lips. A small breathless whisper escaped her.

"Ulrick…"

"You are mine," he growled out.

"As you are mine. Today, tomorrow, and for all eternity," she vowed.

She watched him as his eyes glazed over with a need only she could fulfill. Stepping back from him, she continued to observe his every move while she pulled the linen gown from her body, letting it pool in a puddle of fabric at her feet. It seemed an eternity that she waited for his reaction, until she saw his appreciation in the depth of those mesmerizing eyes.

"By God, you have been sent from the angels above," he said in a voice dripping with the sound of a man struggling to keep his hands to himself.

She went to him in all her naked glory. Reaching for his tunic, she pulled the fabric from his body and tossed it onto his vacant chair. Her eyes gleamed when she inspected that carved muscular chest now exposed for her viewing pleasure. Fingertips reached out to trace his hot skin even while a part of her ached for him to be inside her. She could hear his uneven breathing and rejoiced knowing she was the cause. Her womanly pride soared, knowing he was just as affected as she was considering the next steps they were about to take together.

"You're so beautiful, just as I remember you at that fountain in my own time. Then you were carved from white marble. But now… now I can physically touch you to my heart's content."

"A man is generally not considered beautiful, my lady. Such words are used to describe women," he said, caressing her arms to send shockwaves over her entire body.

"You've always been beautiful to me," she answered honestly. "From the first moment I saw you at the fair in my own time, I was completely smitten."

"Aye… the fountain you spoke of. Mayhap you will tell me more about your time," he said bringing her closer into his embrace. "Your modern marvels… your home…"

"Later…"

Ulrick quickly scooped her up and carried her to his bed and laid her down. His hands roamed the entire length of her body until she was a quivering mess. He seemed to sense her need and began removing his boots, hose, and that crazy underwear called braies. When he, too, was as naked as she was, she could barely breathe. His manhood had blossomed into a thick, swollen masterpiece, growing even more during her inspection. He took her breath completely away, her fierce warrior standing before her with desire shining in his blue-grey eyes. True, neither had spoken the words *I love you* as yet, but hopefully their love would build from this moment on.

She scooted across the bed to make room for him, and he lowered his towering frame next to hers. Minutes quickly evaporated like the morning dew once the sun reached the ground. Time had no meaning as they touched, kissed and explored until Bridgette could no longer stand the exquisite torture that left her wanting Ulrick to fill her completely.

She must have voiced her thoughts aloud for Ulrick moved atop her. Thrusting his hips, he sank into the cleft between her thighs causing her womanly center to tingle and pulsate with pleasure. He set the pace known to lovers throughout time. Slow at first, still exploring what she liked while her hands moved from his broad shoulders to lightly tease her way down his back until she gently squeezed his buttocks. She heard him moan her name in pleasure and Bridgette forgot everything else while she matched Ulrick's rhythm. And then she felt it… that building pressure when you know that a small piece of you is about to die and be reborn. White hot lightening flashed before her eyes when she arched her back as waves of ecstasy pulsed through her entire body.

"Ulrick!" The sound of his name as it burst through her lips echoed in the room until she felt his release timed with her own. Her heart briefly stumbled before falling back into place and, when they both lay there exhausted, Ulrick rolled over onto his back and pulled her into his side. Their breathing, once labored, began to settle once more.

Completely content now they had claimed one another, Bridgette briefly dozed off until she felt Ulrick's hands upon her body once more. With a light laugh, she pulled his head down to receive her kiss. The hours melted away as they began to make love again until they finally found sleep close to the morning's dawn.

CHAPTER 22

For nigh unto a fortnight, Ulrick and Bridgette found solace in each other's arms whilst in the comfort of his bedchamber. Before the sun would rise, Ulrick would gently awaken the lovely lady from her slumber to ensure she returned to her own room. He would not wish for his liege lord to know what they had been doing behind his back. *God's Blood!* Lord Dristan would seek retribution upon the field of honor were he to learn of such a betrayal of trust. And yet... Ulrick would gladly pay whatever the price necessary to have Bridgette with him each and every night.

Aye... she had unconsciously become so important to him that he had no notion to ever let her go. Once Ulrick had acknowledged their connection, 'twas if God himself had blessed their union and yet he was still reluctant to say the words that would bind him to the lady for all time. *Why?* He had asked himself that question a thousand times and mayhap 'twas because he was deceiving Lord Dristan, hiding the truth he had made Bridgette his in every way. He would need to rectify this soon. His honor and the code of chivalry he lived his life by was at stake and his actions had the bitter taste of duplicity.

His gaze went toward the side of his bed where Bridgette had but recently slumbered. He had been reluctant to wake her, for she appeared like an angel with her hand resting upon her cheek on the pillow. But he had had no choice, and with a sleepy yawn, she bid him good-bye and left. The emptiness of his bedchamber and in his heart made him rise to start his day despite the sun only just beginning to make an appearance on the distant horizon.

He threw another log into the hearth until a roaring blaze at last warmed the bedchamber. But hearing the ringing gong had Ulrick quickly dressing. The tower bell sounding out was the call to arms and could only mean one thing. Dristan's lands were under attack. Now where was his squire to assist with his chainmail?

A knock sounded at his door, and he gave the call to enter. His eyes widened in surprise for he did not expect Bridgette to be entering dressed in hose and tunic.

He went to her, giving her arms a slight shake although all he really wished to do was kiss her lips. "Whatever were you thinking returning to my bedchamber? You cannot be found here, Bridgette," he scowled with a frown, only for her to raise her fingertips to caress his brow and the lines that marked his anger.

"I am here because you needed me," she answered looking around his room and seeing his chainmail already laid out upon his bed. "I'm assuming you are needed on some part of Dristan's lands. I saw there is a fire burning in the distance along with a storm brewing off the horizon." Bridgette went to the window to open the shuttler and Ulrick could hear for himself the chaos occurring in the lower bailey below.

"My squire will see to dressing me," he huffed.

"But the lad isn't here yet." She turned from the window and went to lift his gear. "Well? Are you going to let me help you or not?"

"You are most stubborn."

She gave a light laugh despite the hostile situation of where he was about to go. "I would have guessed you already figured that out by now."

Ulrick bent down so she could lift the heavy chainmail over his head. It fell into place with the *chink, chink* of the links. She went on to fasten the leather straps attached to steel plates over other various parts of his body until he was ready to leave. She went over to retrieve his sword, which he pushed into the scabbard at this side.

"Shall we go?" she asked with a slight smile, as though she was attempting to be brave.

"Aye, but we should say our farewells to one another here in the privacy of my chamber. I would not wish to tarnish your good name if I kiss you senseless in front of others." He pulled her into his arms and brushed his mouth over hers as if this might be the last time they would ever kiss again. 'Twas always a possibility. One never knew if one would survive or not in a battle.

When he went to his door and opened it, his squire was there about to knock. Seeing Ulrick already outfitted for war, the lad mumbled an apology.

"Go see to my horse," he ordered watching him depart before holding out his hand as Bridgette linked her fingers through his own. They stood silently in the passageway, her concern outlined and reflected in green eyes.

Hands on hips, she turned to face him. "What do you mean, farewell? I'm coming with you, Ulrick," she fumed. "I'm not some frail female who cannot take care of herself. Surely, you've seen this for yourself on the lists during my training."

"Training with Amiria is completely different than actually going into battle," he warned.

"I am more than prepared to defend myself."

He threw his hands up in the air in frustration. "And to kill? Are you truly ready to take a man's life?"

Her face paled and he knew he had his answer. "Bridgette, you must stay here. For your own safety." Ulrick said, as he placed his hand behind her head. Leaning down he kissed her cheek before he touched his forehead to her own.

She took a step back and jutted her chin out in defiance. "I will not stay behind. I already told you that I'm not great at taking orders," she said, stamping her foot to make her point.

Ulrick smiled. "Aye you have said as much, but your welfare is of the utmost concern to me. I do not know what I would do if something were to happen to you."

"I think the same of you. If something were to happen to you in battle, how would I ever know?"

"Bridgette—"

She put her hand on his lips to interrupt him. "I will stay by your side. No matter what. I will ride into battle by your side, defeat the enemy for you if I must. I will not be an easy person to lose so quickly."

He kissed her lips. "I admire your determination to remain at my side but in this I must insist you remain at Berwyck. You will obey my orders. This is not open for discussion," he warned. "I must leave..."

"But Ulrick—"

He kissed her once more before crushing her into his embrace. "Wait for me, *mon amour*," he whispered his words of love before doing the unthinkable of asking her to come with him. He turned to leave and found his liege lord scowling nearby.

Dristan stepped forward to stand eye to eye with Ulrick. "You and I must needs have a discussion on what the two of you have been doing, once we return to Berwyck. I am not pleased," he warned, before turning toward the turret stairs. "Let us away, Ulrick."

Ulrick gave one last look upon his lady, gave her a brief nod, and left. He had no other option. He would deal with the consequences of his actions with Dristan's ward upon their return.

Bridgette took a step forward then stopped in her urge to follow Ulrick. There was no doubt in her mind that Dristan had observed their kiss. He was furious but obviously had more important matters on his mind than reprimanding them for their behavior. She shouldn't be worried. She was a grown woman, after all. But knowing she was no longer in modern times and clearly failing in her efforts to fit in made their situation precarious as best. She could almost feel the Dragon of Berwyck's fire breathing down her neck on his return. She shivered, even while she caught the last glimpse of Ulrick as he went down the turret stairs. He never once looked back.

How could he just leave her like that? Didn't he know how

worried she would be if she couldn't be near him in case he needed her? A moment of doubt clouded her vision as to her ability to actually lift a sword to kill another human being. But if it was a life-or-death situation she was more than capable of defending herself, and him!

"Ye should follow him, dearie," a woman's voice came inside her head, encouraging her to listen to her instincts and do just that.

"He'll be mad as hell that I defied him," Bridgette answered when Amiria's grandmother appeared in a ghostly vapor. She gave a small curtsey to the older woman. "Hello, Lady Maya."

She gave Bridgette a smile. "So ye know who I am."

"I do," Bridgette said knowingly.

"Then ye should do as yer told and follow Sir Ulrick."

"He asked me to wait for him."

"But ye are a woman who does as she pleases, or so I thought," Maya replied, her brow arched waiting for Bridgette to reply.

She gave a laugh, causing Maya's smile to broaden. "You're quite the instigator, aren't you?"

"Do ye love him?" Maya asked, instead of answering the question.

Bridgette's eyes widened as Maya's words echoed inside her head. She pondered them but an instant. "Yes... I suppose I do."

"And what does that love look like when ye think of yer handsome knight?"

Bridgette momentarily closed her eyes, while memories of her time alone with Ulrick rushed across her soul. "It's like my soul was completely lost, but everything comes back to me when I'm with him. We're only whole when we are together."

"Then what are ye waiting fer, Bridgette? Ye best hurry

before 'tis too late. Find my granddaughter. She will help ye in yer disguise."

"Thank you, Lady Maya, for everything you've done for us," Bridgette said, as the vision of the woman disappeared from view.

"Ye are most welcome, my dear."

Rushing down the passageway, Bridgette entered the turret and ran up to the fourth floor where the family was housed along with her own room. She saw Amiria rushing from her solar.

"Amiria! I need your help," Bridgette said, attempting to calm her racing heart.

"'Tis not a good time, Bridgette. I must needs get to the outer bailey to wish my husband Godspeed."

"I want to ride with Ulrick but need your assistance so I won't be recognized," Bridgette's words rushed out, causing Amiria's steps to falter. She turned to stare directly into Bridgette's eyes.

"Are you certain? 'Tis not a leisurely ride and they will be battling men who have overtaken one of the southern villages on our lands."

"I can't allow him to leave without me," Bridgette insisted.

"Then come with me," Amiria said. "I know a thing or two about disguising myself as a lad. My Aunt Freya actually gave me the idea during the siege of Berwyck. She, too, refused to stay behind when the man she loved rode off without her."

Bridgette listened to the stories Amiria quickly told her and how hard it was to keep her true identity hidden from Dristan's men. Bridgette followed behind Amiria when they returned back to her solar. Inside a chest, she pulled out chainmail and a worn helmet. Bridgette was quickly dressed, and they returned to her bedchamber where she retrieved her sword. At the stables, she was not recognized as anything other than another squire preparing his horse to join the knights who were mounting their warhorses. Bridgette gulped down any last minute thoughts of retreating back to the safety of the keep. Something in her gut kept telling her she was making the right decision as she rode through the barbican gate. Ulrick needed her. He just didn't realize it as yet.

CHAPTER 23

They rode fast and hard that morning, despite the torrential downpour of rain that burst upon them whilst they went south. Clumps of wet mud flew from the thundering sound of the hooves of their horses, covering those who rode behind the front riders. Lightning flashed in the sky above. Ulrick squinted at the momentary brightness. 'Twas not as though they had not ridden in such conditions before. The upcoming battle would only be more difficult, the wet ground making footing hard to maintain.

Despite the conditions, Dristan and his knights were more than prepared when they came across a small army of men making their way in the direction of Berwyck... the fools! Did they not know that Dristan did not take kindly to those who made attempts to harm his lands and people?

As they reached the front line of men, swords were raised to slice through those who would give their lives first to a cause that would ultimately fail. Horses barreled through the men as if they were nothing more than troublesome ants. Some steeds were lost when blades of steel slashed into their flesh, causing the knights atop them to jump from their saddles to fight hand to hand as their horse fell dead to the ground.

Dristan's battle cry rang out and his men began forming into a tight formation that was as well-known to them as 'twas to take their next breath. Shields raised to protect themselves from flying arrows, they began to heavily attack the men, who were unprepared for such a foe. Dristan trained his men well. He would not be merciful to those who attacked what belonged to him and his king.

The steel of Ulrick's blade slashed forward, striking down one man after another as he swung his weapon over and over again. He caught a glimpse of Godfrey as he, too, continued his attack on their enemy. The young knight was proving his worth. But Ulrick had no further time to think how Godfrey would make an exceptional guardsman for their liege lord. There were too many men they needed to conquer first.

The slippery ground beneath their boots began to mix with brown wet dirt and a river of red from the blood of the injured and dying. Moans came from those who had already fallen and still those who remained upright continued to carry on in their efforts to win the day. Their enemy was fierce in their determination, but Ulrick knew Dristan's reputation as the Devil's Dragon would overrule any thoughts of defeat by his army.

The foe in front of him shattered his shield and Ulrick threw the now useless wood to the ground. His sword rang out time and time again as he hacked away at first one enemy and then another. He slipped in the mud beneath his boots and fell to one knee. Before he could stand, he heard his name yelled out from somewhere on the battlefield. His eyes widened in horror at what he beheld.

"Behind you, Ulrick!" The sweet sound of Bridgette's voice rang out over the sounds of battle. She pulled a kirk from her boot and threw the steel in his direction with uncanny accuracy. He heard the sickening smack as the blade made contact with someone behind him. Turning, he saw a knight with the kirk's handle protruding from his forehead. The sword he was about to plunge into Ulrick's back fell uselessly from his hands as his body hit the ground.

Ulrick quickly stood and continued his attack whilst continuing to search for the woman who should be nowhere near a battlefield. But there she was, raising her sword to defend herself time and time again. *By the Blessed Virgin Mary!* The woman should be safe at Berwyck. She had defied him!

For every step he took forward to reach her side, another came to take the place of the man whom Ulrick had just maimed or killed. He was making no progress and yet another was closer to Bridgette and could help.

"Godfrey," Ulrick shouted, pointing to the woman who fought besides Dristan's knights. "Protect Bridgette."

Godfrey appeared just as surprised as Ulrick had been when he recognized Bridgette's small frame and quickly made his way to the lady. There was no further time to consider her fate but at least Ulrick knew Godfrey would protect her. Ulrick's instincts warred within him, knowing he could not be at his lady's side. He was fighting for his own life and refused to be cut down by some cowardly man who thought he was the weaker foe.

Ever onward on their quest to win the day, 'twas not long before the majority of their enemy who yet lived yielded to the Lord of Berwyck. The stench of the dead filled the air whilst

Dristan's men reformed and began looking for their own amongst the dying. Ulrick wiped his blade before putting the sword in his scabbard and, with a determined stride, made his way toward Bridgette.

Taking his helmet off his head, he threw it upon the ground before taking hold of Bridgette's arms. Her chest heaved whilst he shook and shook her, as if the vibration could instill some common sense into this stubborn woman.

"What the bloody hell were you thinking, Bridgette?" Ulrick's voice boomed over the now silent field where only moments ago was a fierce battle. Everyone stopped what they were doing to see what commotion had caused Ulrick's rage.

She took her own helmet off before reaching to cup his face, searching all over his body to ensure he was not injured. "Thank God you are safe!" she said, before hurtling herself into his arms. "When I saw that guy about to stab you in the back, I knew I'd made the right decision to follow along."

He pulled her close before holding her at arms-length for his own inspection. She appeared as well as could be expected, given the woman had also been fighting for her life. His arm wrapped around her waist yanking her forward until she was up against his chest. "You follow me into battle as though your life has no meaning. What would I have done if you had been killed, *ma petite?*"

"You needed me, just as I predicted," she whispered, even as her voice shook as she began to realize what she had done. "Oh my God… I killed all those men…"

"…and lived to see yet another day," Godfrey finished her words as he came to stand next to them.

Dristan had also arrived, and the clearing of his throat caused Ulrick to release Bridgette from his grasp. Steel grey eyes swept over the woman until his brows narrowed. "My eyes must be deceiving me. Is not that chainmail and helmet—"

"Aye, 'tis your wife's," Bridgette answered, with a sheepish look. Since others were listening in on their conversation, Ulrick was pleased she remembered to speak like a twelfth century woman. "Do not be upset with her, my lord. I insisted."

"She will be dealt with on our return to Berwyck, as will you, Lady Bridgette," Dristan warned. "For now, we have the dead to bury, the injured to see to, prisoners to chain, and a village to look over to ensure its survival."

"I am here to help in any way I can, Lord Dristan," Bridgette murmured lowering her head and eyes.

"Then see who yet lives. Godfrey... you did well. Go with her," Dristan ordered.

"Aye, my lord," Godfrey said, taking Bridgette's elbow to steady her as they walked through the muck beneath them.

Dristan and Ulrick stood silent for several moments, watching them begin the task of inspecting the men on the ground crying out for aid.

Dristan's aggravation rumbled from his chest. "You have your hands full with that one, Ulrick. I hate to admit it, but she is much like my dear wife, who I swear will not hear the end of my anger for her part in this fiasco until the end of our days."

"You will forgive her much as I will forgive Bridgette. She saved my life today, Lord Dristan. I never thought a mere woman would show so much bravery in the face of such danger. If not for her, I would not be standing here talking to you," Ulrick replied in awe at what Bridgette had done, all in the name of keeping him safe.

"Aye... well... there is that, I suppose. Do not think our conversation is finished where my ward is concerned, Ulrick, but we shall leave that discussion for another day. Come… there is still work that must needs be done."

"Aye, my lord," Ulrick said, before falling into step with his liege lord. With one last glance at the lady who had risked all for him, he began assisting with the cleanup of another bloody battle. The Devil's Dragon and his men had won the day. Another tale of their miraculous victory would be told for all those who cared to listen upon their return to Berwyck.

CHAPTER 24

The severe downpouring of rain had turned into a dismal drizzle souring the mood of not only Bridgette but the entire company of knights around her. There was a disgusting smell in the air, causing Bridgette to cover her nose with a shaking hand. Burning flesh wasn't something you could easily dismiss. Her gaze fell upon what was left of the village that had been razed to the ground. The sound of dripping rain falling on hot spots sizzled while smoke rose from the charred ashes.

Her heart cried out at the loss in front of her. There wasn't much left. A few men and women walked about, but they clearly were in a stupor at the destruction of their homes and lives. Zombies… they were like the walking dead, even as children wailed out for their missing parents. The fact they still lived must be a miracle.

Pulling on the reins of her horse when Dristan raised his hand for his men to halt, Bridgette could barely sit in her saddle any longer. Her stomach churned at what she had done this day and she was unsure how she hadn't thrown up whatever was in her stomach. She was weary to the bone and beyond exhausted. She knew her legs would fall out from underneath her when she made the attempt to stand upon solid ground. Earlier, Bridgette didn't have the strength to even heave herself up onto her horse. She had to have Ulrick lift her into her saddle. She didn't have much energy left. She had given it all on the battlefield.

Battlefield! Sweet Jesus! If someone had told her a year ago she'd be wielding a sword to keep herself alive, she would have asked what that person had been smoking. Flashes of men falling at her hand caused tears to well in her eyes. She cast her eyes downward, not that anyone was paying much attention to her at the moment. No one would be able to tell if she began sobbing her head off right now, would they? Surely her tears would mingle with the still falling rain. She began to wonder when the shock of the situation she had willingly placed herself in would finally hit her. God help her if she lost it in front of these knights!

Dristan began ordering his men to one task after another and the knights dismounted and began to obey his orders. Their horses were led away by squires who stood ready to perform such a function. She watched in amazement as they went about their duties as though they hadn't just been in the middle of a mighty battle for their lives. Unaffected... they were simply going about what they did on a daily basis. Bridgette, unfortunately, could not erase the day from her mind, nor her actions.

She hadn't noticed when Dristan also dismounted and came to stand beside her horse.

"Bridgette." He said her name softly and she looked down upon him with sorrowful eyes. When he stretched out his hands, she leaned over to place her own hands upon his shoulders. He lifted her down. Her knees buckled and she fell into his chest while his arms of steel wrapped around her to offer her his support until she found her balance. It took longer than she would have liked before she was finally able to stand on her own two feet.

"Thank you, my lord," she whispered raising her eyes to his.

He took off one of his gloves before reaching over to run his thumb across the tears silently leaking from her eyes as they connected with the rain on her cheeks.

"You have done well this day, Lady Bridgette, although you disobeyed your liege lord when you placed yourself in the middle of a battle where you truly did not belong."

"He needed me," she replied in a breathy whisper, hoping Dristan would understand.

"Mayhap, but if you place yourself in danger, then you must needs toughen your heart to what will be required of you and what you have done this day. Tears and signs of weakness do not belong on a battlefield nor amongst my knights."

"Aye, my Lord Dristan," she said, and he gave her a slight smile. She could tell he was proud of her, not that he would say so directly.

"I can see you do not have much energy left within you. Mayhap you can go to the children. See if their parents yet live," he ordered, before turning from her to go about his own assessment of what was left of the village.

Bridgette stood there staring ahead at what was before her and yet her mind continued to relive the ghastly scene of the battle. Closing her eyes, the sound of crying children finally reached into her heart and some motherly instinct she didn't know she even possessed took over, giving her renewed strength. Those poor innocent kids needed her help.

Stepping forward she began gathering them all together and leading them over to a small lean-to that had somehow managed to survive the onslaught of destruction. They were grateful for the protection from the rain and one small girl, no more than two, climbed into her lap, stuck her thumb in her mouth and instantly fell asleep. Bridgette looked upon the remaining children, fifteen in all. Some no younger than the girl cuddled in her lap, some in their early teens or anywhere in between. They all looked to her as if she had the answers to their plight, but Bridgette had no idea what would become of these children.

A few parents came over to where Bridgette had gathered the kids and tears of joy as the families were reunited had even Bridgette crying in relief. Yet there were still at least eight children who weren't claimed, including the girl in her lap. What would become of them?

As Bridgette looked into the frightened eyes of those who were left, she knew she had to offer them some words of comfort. "I know you must be frightened," she began softly, "and unsure of what your future may hold. But Lord Dristan of Berwyck will see to your care. He will not abandon you."

One of the boys who appeared around eight leaned forward. "But 'e's the Devil's Dragon, milady! I 'eard 'e devours children fer 'is noon meal."

She gave the lad an encouraging smile. "Do not judge the man for the rumors you may have heard. He is a fair lord and will not leave you to find your way in the world alone at such a young age." Bridgette could only hope she wasn't overstepping what little authority she had. If she must, she would fight for the welfare of these children.

"How about I tell you a story while we wait for Lord Dristan to finish his business," she asked. Many of the children began to nod and edge closer. "Have any of you heard the story about King Arthur?"

The boy who but moments ago was afraid of Dristan became excited with thoughts of a story. "My da told me the story and 'ow the king 'ad a sword called Excalibur. I never tire of 'earing about 'is knights of the round table and the quest fer the 'oly Grail."

"I am glad you have heard of him, as some think he was only a legend and made up. Shall I begin?" Bridgette asked, and then began to weave the story and more fairy tales from her youth that she thought would be harmless to tell. Minutes turned into what seemed like hours. As the knights began gathering the dead, Godfrey came and took the children one by one to identify their parents if possible. Some came back crying even harder than before, others looked as shocked as Bridgette herself was feeling. Before long, Ulrick made his way to Bridgette, who continued with her stories in an attempt to lighten the situation for these children. He smiled at her as he took in her little flock of lost souls.

"I see you have a captive audience, Lady Bridgette, but we must away and return to Berwyck," he said, reaching out his hand to her. She accepted his assistance even as she placed the girl she had been holding into his arms. His eyes widened as if he had no idea what to do with the child he held at arms-length. Bridgette bit back a short smile when the girl began to squirm until he held her firmly against his chest. A tiny hand reached out to grab a lock of his hair, winding it between her fingers before she rested her head upon his shoulder.

Bridgette turned back toward the other kids still scared and uncertain of what would happen next. "Come along," she ordered. "We will find you a knight with whom you will ride back to Berwyck Castle. You will be safe there until Lord Dristan finds a place for you amongst his people."

Ulrick hesitated only briefly at her command before he, too, ordered the children to obey her. "You will be safe at Berwyck, and no further harm will befall you."

The children began following Ulrick and Bridgette over to the horses and each child was lifted up into the arms of a waiting knight. Dristan gazed back to see all were settled before waving his hand to proceed home. The village eventually disappeared from view, but the day still remained fresh in Bridgette's mind for days to come.

CHAPTER 25

Ulrick awoke to Bridgette thrashing about the bed in her sleep. Before he could gather the troubled woman in his arms, her cry rang out in his bedchamber when she bolted upright to sit upright with frightened eyes. She quickly scanned the room for any signs of danger. Obviously, the only danger was whatever haunted her dreams.

He gave a gentle tug upon her arm until she settled into his embrace, winding her arm around his waist so tightly he instantly knew the fear of her nightmares. They had spoken about them on a regular basis. She had been unable to stop reliving the battle scene she had placed herself in but days before.

"Be at ease, Bridgette. You are safe," he softly murmured, whilst caressing her hair.

"A-am I-I?" she stammered. Her body trembled and he tightened his embrace around her.

"Aye. No harm will befall you ever again," he said placing a kiss on the top of her head.

"You can't make such a promise, Ulrick. Life can be cruel and probably more so here in the twelfth century." Her heavy sigh echoed in his bedchamber, reminding him that the sun would soon rise on the distant horizon.

"Mayhap I should wait until midnight to pledge such a promise."

Her head lifted from his chest and she gave him a slight smile. "Perhaps…"

He gently pushed her head back down. "If I could make a wish, 'twould be that your fears would no longer plague you whilst you slept. I would fight all your nightmares and bring you only peace if I could."

"I wish it was that simple." She sighed again.

"I vow to you that you are safe under my care and that of our liege lord." Silence filled the room whilst he awaited her reply. He knew what tormented her mind.

"I would do it all over again in order to be there when that horrible man was about to kill you," she murmured softly, even as her body shivered again with the memory.

"And I am most thankful you were there to save me, *mon amour*, but promise me you shall never do so again," Ulrick replied. "I cannot lose you to such a fate."

"I promise," she said. "From now on I'll leave the fighting to you and the rest of Dristan's knights. I'm not sure I could kill someone again no matter how much I feel for you."

"Do you not have war in your time?" he asked, taking his hand to gently place her head on his chest. She began rubbing her fingers across his chest and he raised his eyes heaven bound to give him strength not to take her.

"I wish I could tell you the world is a happy place in the twenty-first century, but that would be a lie. Our planet has been plagued with one war after another over the course of its existence. I'm sure that will continue on long after we're gone from this place."

"I am glad to hear you still have worthy knights to help secure your lands."

Bridgette chuckled. "Well... they're not exactly knights as you know them, but we do have military. The Marines, Army, Air Force, to name just a few. I have always been so proud of those who sacrifice their lives for our country, but I was never one who felt compelled to join."

"You have women who fight?" Ulrick shook his head whilst pondering Bridgette's modern world.

"Yes, as a matter of fact, we do. I have the utmost respect for all our military, which now includes you and the knights of Berwyck who keep us safe," she replied, reaching up to grab a length of his hair. She absentmindedly began twirling its length between her fingers.

"Your time must indeed be a wonderous place," he marveled, thinking of some of the inventions Bridgette had told him about.

"It does have its moments, I suppose," she said quietly before leaning up on an elbow to stare into his face. "What's happened with the children, especially the little girl I handed you and the young boy who was scared to death of Dristan? I've been so wrapped up in my own personal misery. I should have inquired about them sooner."

"The boy's name is Eustace and he is eight summers. The little lass is barely speaking and the lad has been calling her Eva. Both lost their parents when the village was razed to the ground," he answered. "The other six were taken in by other family members or friends so they will be provided for."

"I'm glad to know their names, but are they being taken care of? I would like to see them."

"I understand that a family on the far end of Berwyck Village have taken in both of the children since the girl created such a fuss when we attempted to separate them. Eustace will be an adequate worker in the fields and Eva will be able to help with other chores once she is grown. 'Tis honest work and the couple appreciated the extra set of hands since they lost their own son to an illness but recently."

"The boy is to work in the fields? Like as a serf?" she asked, with a furrowed brow.

"There is nothing wrong with the lad tilling the fields and 'tis most likely what he was already doing in his own village in order to survive."

"I want them to more than just survive, Ulrick. I gave them my word they would be taken care of properly," she fumed, before tossing the covers off her naked body and striding to her clothes laying on a chair by the hearth. He appreciated the view of her in all her glory as she crossed the room, and wished she would return to his bed. She tossed a log onto the low burning embers before reaching for her gown.

"They *are* being adequately taken care of, or Dristan would not have placed them with the couple," he argued. He, too, left the warmth of his bed to begin donning his garments. 'Twas apparent that their day was to begin whether he wished it or not.

"*Adequate* is not good enough. Please take me to them," she insisted, as she quickly began braiding the length of her hair.

"I will be more than happy to take you to see them, my lady, but mayhap we can wait until the sun rises to light the way?" His brow rose as if she should have noticed 'twas still dark outside.

"Are you mocking me, Ulrick?" The warning tone was laying just underneath her words. He did everything in his power not to chuckle.

"I would never dare."

She gave him a brief nod. "Good. Then I will see you in the Great Hall to break our fast after I change my gown and attend morning Mass. I wouldn't want anyone to see my walk of shame being dressed in what I was wearing last evening." She went over to him and quickly placed a kiss upon his cheek before she rushed toward the door.

She left so suddenly he had no time to comment on her words. *Walk of shame?* God's Bones, he prayed she was not ashamed that they had been making love. Mayhap he should speak to Dristan and quickly. If Bridgette was having doubts as to his feelings for her, then he would make her his wife, posthaste. Ulrick never wanted Bridgette to have such a feeling again.

CHAPTER 26

As Bridgette left her bedchamber, she began to realize that her words to Ulrick could be misconstrued. Many of those who lived in the castle wore the same garments for days on end. She should be grateful that Lady Amiria had seen to it that she had several gowns to choose from, along with jewelry, or baubles as they told her, to match.

Bridgette certainly wasn't ashamed she and Ulrick had been making love behind everyone's back, especially Lord Dristan's. It wasn't as if she hadn't had sex in modern times so it wasn't that unusual, at least as far as Bridgette was concerned. The word *disgrace* rumbled across her mind but she dismissed it. No matter how many times she reminded herself she was no longer in modern times, she continued to slip back into what used to be her *normal*. She and Ulrick belonged together, and she wouldn't stop sharing his bed. Since the battle days ago, she hadn't been the same. When she relived the horrible scene in her head, the only person who was able to calm her was Ulrick. She needed him as much as he needed her, whether he realized it as yet, or not.

The Great Hall was only just stirring to life and, while Bridgette's stomach growled in hunger, she followed the other knights and ladies who made their way out the keep door toward the chapel. Morning Mass would come first before they would be allowed to eat, and Bridgette was required to sit with Dristan and his family.

The chapel began to fill. It took everything within her power to not look behind her when she took her place next to Amiria and Dristan to see if Ulrick had arrived. Their children weren't present, but that hardly surprised her. Bridgette had been relieved to learn Amiria had a modern approach far ahead of her time where her children were concerned. Bridgette cringed, thinking of infants being swaddled so tightly the poor dears couldn't move. She had come to love spending time in Amiria's solar with Royce and Liliana, who both looked so much like Dristan with their dark hair and blue eyes that there could be no doubt they were his children.

Mass began and once more Bridgette went through the motions of attempting to pay attention to what the priest was droning on about with his sermon. However, thoughts of the lives she had taken on the battlefield continued to wear on her mind and instead she offered up prayers to be forgiven her sins. By the time Father Donovan was giving his blessing to those in the chapel, Bridgette felt as though a great weight had been lifted off her shoulders. Perhaps God had forgiven her after all.

As everyone began to rise to leave and return to the keep to break their fast, Dristan held Bridgette back. At her questioning gaze, he made a motion with his hand and she saw Ulrick moving forward. He bowed before them.

"My Lord Dristan," he murmured before his gaze slid over Bridgette. "My lady…"

Her cheeks flushed at his low sexy tone. Good heavens! They were in the chapel of all places. "Sir Ulrick," she at last replied, before she offered him a brief smile.

Dristan heaved a heavy sigh. "The two of you can forget trying to make it appear as though you have not seen each other yet this morn. Ulrick has confessed all to me along with his desire that you both be wed. Father Donovan will be more than happy to perform the binding of your troth."

The priest stepped forward. "The flesh is weak and your sins will be forgiven. Shall we begin?"

Bridgette's eyes widened before her attention turned to Ulrick who appeared pleased with himself. "Excuse me for just a moment, Father." She pulled at Ulrick's arm and walked with him down the main aisle before taking a seat on one of the rear benches.

"Is there something you'd like to ask me," she inquired while nervously placing her hands on her lap.

"Ask you? Nay. I spoke to Lord Dristan this morn after you left my chamber. He agreed we should wed posthaste," Ulrick said before reaching for one of her hands and bringing it to his lips. "Does this not please you?"

"Yes. It pleases me very much, but don't you think we should be having this discussion between us first before you and Lord Dristan go ahead and arrange a hasty marriage ceremony? It's not exactly the most romantic way of going about things."

"You mentioned your shame, this morn, and your words brought me sorrow that you would think our coupling was anything but a joy to your heart. I wished to remedy the situation," he replied, with a frown. So, her comment had bothered him, just as she thought it would.

"And does it bring a joy to your own heart?" she asked.

"I should think you would know my answer," he replied, looking nervous, which was so unlike him. Ulrick always showed the world an outward appearance of being in control, but the emotion of love was apparently new to him.

"Sometimes a woman likes to hear the words that will make her heart sing." She waited for his answer, but he only continued to stare at her. She gave a heavy sigh. Obviously, he wasn't quite ready to declare his love out loud. "I am sorry for my words this morning. It's a modern saying and I shouldn't have said it. I'm not ashamed to be sharing your bed, Ulrick. Please forgive me."

"I do not wish to dishonor you or your name by continuing to go on as though you do not mean all to me."

Ah… there it was. The beginnings of learning what was in his heart. Her heart swelled to near bursting at his declaration, but she wasn't about to let him off so easily. "Your words bring me much comfort, knowing that you care for me."

"Of course, I care for you, my lady. Why else would we be getting married?"

He was adorable when he became flustered, but she would in no way be getting married to a man who had not asked her for her hand first. "We will not wed today," she said before standing.

"Why ever not?" His frown marred his otherwise handsome features.

"Because you haven't asked me to become your wife," she declared in a huff. "Besides, we have another priority and that is to see Eustace and Eva today. You did promise me you'd take me to them, didn't you?"

"I had plans to take you after the ceremony."

"Since I won't be rushed into a hasty marriage, then we'll have more time to spend with the children," she replied, before leaving the pew to curtsey before Lord Dristan and his priest. "My lord... there shall be no wedding today. There are certain things between Ulrick and me that must needs be clarified first. I am certain you understand."

She gave them no time to discount her words and headed out of the chapel to return to the keep. She had a feeling she was going to need a full stomach to survive whatever else would get thrown in her direction this day.

CHAPTER 27

The woman was near impossible! Frustrated that the lady of his choosing had decided they would not wed this day, he watched her walk ahead of him through the village. She had become familiar with those in the market who sold their wares, chatting with one person after another and calling them by name. Ulrick had never taken much time to learn or care what these people were called. He had other more important things to do each day, like his training.

And yet, as he watched her flit from one person to the next, Ulrick held back his smile. Bridgette brought so much light into his life, even though he had not confessed as much to her as yet. He could easily see her at his own home at Dunster Castle. God's Bones... how long had it been since he had been in his own hall? His, as he had been born there, and even more his since his older brother died, leaving him to take up the demesne. He knew his mother continued to receive the monies he sent for its upkeep, but he had yet to set foot on his lands. Would he even recognize Rowan and Seraphina after all this time?

Thoughts of home made him long for a time when he would be raising his own family within its walls. He had always felt he had time to find himself a wife. Now that he took a step back and looked at his own life, he realized that time was swiftly passing him by. Ulrick had been with Dristan since their early days together as squires for Sir Fletcher's father. That seemed as though 'twas but yestereve, but it was more like a decade and a half. At the ripe old age of seven and a score and a half, he was unsure how many years he would still grace this earth.

He shook his head to clear his memories of simpler days gone by and returned to watching Bridgette. She would marvel at one trinket or a bolt of cloth and when she moved on, he would pass a coin to the merchant and a servant readily gathered the items that had been purchased. When the man's hands were full, Ulrick motioned for him to return to the castle and Ulrick caught up with his lovely lady. He offered her his arm as they neared the outskirts of the village. The well where they first met became visible and Ulrick suddenly had an uneasy feeling in the pit of his stomach.

"Look, Ulrick!" she exclaimed happily. "This is where I first met you."

She began to rush forward and, of a sudden, the well began to glow whilst golden light burst from its depths. Bridgette skidded to a halt and turned back to face him with fear etched on every feature of her face.

The pull of *Time* must have been strong as she began walking backwards toward the well, her face showing it was against her will.

"Ulrick," she shouted, with her arms outstretched for him to reach her.

He wasted no time lessening the distance between them. Catching hold of her hands, he gave a fierce tug, bringing her into his embrace. Her head upon his chest, they watched in amazement when the well hummed as if in protest that Bridgette was not returning to her own time. The glowing ring around the stone edges soon disappeared and it looked like an ordinary well and not a vessel for time travel.

He leaned down, pressing his lips over her mouth, her cheeks, the tip of her nose, and finally her forehead. Cupping her head, Ulrick gently pushed it back down upon his chest whilst he stroked her hair. Her body shook within his arms, telling him she knew just how close she had come to vanishing right before his very eyes. "By *St. Michael's Wings!*" he swore. "I cannot bear the thought of losing you to *Time, ma cherie.*"

Her arms circled his waist and she held on tight. "I had no will of my own, Ulrick," she whispered with a catch in her voice. "It was as though the twenty-first century was telling me to get myself back where I belong."

"You belong here with me, Bridgette. For now and for always. 'Tis my fondest wish that you become my wife. I adore you, *mon amour*, and will love you until the end of time itself," he declared honestly. If she did not understand his heartfelt plea for her to become his, he had no notion of how else to verbalize his feelings. Her head raised from his chest, and he saw tears brimming on the edges of her eyes.

"You love me..." The awe in her words were like a calming balm to his soul.

He traced the tears that ran down her cheeks before kissing them away. "Aye. A thousand years could pass by and my soul would always find yours," he vowed, bending down to seal his promise with a kiss. 'Twas not a kiss born of passion but one of a commitment to her if she but chose to accept him as her own.

"Ulrick..." his name escaped her lips when he at last let her take a breath. "I love you with all of my heart and all that I am, or will ever be, while at your side."

"Then mayhap now is a good time to ask you to take me as your husband," he said, with hope for his future residing in her answer.

"You honor me with your request, Sir Ulrick," she answered, so formally he thought mayhap she thought him incapable of the riches that might see to their life together.

"If you are worried that I cannot provide you with monies to see to our future, have no fear. I have an estate that I have neglected but 'twill be a good place to raise a family."

Her eyes twinkled in delight. "You wish for a family."

"You do not wish for children of your own?"

"Nothing would make me happier than for us to have children together. I was only teasing you, Ulrick. Now ask me again, so I might answer you properly." Her smile brightened his day as though he already knew her reply.

"Will you wed with me, Lady Bridgette. Be mine... and I shall be yours for all eternity."

"Yes... aye... I will marry you, Ulrick." Standing on the tips of her toes, she kissed him. He lifted her up and swung her around and around whilst their laughter rang out in the air.

"You have made me truly happy," he finally said, setting her back upon the ground before kissing her forehead once again.

The sun burst out behind a cloud and Ulrick shielded his eyes from the brightness before he realized they were no longer alone.

Amiria's grandmother showed herself to them in a vague whisper of a ghost. The woman appeared very pleased with herself. "'Tis about time the two of ye finally declared yer love. I was about tae give up hope of such a union. But beware... there are still obstacles in yer path tae happiness. Do not allow them tae settle into yer hearts tae tear ye apart. They will be yer test lest ye ferget what ye have pledged tae each other this day."

Just as quickly as she appeared, she was gone and Bridgette shook her head. "What more could *Time* have in store for us other than what we just went through?"

"I have no idea, but we best heed Lady Maya's words. Her matchmaking brought you to me and I am most grateful for her meddling."

Bridgette chuckled. "As am I."

"Shall we continue on our way to see the children as I promised you?"

"Yes... and let's never come near this well ever again."

"I could not agree with you more, my lady," he said, offering his arm. "We can return to Berwyck on a different route."

They made a wide berth away from the well and continued on their way past thatched covered roofs for the dwellings of the serfs who lived near the fields they tilled. Ulrick could see that Bridgette was anxious to see the children, as her gaze continued to seek them out.

They came to one of the last huts and an older woman sat outside sewing some garment in need of attention. When she saw them approach, she dropped what she had been doing into a nearby basket and stood, lowering her head.

"We have come to see Eustace and Eva," Bridgette began. The woman pointed toward the field.

"The lad be out there where 'e belongs. The lass be nappin'.'"

Ulrick took Bridgette's elbow. "Shall we go see the boy, my lady?"

Bridgette appeared as if she were about to protest before she decided against the outburst. "Aye, of course, Sir Ulrick."

Ulrick nodded to the older woman who once more sat and took up her sewing. "We shall return shortly to see Eva."

The woman gave them no mind and Ulrick dismissed her before leading Bridgette toward the field. Many serfs were busy attending to the sprouts that were rising from the ground. Eustace was among them and, when he saw them approach, he waved his hand in greeting before rushing forward.

"Sir Ulrick! Lady Bridgette! 'Tis good tae see ye," he said happily, before his enthusiasm lessened. "Lady Bridgette... are ye unwell?"

Ulrick looked down upon his lady who was scowling in anger. Only God above knew what was going through her mind but he knew he was about to find out.

"What is the meaning of this, Ulrick?"

"I do not understand your concern," he replied not liking that she chastised him in front of the boy.

She went to Eustace, taking him by the arms inspecting him as she turned him around. Her eyes narrowed. She gave Ulrick a sideways look of disgust. "The boy looks as though he's gone from his burned village straight into the fields with no thought to his wellbeing."

"I do not see the prob"

She cut off Ulrick's words, turning her attention back to the boy. "Have you even had a proper bath since you have been brought here?" she inquired firmly with a raised brow.

"I dinnae care for bathin', milady. 'Tis not good fer ye,"

Eustace answered, before turning his gaze to Ulrick. "Have I offended ye, Sir Ulrick, or the liedy?"

Ulrick shook his head. "Nay, you have done nothing wrong, Eustace."

Bridgette grabbed Ulrick's hand and took him a few steps away from the lad who shuffled his feet in the dirt. "This will not do. This is not how I expected the children to be taken care of."

"He is fed and is working hard for the food that he eats each day. What more do you expect of him?" Ulrick asked, wondering what this woman would now come up with as a solution to the children's plight.

"They're coming back to Berwyck with us."

"'Tis not how things are done, Bridgette," Ulrick declared attempting to calm his lady's tirade before it erupted.

"Mayhap not," she said keeping her language correct, now that they now had a growing audience intrigued at what was transpiring, "but I gave my word these two children would be taken care of and this is not what I foresaw for their future."

"'Tis more than adequate…"

"I think we have had this conversation before, Ulrick. Adequate is *not* enough! Eustace… come with us," she ordered, before she began making her way back to collect Eva.

"We best listen to her, lad. Come along now," Ulrick said, placing a comforting hand on the lad's shoulder.

By the time they caught up with Bridgette, she was in the middle of a heated argument with the woman, who was complaining loudly about the loss of monies after she planned to sell Eva to another couple in a nearby village.

Furious, Bridgette turned to Ulrick. "Compensate her what-ever you think will keep this woman from ever thinking of selling the services of another child that may come into her care."

Bridgette pushed her way inside the hut while the woman continued to haggle for every bit of coin she felt was due her.

Ulrick reached into the pouch on his belt and handed the woman several coins. "You best heed my lady's words and never think of selling another child. I do not believe Lord Dristan would be pleased with such an outcome for a lad or lass he placed with you."

The woman's eyes momentarily widened in panic before she bit into each coin and nodded her agreement. Bridgette soon came out of the hut cooing to Eva who looked very happy to be reunited with his lady.

"Shall we go home, Ulrick?" Bridgette said calmly, as though she had not just been in an argument over the children.

"I suppose we now have a family to take care of?" he asked, with a slight smile. Bridgette had been like a lioness defending her cubs. He would not dare try to part them from her.

"Is this a problem?" she asked, her brow arching again.

"Nay, 'tis not an issue. I only make mention of it since we are not as yet wed and you plan these children's future as if they are your own."

She came over to him and with a crook of her finger, he bent down. "It's called adoption in my time," she whispered in his ear, before kissing his cheek. "Thank you for agreeing for us to become their guardians."

She began walking back through the village with Eustace at her side chatting away about how their lives were about to change. Ulrick laughed, realizing he had never agreed to anything, but if this made his lady happy, then so be it. He would move heaven and earth to see her content.

CHAPTER 28

Bridgette made her way through the kitchen and out the rear door into the garden. A servant had come to her bedchamber stating a knight had requested her presence and she assumed it was either Lord Dristan or Ulrick. She was surprised to see Godfrey rising from a stone bench situated beneath an apple tree.

Her footsteps faltered only a moment before she continued forward until Godfrey bowed before her. "Sir Godfrey," she began with a small measure of concern, "you asked me to join you?"

"Lady Bridgette," he said taking her hand and raising it to his lips. "Thank you for seeing me."

"To be honest, I did not realize 'twas you who was asking," she replied while curious as to his reason to see her. "What do you wish to discuss?"

"My lady... I wished to make amends for my earlier

behavior upon your arrival at Berwyck. 'Twas not the conduct of a knight under the supervision of our liege lord and I must needs ask your forgiveness." He motioned toward the bench and they sat.

"There is nothing to forgive and perchance I must also ask your forgiveness for my conduct." She watched him intensely, but she no longer saw the lust or hunger lingering in his gaze. "You reminded me of someone from my past, you see. 'Twas not a good memory."

"Mayhap this is why I also felt drawn to you," he replied with a slight smile. "I cannot explain my initial reaction to you, but I felt this overpowering urge to make you mine. Such a feeling made no sense and the more you withdrew the more I needed or wanted to be near you."

Bridgette had a sense of *déjà vu* and her time with Brad. He had always been possessive of her time, expecting her to put everything from her life aside to spend every waking moment with him. He had been obsessed, not only with her but with his own good looks, as though he was God's gift to women. It hadn't taken long for Bridgette to realize their relationship was unhealthy. Perhaps this initial meeting with Godfrey had somehow overflowed into the modern-day reincarnation of the knight now sitting beside her. She could in no way dismiss they were somehow related, although many generations apart.

"Mayhap we can start anew," Bridgette said with a smile. She could not fault the man before her for her past relationship with his descendant. If Godfrey was honestly seeking her forgiveness, then she could do the same.

"You honor me, Lady Bridgette," he replied. "My thanks for accepting my apology."

"And I as well. I should also offer my thanks for assisting me after the battle. I must admit I was in a bit of a daze afterwards and was mainly going through the motions of tending the wounded."

A chuckle left him. "You have no notion how shocked I was when Sir Ulrick called out for me to help you during the fight. You are a rare woman, my lady. 'Tis no wonder Ulrick is in love with you."

"I am in love with him as well, which is why I had to do all in my power to save him, even if it cost me my own life," she replied, with eyes downcast.

"He is lucky to have such a steadfast woman at his side. My prayer will be to find one for myself one day with the same conviction as you show to Sir Ulrick," he said, but then gave a short laugh. "However, I am not of the mind to wed as yet. Plenty of time for all that later in life. I wish to now fulfill my obligation to prove my worth to Lord Dristan and become one of his knights."

"I am certain you have already proven you are worthy, Sir Godfrey, if not in the battle then on the training field." She could tell her words pleased the young man before her, as he appeared to puff up with pride. He reminded her of a peacock shaking his feathers to attract a mate and she did all in her power not to laugh at him and spoil this fragile newfound friendship.

"Your encouraging words and praise will provide the inspiration for me to do all in my power to prove you are correct," he beamed before rising from the bench. "Now I have taken enough of your time, and I am certain you are busy now that you have two children under your care. I bid you good day, Lady Bridgette, and again my thanks for your graciousness." He bowed once more before her and at her nod, he left.

Bridgette felt a fair amount of satisfaction with his parting. She hoped that maybe the future version of this knight would perhaps benefit from the understanding that Godfrey and Bridgette now shared. She was about to rise when Lady Ella entered. Wife to Killian of Clan MacLaren who was like a father to Lady Amiria, Ella was one person she had been meaning to speak with since Bridgette found herself in twelfth century England. Since today was a day of apologies and a hope for the future, there was no time like the present to have a talk with the woman. After all, she, more than anyone else here at Berwyck, knew a thing or two about traveling through time.

"Lady Ella… might I have a word," Bridgette called out and watched the middle-aged woman approach.

Ella sat down next to Bridgette and took her hands. "Please… just Ella, my dear. I still cannot get used to being called lady even after all this time." She squeezed Bridgette's hands before continuing. "What did you wish to have speech about?"

Bridgette stared at the woman whose soft brown eyes twinkled in unsuppressed merriment. "I must apologize for not reaching out to you sooner. If I had done so, then perchance you might have answered some of my original questions."

Ella patted her hand. "Time travel takes a bit of getting used to, does it not?" she laughed quietly. "Take it from someone who has done it a time or two."

"More than once?" Bridgette gasped. She had known Ella had travelled through time but to go through that more than once? Unbelievable.

"'Tis a long story, as was my journey to finding my true love and my reason for slipping through time in the first place."

"Will you tell me? That is… if you would be so kind?" Bridgette asked, settling herself back against the stone wall behind her as if she needed the extra support.

"Since you, too, have traveled from another place in time, I know my secret is safe with you," Ella began closing her eyes as though reliving it all over again. "It all began on a hot summer day in St. Augustine, Florida…"

As Ella began to weave her tale, Bridgette considered herself lucky to have not had to go through all that the lady before her had. Imagine falling through time and finding love, only to lose that love and slipping through time again and reliving your entire life all over again. Bridgette wasn't sure she could accomplish such a feat.

"So, you see," Ella continued, "my story had a happily ever after with Killian who was right before my very eyes for years. I was so blinded by my determination to return to Henry that I completely forgot why I ran from him in the first place. I thought I could change my past when really, I needed to change my future. My son Conrad is a result of my time with Killian. I would do everything all over again in order to have my son."

"It was worth it in the end?" Bridgette asked softly.

"Aye, of course. Love is worth everything we do in life and what give us purpose. And I heard all you had to do was make a wish… if only I could have been so lucky," she murmured. "But I suppose I had more of a lesson to learn from my experience than you."

"Amiria's grandmother played matchmaker between me and Ulrick. She told us we will still be tested."

"Then hold strong to the love you have between you, Bridgette, and never forget the binding tie that brought you together in the first place. Miracles do not happen every day, but they do seem to occur more frequently with the knights of Berwyck."

Ella leaned over to kiss Bridgette's cheek before taking her leave. Today had been full of conversations that would shape her future. She only had to hold on to the love she found with Ulrick in order to have her every wish come true.

CHAPTER 29

Amiria's solar was usually a place to find quiet solitude. This day, however, was a bit different as 'twas filled with several of Dristan's most trusted knights and children. Amiria and Dristan's son Royce, who was eight summers, was playing with Eustace in a corner as they thrust wooded swords at one another. Liliana, their daughter of only three summers, paid close attention to Eva who was being held in Bridgette's arms. Killian and Ella were also present as was their son Conrad who stood proudly next to his father. All in all, 'twas quite the domestic scene and one Ulrick never thought he would be included in... family spending time together. 'Twas all possible because of Bridgette.

A knock sounded at the door and, at Dristan's call to enter, Godfrey opened the portal and stepped inside heading straight to his liege lord.

"A runner just arrived from Bamburgh Castle, Lord Dristan.

The missive has the king's seal," Godfrey explained, handing over the parchment.

The once noisy room quieted. All eyes turned toward Dristan who broke the red wax. A slight frown marred his brow before he passed the message to Killian, who read it quickly. Amiria came over to the men and the missive was given to her outstretched hands.

"I have been summoned to Bamburgh," Dristan announced to the room before he continued, "along with many of my guardsmen."

"'Tis some time since you needed to attend the king," Amiria said, turning her eyes toward her husband. "I had hoped he would leave us in peace."

Dristan pulled her into his arms and kissed the top of her head. "He does not specifically say I must travel with my contingent of men to wherever he wishes them to go. Only that I join him at Bamburgh. We can hope for the best, but I still must answer his summons. I am certain we shall learn more upon our arrival."

Ulrick watched Bridgette's eyes light up before she handed Eva to one of Amiria's ladies in waiting. He knew that look and could only assume they were to get into another argument as to their fate. She crossed the distance between them and he pulled her close and held onto her waist. He did not dare look down upon her.

"Nay," he responded in a hushed whisper before she had time to ask him anything.

"You do not even know what I was going to ask," she replied, just as quietly although he was pleased she remembered not to use her future way of speech.

"You wish to join us as we travel to Bamburgh. 'Tis not going to happen. You shall remain here with the children at Berwyck where I know you all are safe."

"But it is *Bamburgh Castle*, Ulrick," she said urgently. "I have only seen pictures of the place and I would love to see what it looks like in this time."

His brows narrowed and she covered her mouth at what she had confessed. He shook his head. "'Tis but a keep and some outbuildings. Nothing special." Ulrick crossed his arms over his chest with feet spread apart. Most would notice his formidable stance and stop trying to bend him to their will. He somehow doubted his lady would see him as anything other than stubborn.

She assumed the same stance and lifted her chin in defiance. Inwardly, he gave a heavy sigh. This was becoming a standard for her… standing up to him whenever she had a point to prove. "We are better together than apart," she retorted, "or have you forgotten this already?"

"Nay. I have not forgotten something of such import."

"Then why do you wish for me to remain behind while you go south without me?"

All eyes were upon them and Ulrick knew this discussion was not for everyone to hear. He turned toward his liege lord. "Lord Dristan… if you would but excuse Lady Bridgette and me?"

Dristan looked upon the pair and nodded his acceptance with a wave of his hand. Ulrick took Bridgette's elbow and escorted her from the solar, down the torch lit passageway until they entered her bedchamber. He bolted the door behind them.

She quickly turned to him, a small burning flame flaring in her brilliant green eyes. "What can you say to me here in private that could not be said before the others?"

"You do not understand why I wish you to remain behind and why Bamburgh is not safe for you."

"I am not safe anywhere if I am not with you. Can't you understand this yet?"

"*Mon amour...* 'tis not that I do not wish for you to join me—"

"—then what could possibly be your reason to keep us apart?" she fumed. Tears threatened to spill from her eyes. 'Twould surely be his downfall.

"Because there is a *Time* gate in one of the turrets at Bamburgh," he yelled as frustration got the better of him. "I refuse to take the chance on your welfare that *Time* may decide our fate and take you from me!"

"What?" Bridgette took hold of his hands, and he rubbed his thumbs across the back of her soft skin. Her tender touch calmed his rising anger, or mayhap 'twas fear. Aye... fear of losing her had begun to consume him.

"'Tis true. Lady Katherine and her friends traveled through *Time* in one of the turrets at Bamburgh just as Lady Jenna landed on the beach north of Berwyck. 'Tis the reason why I never take you in that direction. I will not lose you to *Time*, Bridgette."

She loosened her hands from his and brought them to his cheeks before he bent down to place his lips upon her own. His arms wound around her, bringing them chest to chest and he forgot all else except this woman who meant all to him. His heart began to beat a rapid staccato and he was amazed that a woman could completely melt the ice that had surrounded his heart. He had kept himself guarded for years whilst women of all sorts tried to persuade him to marry them. None had captivated him or even interested him in offering for them until Bridgette had fallen into his life.

He heard her moan of pleasure and became aware she was attempting to draw his tunic off his body. He stilled her hands, not because he did not want her, but because he knew Lord Dristan's patience would only last so long. If they did not return to the solar, his liege lord would certainly come looking for them.

"Ulrick..." His name as it escaped her lips was a calming balm to his soul and he brushed her black hair from her face to caress her cheek.

"*Ma cherie*," he began before brushing a quick kiss upon her swollen lips, "we must needs return or I fear Dristan may never forgive us."

"I'd rather stay here with you," she answered pulling him close.

"As would I, but may I offer a suggestion?" he asked quietly before he pulled her away to stare into the brilliance of her eyes.

"Of course," she whispered whilst offering him a bright smile.

"Marry me after the evening Mass tonight. I know 'tis rushed but I do not think I can go another night without you as my wife." He waited breathlessly for her answer. When none came, he gave a heavy sigh. His sorrow was short lived because she suddenly laughed. The sound gave him hope for their future.

"Yes, Ulrick. I will marry you. Nothing would make me happier!"

She threw herself into his arms and joy that she would finally be his wife surrounded his entire being. His body reacted to her nearness as never before, and he knew without any doubt that he had found the missing half of his soul. He tried to dismiss Lady Maya's warning, because nothing would ever tear them apart again. Nothing could possibly go wrong as long as Bridgette was by his side… or could it?

Bridgette fidgeted with the ribbon that had bound hers and Ulrick's hands together when Father Donovan had sealed their fate. She had asked to have the keepsake and Berwyck's priest happily nodded his approval. It was most likely because he had married another couple together who would otherwise be living in sin. Not a big deal in modern times, but obviously a problem in twelfth century England.

She had thought their hasty ceremony after the evening Mass would be a small affair. However, word must have quickly spread that one of Lord Dristan's personal guardsmen would wed that eve. All had turned out to witness their union, causing Bridgette's heart to swell with uncontained joy. She had grown fond of many of these people who thrived at Berwyck Castle. She could only wonder what their future held in another place in time.

When the priest had called for an accounting of what Sir Ulrick would bring to their marriage, Bridgette had been astounded to learn that her soon-to-be husband was an extremely wealthy man, with lands in both France and England. She realized she would never want for anything for the rest of her life. Not that she needed physical objects and massive wealth. Truly, she would have been perfectly content with Ulrick at her side along with Eustace and Eva. She had lots of questions but those could wait for another time.

Bridgette had a moment of panic when asked what she, in turn, would bring into Ulrick's coffers but this, too, was quickly squashed as first Dristan and then Bertram stepped up and dropped a sizable pouch filled with coins. The jingle of monies when the leather bag settled onto the table left no doubt that these men would see that she was sufficiently dowered. Drake and several other guardsmen followed in their wake, leaving Bridgette standing on wobbly legs as their generosity touched her heart.

"Bridgette..." her name being whispered brought her attention back to the present while Ulrick held a quill in her direction. He silently nodded toward the parchment for her to place her signature.

She squinted in the dimly lit chapel since she really couldn't make out the medieval wording. Such was the drawbacks of being a woman from another place in time. However, she did make out the word *countess* scrawled beneath where she was to sign.

She raised a questioning brow to her husband. "Countess?" she asked, her hand trembling as her fingers took the quill.

"Aye, of Somerset," he replied, before leaning down to whisper in her ear. "There is no cause for alarm, and I will reveal all later, *ma cherie*."

"You have been keeping secrets from me," she teased while a smile turned up at the corner of her mouth.

He bent forward to kiss her lips. "I will make it up to you later," he murmured. The rich vibrato of his husky tone caused a warm glow to seep into her body. His eyes held the assurance of what their evening would entail once they were alone in his chamber.

"Promise?"

"Aye... now sign the document before these people starve to death at our delay to fill their bellies."

Taking a deep breath, she dipped the quill in the ink pot and signed her name. A cheer arose in the chapel before Lady Amiria announced for all to head to the Great Hall to feast.

Ulrick offered her his arm and Bridgette gladly accepted his support. She had the feeling she would never make it across the inner bailey on her own. Life had just taken a sudden wide turn she had been unprepared for, but she would look forward to their next adventure together.

CHAPTER 30

Ulrick stood at the hearth, a cool tankard of mead in his hands. His friends of many years gathered around him to offer their congratulations on his marriage. He gazed from one knight to the next whilst memories of their time together as Dristan's personal guard flitted briefly across his mind. They had formed a brotherly bond during their time together and had saved each other in one battle after another more times than he could count. 'Twas hard to image not having them in his daily life. But all things must change and Ulrick's course had been set. 'Twas time for him to return home to Dunster Castle and assume his entitled role he had neglected over the years.

His eyes drifted to Dristan and Ulrick inwardly chuckled. The man's reputation as the Devil's Dragon was still alive in England and abroad, and yet his liege lord had been living a more domestic life of late. With two children and another on the way, his role as husband and father suited the man and Ulrick could only hope he and Bridgette would be as blessed.

A silent understanding passed between the two men, and for the briefest moment in time, Dristan appeared sorrowful, as though he knew where Ulrick's life would now lead. His liege lord, and more importantly friend, gave the slightest nod before he raised his goblet in a toast to those who stood nearby.

"My brothers-in-arm... my comrades... Let us lift our cups in a salute to Ulrick and his life with the fair Lady Bridgette. May their lives be blessed as they begin their journey through life together," Dristan proclaimed before he downed the contents of his drink.

A round of *aye, ayes* was chorused among Dristan's guardsmen and more than one came to slap Ulrick upon his back before they, too, took a sip of the contents of their cups.

"My thanks to you all," Ulrick replied, wondering how he would manage to say farewell to his friends. "Lady Bridgette and I appreciate your well wishes. I will always remember our times together with great fondness."

Drake's brow rose at Ulrick's implication that he was leaving. "What the bloody hell is that supposed to mean?' he snapped whilst he lowered his cup.

Lord Dristan raised his hand when the knights around him all began speaking at once. "It means that Ulrick and his bride will be leaving us. 'Tis time for him to return home to his estate. 'Tis the way of things and should not be questioned. One day you, too, shall leave to return to the lives you left when you joined me."

Several of the men grumbled a reply and the mood between them took a downward plunge. However, 'twas not long before one spoke up in an attempt to brighten their mood.

Turquine winked at his brother Taegan. "Perchance we will

SHERRY EWING

be as lucky as our comrades who have found one of these future women who continue to appear at Lord Dristan's gates!"

Taegan gave a warning glare to his brother who only laughed at his expense. "I have no desire to look for a woman to wed. There are plenty of women to see to my needs that I do not need to marry," Taegan muttered into his cup, causing those around him to burst out in laughter.

"That is because you have found her, you fool. I honestly do not know why you are still here at Berwyck. You should be high tailing it back to Lancashire to make amends with Lady Amy!" Drake announced to another round of loud guffaws.

Taegan growled his frustration. "The lady must needs cool her temper and learn her place in life."

The knights all took turns at calling Taegan one name after another for his foolish comment.

Nathaniel also had his cup refilled. "Personally, I continue to ponder if there will be any of us left to guard Berwyck's walls. We seem to be diminishing as the recent months pass us by whilst those around us find wedded bliss."

Cederick nodded before pointing toward one of the knights who was dancing with his wife Kenna. "At least Geoffrey will remain."

Bertram held out his hand to a passing servant who refilled his goblet. "The night is yet young and this is no place to become melancholy like a bunch of old warriors who have nothing better to do than relive their days of glory. This conversation can wait for another day. We must continue to celebrate!"

Morgan laughed. "Mayhap not for Ulrick. If I was in his place, I would not be wasting time drinking here with us when he has a beautiful woman waiting for him!"

Ulrick smiled, whilst his eyes wandered throughout the hall

before they landed on the woman who now held their attention. Aye, he was indeed a blessed man, and perchance 'twas time to leave the men to their drinking and for him to enjoy time with his wife. Her smile when their eyes met across the hall was as intoxicating as the lady herself and when she gave him a come-hither look, Ulrick had no hesitation about what was in store for the rest of the eve.

Ulrick was not the only one who had noticed the unspoken command for Ulrick to follow his lady to their chamber.

"You lucky sod, Ulrick," Turquine said with a laugh.

Taegan turned away from the sight of Lady Bridgette looking over her shoulder with a beguiling smile before ascending the turret stairs. "Another damn happy couple. I need another drink," he snapped, before leaving the group.

Ulrick chuckled as he gave a nod to his friends. "Gentlemen... if you would excuse me..."

His words trailed off and he did not wait for their answer. There was no need. They were well aware a knight should never keep a lady waiting!

CHAPTER 31

Bridgette entered Ulrick's chamber, removing the floral circlet from her head and placing it on a table that served as his desk. She had never paid much attention to the parchments that were there but a quick glance revealed the word *Dunster* in several places, the only words she could read of the medieval writing upon it. She shouldn't have been surprised that her husband had been receiving reports from his home... her home... their home.

A shaky breath left her and she strode to the hearth where she poured wine into a chalice. Taking a sip of the red heady brew briefly calmed her nerves, although why she was nervous she couldn't say. Was it because she had learned that a title was now linked with her name? She was an American. A title was only associated with royalty for those who lived across the pond. She never could have imagined that Ulrick was an earl. He never mentioned it and Bridgette had never thought to ask. Why would she?

Wondering how long it would take before Ulrick joined her, she quickly began removing her gown and carefully folded the lovely green fabric. One of Amiria's ladies had done an amazing job of embroidering a floral pattern at the wrists, neckline, and hem and Bridgette took another moment to marvel at the work. She had always admired people who had the ability to sew their own clothes, which would explain why Bridgette had always bought her own outfits for the fairs she attended. It was expensive, but a girl had to do what a girl had to do when your abilities to create something so beautiful was not in your wheelhouse.

She reached for the dark red robe that had been placed on the bed for her. Wrapping the soft linen around her body, she then went to sit by the hearth before undoing the small braids that formed a crown around her head. Giving her hair a shake made her black tresses fall free down her back in a cascade of heavy black waves and she gave a heavenly sigh. It was this scene that her husband witnessed when he walked through the door. Ulrick's gaze went to her and his eyes practically sizzled with desire.

He turned to bolt the door but didn't lessen the space between them. Instead, he leaned against the wood and looked his fill before a wicked smile graced his face. Bridgette gulped at the sight of him. Seeing him from across the room made her entire body quiver with longing. My God… this man was really and truly her husband. How had she ever gotten so lucky, and would this turn of events shape her future self? She dismissed the notion. Now was not the time to worry over such matters. She gave Ulrick a welcoming smile before crooking her finger for him to come to her.

He finally crossed the room and took her into his arms. "I

have never seen such beauty in all my life," Ulrick murmured into her ear and she trembled to hear the rich vibrato tone. Her knees weakened and he pulled her closer into his embrace to steady her. "And to think that you shall be mine until the end of time itself."

"Hello, my love," she whispered, running her hands up his massive chest. She could feel the muscles beneath the fabric and her tongue ran across the seam of her lips in anticipation of what the night would offer.

"Hello, indeed, my lady. Was it only me or did the festivities last entirely too long before we could make our excuses in order to retire to our chamber?" he asked, continuing to stare upon her face as though memorizing every feature.

"Far too long," she answered before cupping his cheek. "You are here now and that is all that matters."

"I can now officially make you mine by claiming you as my wife," he said, with a twinkle in his vivid blue-grey eyes. He took one of her hands and placed a kiss on the inside of her wrist. She sighed again in pleasure before a short laugh escaped her.

"I thought we did that when Father Donovan joined our hands in marriage," she teased, as she once more felt the bulging muscles beneath the fabric of his tunic.

"Aye, that he did, but I was talking more about taking you to our bed and making love to you until you tire of this old warrior," he chuckled in return to her comment.

"Even when I'm old and grey, I'll never tire of making love with you, Ulrick."

"I may hold you to such a vow, wife."

Bridgette turned from him to pour him a cup of wine. She offered the chalice and watched him take a sip. "You could have mentioned you were an earl," she said, with a raised brow.

"Would that have made any difference to your agreeing to become my bride?" he asked warily, and she did a double take to see if he was joking with her. The seriousness of his features told her much. Obviously, this was a subject of much contention with the women he may have considered for his bride in the past.

"You know it didn't. To me you were just a knight. I would have been perfectly happy to make our home here at Berwyck as long as Dristan and Amiria didn't mind that we continued to live here. I don't care about titles or whatever wealth you may or may not possess."

"Which is why you, more than any other woman who may have crossed my path, are worthy of being my wife, Countess," he replied, before setting the chalice down and pulling her into his arm once more.

"Countess... that's going to take some getting used to," she said while sliding her arms around his waist.

"Countess is hardly worthy of you. I would call you my Queen for all our days together, which would be more fitting."

"Maybe while we're alone together," she laughed, "although that, too, makes me uneasy."

"Then mayhap I should just continue to whisper sweet endearments, *mon amour*," he said in a husky whisper, while the soft Norman French accent sent shivers throughout her body.

"No more talking, Ulrick," she exclaimed, quietly. "I think there are better things you could do with your mouth right about now."

She ran her fingers down his muscular chest, watching his wicked eyes urge her further in her exploration of his body. He pulled his tunic from his torso, revealing what was now avail-able for her viewing pleasure. Ripple upon ripple of his six pack proved her husband spent many an hour with his training, and now his body was all hers to enjoy and explore. She took a cursory glance at the magnificent bulge outlined through his hose. An arched brow rose when she looked up into his hand-some face.

"See what you do to me, *ma cherie?*" he asked with a roguish smile.

She only returned his smile with one of her own before she watched him strip away the rest of his clothing. When he stood naked before her, his fingers softly trailed over the skin outlined at the neckline of her robe. A simple tug of the tie at her waist with one hand loosened it, and his other pushed the fabric from one shoulder until the linen fell to the floor at her feet. He trailed his fingertips down her back and found her soft buttocks, giving them a gently squeeze. Her breath hitched and a chuckle escaped him. He pressed a kiss to her temple. She gulped hard when he turned from her to stride toward the bed as she watched the muscles of his back and waist and his own toned bottom in fascination. The mere presence of him caused her stomach to clench in anticipation.

He drew back the coverlet of the bed, not caring that some fell to the floor in his urgency to see to their needs. He sat on the edge and his look held her spellbound until an unspoken command for her to join him had her moving forward. She ran her fingers through his shoulder-length hair while his mouth suckled at her breasts. Her back arched, begging him to take her and she felt his powerful hands reaching for her waist until she lay atop him. Skin to skin, a rush of heat flooded her body and she leaned down to receive his kiss.

Ulrick devoured her mouth with deep sweeping strokes of his tongue. It was a hungry possession as though they had been waiting an entire lifetime to at last find the missing half of themselves. She became lost in his kiss until she could wait no longer to seal their fate together. She moved above his manhood and lowered herself upon his shaft. The exquisite tightness while he filled her completely made her head arch backwards before she once more lowered her mouth to his own. They began to move in unison while their tongues danced as each of their bodies melted together in this sacred union.

He urged her on, letting Bridgette take control of their love-making before he at last rolled her over. Where his body began, hers ended. They were one with *Time* and never before had she ever felt this loved. The furious beat of her heart echoed with his as Ulrick brought them closer to the heavens. Every muscle in her body tensed in expectation before she screamed out his name when she found her release. With one last pulse of his body into her own, his seed filled her before his lips came crashing down upon her mouth again.

Their chests heaved against one another until their breathing at last returned to normal. Ulrick rolled over and he pulled her into his side while her head rested upon his chest. Her fingers rubbed at the hair tickling her nose before she snuggled into his warmth. Their fate had been sealed. They were as one. Their lives were complete.

CHAPTER 32

U lrick quietly opened his bedchamber door so as not to awake the beauty who still slumbered in his bed. Stepping inside the room, he gently shut the door before moving forward to watch his sleeping wife in the candlelight of the chamber. She appeared as an angel. Her perfection whilst resting caused his heart to fiercely beat inside his chest. Her hand resting beneath her cheek, a slight smile curved her lips and he pondered what she was dreaming about to cause the serenity of her features.

He sat down and reached over to carefully brush the silky black tresses from her face. He must have infiltrated her dreams, because her eyelids began to flutter open and the candle next to the bed became reflected in the green of her eyes. She began to stretch before she once more relaxed, holding out her hand for him to join her.

"You're already dressed, Ulrick. What was so important that you left our bed before the sun has even risen for the day?" she asked in a breathy whisper whilst tugging upon his hand. Instead of joining her, for he knew he would not be able to resist the temptation she presented, he gathered her in his arms and nuzzled her neck, smelling the light floral scent that had parts of him rising to the urgency of his need if he but let the morning take its natural course.

"Good morning, my sweet," he said in return. "We must rise if we are to begin our journey."

She pulled back from him to stare at him intently whilst her puzzlement etched itself across her visage. "What journey? You did not mention we were leaving Berwyck so soon for Dunster Castle."

He kissed her forehead before leaving her clutching the coverlet over her naked breasts whilst he made his way across the room. Aye. She was too tempting to continue to gaze upon her and there was much to do if they were to leave this morn.

"Yesterday's festivities must have caused you to forget we have been summoned by the king, although I must admit I, too, would like nothing better than to continue our wedding celebration." He gave her a wicked grin before turning his attention to the parchments upon the table.

She gave a sleepy yawn. "We did keep one another up for most of the evening," she teased with a seductive tone, suggesting she would like nothing better than to continue where they had left off but hours ago.

Alas, there was no time to give in to his baser needs. He ran his hand over the back of his neck. "I have just left Lord Dristan's solar. I have been asked to ride one last time with him and his men to Bamburgh Castle to meet with the king. The journey will not take long but there is much to pack. They will not wait for us if we are not ready to ride when the company is ready."

"You're taking me with you?" she asked as if she doubted his words.

"Aye and the children, as well, so we must needs pack and quickly. We will not be returning to Berwyck and can send for anything we must leave behind. From Bamburgh we will continue on to Dunster so I can claim my lands that have been neglected for many a year."

"Berwyck has been all that I've known since I slipped through *Time*, Ulrick," she said in what sounded like shock. He stopped rolling the parchments on the table before him to watch his wife's eyes flit around the room. 'Twas not like her to panic, for she had always appeared up to the challenges of being thrown into a time not her own.

He returned to her side and took her cold shaking hands in his, bringing them to his lips. "There is nothing to fear, *mon amour*," he whispered, before bending forward to place a quick kiss upon her mouth. "We are only beginning a new adventure, you and I together, as husband and wife."

"I know. It's just that I guess I never thought we'd be leaving here and all the people I've come to care for," she answered before he pulled her from the bed.

He gathered her into his arms, his chin resting on the top of her head. "I shall keep you and the children safe, and you have no need to fear, Bridgette, but please hurry. Lord Dristan does not like to be kept waiting, especially when he must needs appear before the king."

"Of course, Ulrick. As you are aware, there's not much for me to pack since I came here only with one gown that wasn't even for the right time period," she proclaimed, before leaving his arms and scurrying around the room to gather what she felt must be packed.

"I will rectify that upon our arrival at Dunster. No wife or children of mine shall ever go lacking in the basic necessities of life," he answered, feeling guilty he had not adequately provided for her.

She must have known the bitterness of his words for she rushed to him. "I only need you, Ulrick," she said putting her hand around his neck, gently pushing so he leaned forward. She quickly kissed his lips. "The rest doesn't matter in the least to me. As long as we are together, that is the only necessity of life I shall ever need."

Her words reassured him, and he gave her another kiss. "Then off with you now and see to packing else I shall take you over to that bed and make love to you, which will surely irritate our liege lord."

He heard her giggle and mutter something about him making it up to her later. He went back to the task at hand. He had much to see to and as the room began to empty of his belongings he, too, had a moment of melancholy fill his heart. He put on his black tabard with a red dragon embroidered on his chest, a dark blood red cape flowed from his shoulders… the last time he would wear Dristan's colors before he began to wear his own. He had followed Dristan since his youth, but Berwyck had been his home for the past nine years since the siege. Now 'twas time to move on with his life and leave the past behind. 'Twas a new beginning and at last he had a woman whom he loved to share his life with. He was blessed.

Bridgette went to a nearby wagon, two blankets in hand. Stepping into the conveyance, she began tucking the wool around Eustace and Eva to ensure their warmth from the coolness of the morn. Eva was snuggled into the boy's side, her thumb sucking away inside her mouth. Bridgette smiled at the cuteness of the both of them. Eustace had become quite attached to the little girl and she prayed there would come a time when they only thought of each other as brother and sister.

"Will the journey take long, Lady Bridgette?" the boy asked, as he looked around the busy outer bailey filled with knights who were beginning to mount their steeds.

She reached over to caress his cheek, knowing there would come a time when such a sign of public affection might be considered a sign of weakness as he grew. "Nay, the ride will not take long but I do not know how much time we shall remain at Bamburgh before we continue on to our new home."

She gave his cheek a little pat and began to withdraw but he grabbed her fingers in a fierce grip for one so young. Fear flickered in his brown eyes, and she bent forward to kiss his forehead.

"There is nothing to fear, Eustace. Lord Ulrick and I now consider you and Eva our children. You shall be taken care of as befits your new station in life. Never doubt we care for you as if you had been our very own."

He gulped hard. "Aye, milady."

She gave him a reassuring smile and leaned forward to whisper in his ear. "I know that we can in no way replace your parents, Eustace, and I am sorry they were not among those who were spared. But when the time is right and you are ready, nothing would please me more than for you to call me *mother*."

Sitting back on her heels to watch the lad, his eyes misted up before he wiped them with his sleeve and a sniffle. "Aye... mother," he replied with a nod.

Her heart melted right there on the spot and Bridgette had her own moment of weakness, knowing these two precious souls were her responsibility.

"Very well, then. Now take good care of your sister, Eustace, and let any of the guards know if there is anything you need. I will be riding nearby with your father," she said before jumping down from the wagon.

"I shall take good care of her, mother," the boy beamed.

"Thank you, son."

With a final look at the children and knowing they were settled, she made her way to Ulrick, who was talking with Lady Amiria. She would miss this woman, who had become her first friend since the unexpected arrival at her gates. When she approached, Amiria wrapped Bridgette in an unexpected hug.

"You shall be missed, Bridgette," Amiria said, her violet eyes reflecting her emotions that were usually kept hidden from view. "Who shall I spar with when my husband deems I am once more capable of lifting a sword after this babe is born?"

Bridgette laughed. "I am certain any one of Lord Dristan's guards shall be up to the task, my lady, as they were before my arrival."

"Aye. I suppose this is true. However, I enjoyed training you to become the swordswoman you are today," she said sweetly.

"I am far from being of the same caliber as you are, my lady," Bridgette answered, with a blush rushing across her face.

Ulrick put his hand around her waist. "I shall make sure she continues to do you proud, Lady Amiria."

Amiria nodded. "See that you do," she said, reaching out for his hands. "You and I have been through much, Ulrick, and, while we may have started out as enemies many years ago, 'tis an honor to now call you my friend."

"The honor has been mine, my lady," Ulrick said with a bow.

Amiria shook her head, and she moved a lock of her red tresses behind her ear. "Do not be strangers to Berwyck. I expect you to return for regular visits."

Ulrick brought her fingers to his lips. "My lady… Bridgette say your farewells. We must ride."

He left the two women alone and Bridgette felt over-whelmed with their departure. Amiria must have felt the same, for they enveloped each other in another hug.

"You shall take good care of him… and yourself, of course," Amiria stated.

"Yes…" Bridgette whispered.

"And you will send a runner if you ever have need of us." Amiria continued holding onto Bridgette's hands.

"Yes." Tears welled in Bridgette's eyes before they began to fall down her cheeks.

"There are not many women whom I call friend, but I am glad you crossed through *Time* and became mine."

Bridgette gave her friend another hug. "So am I. Thank you for everything you have done for me and, when you next see your grandmother, please thank her for giving me that coin so I might make a wish. If it wasn't for her, I wouldn't be here now."

"I am certain she is pleased that all has worked out as it should. Now off you go, my dearest friend. I can see my Dragon is impatient to be on his way and 'tis never good to keep my man waiting."

"Take care of yourself, Lady Amiria," Bridgette said.

"And God speed to you, Lady Bridgette."

Before there were more tears to spill with their departure, Amiria left her to go to her husband to say her own farewell whilst Bridgette made her way to her horse. Ulrick stood next to the steed.

"All is well?" he asked.

"Yes, but I shall miss her company."

"We shall return one day for a visit. Are you ready to depart?"

"Let us be on our way to a new adventure, my husband."

She gave him a bright smile before he lifted her into the saddle. Once she was seated, he handed her a pair of soft leather gloves along with the reins. With a nod of her head, Ulrick went to his own horse and Bridgette marveled how Dristan's knights were a force to be reconned with. Seeing them all together, she would certainly understand how Dristan had earned his reputation as the Devil's Dragon. She was glad that, for her own part of this journey, she at least wouldn't be sending Ulrick off to some battle.

CHAPTER 33

The thunderous sounds of hundreds of horses cantering across the packed sand of the beach left Bridgette in awe. They had travelled fast today and Ulrick had told her that the wagon carrying the children and other supplies would eventually catch up. She had a moment of panic with worry for Eustace and Eva but her husband reassured her they were well guarded. It had taken several miles of their journey before she could finally relax and trust that they were well taken care of, especially since she had given Eustace her word that she would be nearby.

Now, with the keep of Bamburgh seen in the distance, she marveled at the sea of dark red capes that fluttered in the breeze of Dristan's personal guard riding ahead of her. Witnessing such a force, she could understand how they would scare anyone with half a brain into surrendering. Luckily for her, she had no worries about a possible invasion, but her thoughts lingered on Maya's words that she and Ulrick would still be tested. Wasn't the incident at the well enough that *Time* would now leave them in peace to begin their lives together?

She kept her focus on handling her mount and the keep that rose majestically on the rise of land in the distance. She briefly closed her eyes and, when she opened them again, she swore for the briefest of seconds she saw a modern-day Bamburgh in its place. The vision disappeared quickly to the twelfth century keep and outer walls that now existed. It hardly appeared like the pictures she had seen on the internet, and she had to admit she was a little disappointed. Inwardly she laughed at her own stupidity. It had taken years for Bamburgh to become the place of the land of kings it was later known. It would be an important castle to defend the land, thanks to the architects that rebuilt the structures over the centuries. Henry II may have started this place but would not be around to see its completion, let alone what it had become in modern times.

As the distance lessened between Bridgette and a place where she knew others had traveled through *Time*, her heart skipped a beat at the possibility that this had been a horrible mistake. She should have stayed at Berwyck until Ulrick's business was completed and Dristan released him. Or he could have just sent her ahead to Dunster. Either way, something in her gut told her they needed to get the hell out of Bamburgh as quickly as possible.

When they finally reached the outskirts of the castle, Bridgette could see for herself that the king had been summoning his army for something major happening in some unknown place. Tents and camp life were everywhere before her eyes, but she didn't remember British history well enough to know what event was going to change the course of the country. They came to a halt and Dristan began ordering the majority of his men to set up camp before he gestured for his personal guard to accompany him to the keep. A motion of Ulrick's hand indicated that this included Bridgette. With a nudge of her heel, she put her horse back into motion.

When they arrived inside the courtyard, or inner bailey she supposed, lads came to take the reins of their horses to lead them to the stables. Bridgette could only assume they must be overflowing if the king had summoned his noblemen for their support. Ulrick came and lifted her from the saddle and her knees buckled before he pulled her into his chest. The familiar scent of him calmed her frayed nerves, especially when he pulled off his gauntlet and caressed her cheek.

"Are you unwell?" he asked, his brow furrowed in concern.

"I am uneasy," she replied while her voice quivered in uncertainty. She watched his shoulder-length black hair moving with the afternoon wind and she wished with all her heart they were back in their bedchamber at Berwyck. "This was a bad idea."

"What do you mean, *mon amour*?" he whispered while searching her face.

"I think you were right all along that I have no place being at this castle. The closer we got to Bamburgh, the more I began to feel apprehensive, as though the castle was warning me to stay away... or maybe it was *Time* itself." She shook her head before she felt him kiss the top of her head.

"We cannot change our decisions, unfortunately, Bridgette. We are here now, and we will do our duty by paying homage to our king," Ulrick said, before lifting her chin and kissing her lips.

"The king? I am to meet the king?" Shock gripped her innards right down to the very tips of her medieval boots. "I can't meet the king, Ulrick!"

"Aye, you can and you will. 'Twill be expected of you, my lady. Be certain to remember to watch your manner of speech whilst you are here. There are those who would like nothing more than to cut us to the quick if 'twill make them appear far more favorable in the eyes of His Majesty."

"I think I'm going to be sick," Bridgette groaned. "You mentioned nothing about us meeting with the king, only that Dristan had been summoned."

"Since I am to take over my lands and you are my Countess, we are required to submit to the king's rule. Hopefully, the amount of coinage I have will be sufficient that I will not need to be a part of whatever plans he has for the army he has amassed outside of his gates."

"I'm never going to be able to pull this off with a court full of people, Ulrick." She cast leery eyes around at the people wandering through the courtyard.

He took both her cheeks in the palms of his hands. Their warmth seeped into her soul giving her the comfort she stood in need of. "Aye, you will, wife. I have seen for myself your courage and strength during our time together. You will not falter in your resolve to firmly place yourself in this time and place."

His words were like an order for her to get her act together but also a balm to the part of her that was scared to death. She could do this. She really didn't have much of a choice. She gave him a brief nod, words having left her, and he took her acceptance of her fate in this life.

Offering her his arm, she grasped at the life support as if he were the anchor she needed to keep her grounded. He placed his other hand over her own while she moved her thumb back and forth across fabric beneath her fingertips. Each step brought her closer to the stairs leading up into the keep and whatever new challenge she was about to face.

The wooden portal opened before them as if by magic. Dristan's entourage continued to file into the building and, as Bridgette entered the keep, a servant gave them a brief nod. The Great Hall came into view, its timbered ceiling high above their heads. Walls were covered in intricate tapestries and Bridgette couldn't even begin to imagine how long it must have taken someone to create such masterpieces. A huge fireplace was inlaid into one wall and Bridgette was certain she would have been able to stand upright in the hearth, it was that big. She gave a brief sigh of relief but was still a little surprised the room wasn't filled with people. She looked up at Ulrick and he nodded to the far end of the hall where another room containing a throne sat empty. Since the king wasn't in attendance, she assumed other courtiers were seeing to their own amusements until they were called upon.

Ulrick squeezed her hand. "We will be shown to a room where we can rest after our journey. I am certain we will be called to attend the king with the evening meal."

As they moved forward toward a nearby turret, Dristan raised his hand to halt their progress. "Nay. We shall use the other stairs in another wing," he replied to the servant leading them to their rooms.

"As you wish, my lord," the man answered before moving down another passageway while Dristan's men began to follow.

Ulrick and Bridgette looked upon each other as they brought up the rear of their group. When they moved near the turret stairs, a slight rumbling beneath their feet halted them from continuing. Bridgette gazed into the turret and she swore she saw modern day lights along with a soft twinkling glow. She grasped Ulrick's arm in a tighter grip even as he pulled her closer into his side.

"Ulrick," Dristan called out. "You would be wise to keep yourself and your lady away from that turret in particular if you understand my meaning."

"Aye, Lord Dristan," Ulrick replied before he pulled Bridgette away from the stairwell.

Curiosity got the better of her when she turned back to look at the place where the modern world waited for her return. A sucking sound diminished the lit turret and once more a torch was placed in a sconce at the entrance.

"We need to get the hell out of here, Ulrick." He lengthened his stride as though he now understood her need to leave Bamburgh, while Bridgette raced to keep up with her taller husband.

"Aye," he murmured. "As soon as 'tis permissible, we shall leave and never step foot here again," he replied, while raising her hand to his lips.

Bridgette could only pray that their time here at Bamburgh would be brief. She had no intention of allowing *Time* to take her from the man who meant everything to her!

CHAPTER 34

U lrick stood near the steps leading up to the area where
the king now resided, Bridgette fidgeting at his side. He
linked his fingertips through hers, hoping to try and calm his
wife. When he glanced down upon her, she appeared as though
she was about to flee from the room, and he could hardly blame
her. Dristan and his men held the attention of all those who now
filled Bamburgh's Great Hall. 'Twas not often the Devil's Dragon
was summoned to court, and jealousy leaked from these people
like water from a spout.

Ulrick listened intently to the reason the king required
Dristan and the small contingent of men he had brought with
him to Bamburgh. Henry the Young King, the eldest son of
Henry II and Eleanor of Aquitaine, had been waging a campaign
against his father in France. Ulrick knew a bit of the young
man's history. At the age of fifteen summers, Henry the Young
King had been crowned during his father's reign. However, he
had apparently grown frustrated by his father's refusal to grant

him meaningful self-ruling power. Ulrick had not been aware that father and son had fallen out with one another in the year of our Lord's Grace 1173, around the same time as the siege of Berwyck. However, they reconciled after the capture of his mother and the failure of the rebellion.

Henry the Young King then spent many years in his enthusiasm for attending and competing in tournaments until last year when he fell out with William Marshal, the leader of his tournament *mesnée*. Now, he had been waging another campaign against his father and brother Richard in Limousin, France, and had been pillaging local monasteries to raise coinage to pay his mercenaries. Henry II wanted reinforcements from his noblemen.

Ulrick watched when Dristan bowed before their king before striding backwards a respectable distance. He then made his way to stand on the other side of Ulrick's wife, so that Bridgette stood between the two towering men. He heard her give a heavy sigh, as if the added reinforcement of the Devil's Dragon next to her gave her the extra bit of comfort she needed. Ulrick took her hand and placed it at his elbow, knowing what would come shortly.

"I will be heading to France with most of the men," Dristan began whilst peering straight ahead. "Luckily, I left Bertram and Killian at Berwyck with enough guards to see to its protection, but I am not happy that the king would not listen to my petition for me to return home."

"'Tis hardly surprising, Dristan," Ulrick exclaimed. "The king wants his best men on this campaign, and you are one of his fiercest warriors."

"Aye. My reputation still stands in place no matter the years since I have had to defend it. I suppose there is an advantage to having made a name for myself in my younger years."

Bridgette chuckled. "You are hardly old, Lord Dristan. However, I must admit that seeing all your personal guardsmen together is quite the site to behold. Did you all realize how much you have in common with your similar long black hair and your garments that look like they've been given to you by the Devil himself after a trip to hell?"

The two men laughed together and a looked passed between them before Dristan crossed his arms over his chest. "'Twas not intentional but, as knights began to follow me from one tourney to another, it became a requirement in order to show our unison, I suppose. I think those days are long gone now, with Sir Godfrey joining our ranks."

"He has proven himself more than worthy to wear your colors, my lord," Ulrick replied, satisfied with the young knight's training and how his attitude had turned around for the better. Aye, 'twas as though Godfrey was a completely different man than the one who first showed up at Berwyck's gates.

"And he will be presented with them before we leave for France. I must send a runner back to Berwyck to give Amiria what small measure of comfort it may be to have news, though she will not be pleased to know I am departing from England's soil. I will also not leave you without enough guards to watch your back whilst you return to Dunster," Dristan said, widening his stance.

"I appreciate the reinforcements," Ulrick replied, "especially since we have the children to protect."

Bridgette poked her finger into his chest. "What about my protection?" she teased playfully.

Ulrick lifted her finger to his lips. "You are a treasure beyond compare, *ma cherie*, and I would die to protect you. However, I would not wish to say you could not defend yourself if the need arose. Not after you spent so much time upon the training field with the Lady Amiria."

"My wife did amazingly well with your training, Lady Bridgette, even though she dismissed my words given her pregnancy. She is most stubborn," Dristan complained, although Ulrick could see how proud Dristan was of his wife before his gaze turned to those in the hall. *"God's Bones,* how I hate court life. Do these people have nothing better to do than wait for the scraps the king might throw at their feet?"

Before Ulrick could comment, he heard what he had been dreading all eve.

"Come before your king, the Earl and Countess of Somerset," a voice echoed throughout the hall

"Oh my God!" Bridgette moaned.

"Take a deep breath, my lady," Ulrick said, before ushering his wife to stand before Henry II. They made their bow and awaited the king's command.

"You have married," the king exclaimed, more in a statement than a question.

"Aye, Your Majesty," Ulrick answered, waving his hand to the lady at his side. "May I present my wife, Lady Bridgette of Dunster."

Bridgette curtsied before their king. He waved her closer. She stood before him as he inspected her from head to toe and Ulrick was proud of Bridgette when she appeared as confident as he knew she could be, despite her apprehension of this meeting.

"She is exquisite, Lord Ulrick," the king finally replied, before pointing his finger toward the lady. "And will you swear your fealty to your king as you have sworn to obey your husband, Countess?"

Bridgette stepped forward before kneeling down, taking the king's hand, and kissing the ring upon his finger. "Aye, Your Majesty, with all that I am, I vow you my fealty."

"Rise, Lady Bridgette," the king exclaimed. He appeared satisfied with Bridgette's response, although what other answer did he expect? Of course, she would swear her loyalty to their king. He returned his attention back to Ulrick with a nod. "May I assume you are finally done following at the heels of my Devil's Dragon and will now take your rightful place at Dunster Castle and begin to manage your estates?"

"'Tis my plan, Your Majesty, with your blessing, of course," Ulrick said, taking a heavy pouch tied at his belt. "Mayhap this will help with your cause in France to adequately fund your army whilst I continue home instead of joining the campaign."

A man standing behind the king came to take the pouch, bouncing the leather bag as if to weigh its contents. Opening the strap, he peered inside before he nodded to the king that the offering was substantial and more than sufficient.

"It appears you have given enough coinage to satisfy my steward. Proceed to your estates, Lord Ulrick, and protect the castle in my name," Henry declared, with a wave of his hand, dismissing them. Their audience with the king had been brief but luckily over.

"Your Majesty," Ulrick replied, taking Bridgette's elbow whilst they both bowed, paying homage to their king.

They returned to Dristan and his men who had gathered around him. Bridgette turned toward Ulrick and her hand shook upon his arm.

"Can we now get the heck out of here?" she asked quietly, looking upon him with worried eyes.

"Only after the king has retired. We can then return to our chamber for a good night's rest. We shall leave come the morn," Ulrick said giving her hand a gentle squeeze.

"Dawn cannot come soon enough," she whispered.

It would be hours later before they could at last seek their chamber. With the dawn they would finally travel toward home. Ulrick could only ponder what awaited them upon their arrival.

CHAPTER 35

S wirling images of Bamburgh's past floated across Bridgette's dreams. One... a young woman in a shimmering pink gown calling out for the boy she loved and who was lost to her; another... four women falling down in a turret as they were swept back in Time; one more... of one of those same women, heavily pregnant, praying upon the identical set of stairs begging to go back to her own place in Time; and lastly... her best friend Megan who appeared out of place around the ancient stones of the castle as she called out to... her.

"Bridgette! Where are you?" her voice rang out in an eerie faraway tone. "Come home!"

A robe wrapped around her, Bridgette's feet ran down the cold passageway while she became lost in the twist and turns of an unfamiliar castle as she followed the sound of her friend's voice.

"I'm coming, Megan," Bridgette called out, as she continued to dart down one corridor after another. She went down one of the turrets with a sensation that this particular one was only a set of stairs and not a connection to modern times. She continued onward.

Turning around, uncertain of which way to go, she distantly heard her friend's voice once more calling out to her. "Hurry, Bridgette, before it's too late!"

Left! She needed to go left and she took off once more before coming to a sudden halt before a glowing turret. Dristan had warned her about not going near this one, and Bridgette now understood why. This was the place where Katherine de Deveraux and her friends had traveled through Time and Bridgette assumed these were the women she saw in her dream.

Hesitantly, she approached and saw a vague ghostly image of her friend as though she was floating in thin air.

"There you are, Bridgette," Megan exclaimed with a smile, her hand outstretched for Bridgette to take. "Are you ready to come home? You've been missed."

"I am home, Megan," Bridgette insisted taking a step forward before she stopped. The urge to enter the stairwell was stronger than she thought it would be.

Megan frowned. "Home is here… with me. Zoe and I need you."

Bridgette shook her head. "But I've found love here, Megan. I've married a wonderful man."

"You don't belong there, Bridgette, and you are messing with the fabric of Time! Come with me now," Megan shouted, reaching out her hand once more.

"I cannot leave him," Bridgette cried out, even as her feet unwillingly took another step closer toward the turret. She watched in fascination as her friend's hand pushed through the barrier between the past and the present, appearing as real as her very own.

"That's it, Bridgette. Just one more step," Meagan urged and Bridgette raised her own arm. Her fingertips were still barely out of reach from her friends.

She hesitated once more, tears rushing down her cheeks. "I love him. He'll never understand why I left him," she sobbed, as she inched her way forward and watched her friend's smile of encouragement.

"You will learn to love again," Megan replied as she took Bridgette's hand in a firm grip.

"Never..." Bridgette said with a mournful cry. "I will never love another as I have loved Ulrick."

Hearing his name out loud caused Bridgette to break contact with Megan as she pulled her hand away. My God! What had she almost done? With the spell that had been woven around her broken, Bridgette gazed once more into the turret. It was no longer Megan urging her to go back to her own place in time but some unknown ghostly vision of someone long past dead. The empty space inside the skull where its eyes should have been, began to glow a deep horrifying red.

"'Tis time fer ye tae go home!" The skeletal bones once more reached out to grab Bridgette by the hand and she heard the abominable tone of the repulsive being that had her in its grasp begin to chuckle. As it pulled her closer to the turret and away from Ulrick, Bridgette let out a terrified scream!

✖

Startled awake, Ulrick reached over for his wife, only to find her place beside him empty. He turned toward the hearth expecting to find her there, only to see the low glowing embers left by the untended fire instead. Bolting upright in their bed, he searched the chamber. She was gone.

He wasted no time getting dressed. As he tightened a belt around his waist, he reached for his sword that was propped up near the head of the bed. Pushing the blade into the scabbard at his side, he rushed toward the door and swung it wide.

Which way? A moment's hesitation brought him the only

conclusion he could rationally think of. Bridgette was leaving him! Running down the corridor, he remembered Riorden de Deveraux once telling him about the tale of his wife, Katherine, and the unbelievable method by which she and her friends had traveled through time. He hurried down a turret, remembering how they reasoned that going down in one particular set of stairs brought the women back into the twelfth century and to go up them surely took them back to the twenty-first. With nothing else to go on, he had the distinct notion he would find Bridgette at the bottom of that particular turret.

He heard her scream just as he rounded a corner. His eyes widened as he watched his wife wrestle within the grip of a skeleton pulling her toward the interior of *Time* itself. With no further hesitation, he ran to his wife, grasped her about the waist, and yanked her into his chest with all his might. They fell backwards onto the floor and the connection to the future was gone. The skeleton threw back its head, giving off a startling scream before it vanished, along with the glowing lights writhing in the turret. Once more, the stairs appeared as any other inside of Bamburgh's walls.

Bridgette turned into his arms, sobbing and muttering words that were incoherent, as Ulrick continued to grasp the meaning of her being in this predicament in the first place.

"You were leaving me?" His words bitterly escaped from his lips while her betrayal was like a knife wound to his heart.

"No!" she managed to say, pulling back from his arms to stare into his face in the dimly -lit passageway. "I thought I was dreaming and must have been sleepwalking."

A muffled curse left his mouth and he began to untangle himself from his wife before standing and offering her his hand.

Helping her from the floor, he took her elbow to usher her down the corridor.

"Ulrick?"

They passed a guard standing near one of the doorways leading out of the keep.

"Not now," he fumed, whilst he continued to take her up to the next floor. "I do not wish our private conversation to be overheard by someone who could mayhap use such information against us."

They reached their chamber and the door slammed against the wall with the force of its opening. He pushed Bridgette inside before bolting the door. His head rested upon the wood, and he took a deep breath. "Explain yourself," he growled out in frustration before he at last turned to face her. His heart hammered inside his chest, and he knew he was barely holding onto his effort to control his temper.

"I was sleeping and—"

"—and leaving me, Bridgette!" he yelled out and he watched her jerk away from his outburst. "You nigh unto broke my heart to see you—"

"—and I can mend the hurt I caused you but I was *sleeping*, Ulrick," she shouted back at him, her hands placed on her hips in defiance. "You can't hold me accountable for something I unknowing did when I wasn't myself and asleep."

"Aye! I can. 'Tis clear that subconsciously you wish to return to your own time," he assumed, crossing his arms over his chest.

"You're being unreasonable," she stated, tears beginning to rush down her cheeks. She turned away from him to go to a table, resting her hands on the edges whilst he watched her shoulders heave in her grief. "I would never intentionally cause you pain, Ulrick, nor do I wish to leave you to go back to modern times and the empty life that would await me there at my return."

He took a step forward before he halted in indecision. Aye, perchance she was right when she told him he could not hold her accountable for something she had no control over and yet... something in the pit of his belly said he needed time to sort out his thoughts. He shook his head and for the first time since she all but fell into his arms, did not offer to comfort her, even though every part of him warred within him to go to her.

Nay. He was upset and need to clear his head. "Dawn approaches. I will send someone to assist you with dressing and meet you in the Great Hall to break our fast with the children. Must I needs warn you to stay away from *that* particular turret?" he snapped heading toward the door.

"No." Her quiet response satisfied him, and he left her to her own thoughts. He had the notion that, by not going to his wife, he had just made a horrible mistake even whilst he ignored Lady Myra's reminder to beware of happenings that may tear his wife and him apart.

CHAPTER 36

Bridgette stood silently at the rail of the ship lost in thought. Leaving Dristan and his men at Bamburgh had been bittersweet, although she had been glad to be a part of the short ceremony when Godfrey had received Dristan's colors. Although there had been plenty of ships bobbing in the waves of the sea, they were bound for France and none were available for Ulrick's party to take them down and around the coast of England to Dunster. It was a journey of roughly four hundred miles by land.

After a final farewell to Dristan and everyone who had been a constant in her life since arriving in the twelfth century, Ulrick's party rode south for several miles before her husband hired a ship in North Sunderland. The brothers Turquine and Taegan had joined their party, along with several other of Berwyck's knights she was unfamiliar with, since Dristan had more knights in his service than Bridgette could count.

With her excited children now at her side, Bridgette stared

off into the distance while the ship began to unload in the fishing village of Dunster near the river's inlet and not far from where they were now anchored. The castle rose some two hundred feet up from the motte and bailey hill where the sea provided a natural defense. Her new home. This should have been a happy time in her life, but unfortunately her mood was anything but happy.

Ulrick had been irritable the entire trip and had given her nothing but the bare minimum response to any question she asked of him. She finally gave up for the time being, since living on board a ship, no matter how brief, tended to not give them a whole lot of privacy. Their cabin was small and even more so with the children nestled in their own cots and, although they shared a bed, there certainly wasn't an opportunity to either discuss the problem that had caused a rift between them or to have sex... not that she was about to have Ulrick make love to her when he had barely spoken a word to her in days.

A heavy sigh escaped her with the realization that she had no clue what to expect upon her arrival at the castle. She knew Ulrick's mother lived there, taking care of his younger brother and sister. She didn't even know their names for heaven's sake! The eldest son had passed away, leaving Ulrick with the title. Bridgette had been surprised that her husband hadn't returned to his lands sooner. She didn't have the answer as to why he hadn't, nor any information about the place she would now call home.

The brothers joined her at the rail before Taegan took the children to disembark the ship. Turquine leaned his elbows upon the railing, clasping his fingers together before casting her a quick glance.

"You have fallen out of accord with Ulrick," he said, his tone flat, as though his words were as distasteful to him as they were to Bridgette.

"Aye," Bridgette answered, unsure she would be able to say more... not that it was anyone's business.

"Why?" he asked giving her his full attention.

Bridgette turned toward the knight who was so similar to Ulrick that it was almost painful to gaze upon him. Her brow lifted in annoyance. "Why do you not ask him yourself?" Her sarcastic tone surprised him.

"I tried. He told me to mind my own business," Turquine replied, with a frown.

"Sound advice," she replied, before returning her gaze back to the castle. She pointed to the structure off in the distance. "Have you been here before?"

"Once, many a year ago. I met Ulrick's father before his passing, but we were young then and I cared not for learning the history of the place," Turquine said with a slight smile.

"I am certain 'tis a place of importance if King Henry is asking Ulrick to see to its keeping," Bridgette said, trying to think of something she might remember of the history of this time.

"I do know the castle survived a siege in the war for the throne between King Stephen and the Empress Matilda," he explained off handedly.

Something sparked a memory inside her head. "Are you talking about the Anarchy?" she asked, now far more curious about the history of the keep than she was before.

He nodded his head, possibly in approval. "Aye and depending on whose side you were on, either one could have very well been considered the ruling monarch of England."

"And is not King Henry the son of the Empress?"

Turquine's mouth lifted into a small grin. "You know our history well. I am surprised Ulrick has not mentioned all of this to you. After all, 'tis a part of your own history now that you are married and shall call Dunster your home."

"There is much my husband has yet to inform me about the place," she replied, still frustrated about not knowing what awaited her. "Did you know his older brother?"

"Aye. Briefly. 'Twas an unfortunate accident that took his life."

"I was not aware he had died from an accident," Bridgette exclaimed, feeling sorry for Ulrick at the loss of his brother.

"We were at Berwyck at that time. A riding accident, or so Ulrick was told," Turquine said before continuing. "'Twas very tragic, for he was in the prime of his life."

She was about to respond when Ulrick came into view and began to stride in their direction. Her breath hitched at the sight of him because, no matter how sad or angry she was with him, she still loved him with all of her heart. He must have seen something in her face for his features softened for the first time since the incident in Bamburgh's turret.

"Are you ready to go ashore, my lady?" he asked quietly, offering her his arm.

Her fingers trembled as she felt the muscles beneath her fingertips. "Aye, my lord," she answered for those close enough to hear their conversation.

Ulrick nodded as he began to escort her from the ship before speaking over his shoulder to his friend. "Turquine, ensure our horses have been offloaded and have been well seen to. I will ride with my wife and the children to the castle."

"Aye, Ulrick. Taegan and I will see you there shortly."

The wagon was nearby, and it took a moment for Bridgette to

get her footing once on solid ground, since she had become used to the swaying of a ship beneath her feet. Ulrick's arm swept around her waist for support, and he looked down upon her in concern. So, there was something there that hadn't vanished after all. She had begun to wonder if he was lost to her, and she shouldn't have doubted the connection that still existed between them.

"Are you unwell?" he asked, while holding her firmly against his own body.

"Not from the journey but only with what awaits me upon our arrival. You have told me nothing of the place that shall be our home." She lifted her head to stare into those blue-grey eyes and saw for herself the tension he had kept hidden from her.

"My apologies, madam," he replied, before continuing their walk to the wagon. He lifted her up onto the bench, noted the children were settled, and came to sit beside her while taking up the reins.

"We have barely spoken to one another since Bamburgh, Ulrick," she frantically whispered. "How long do you plan to punish me for something that I unwillingly did?"

She heard him curse beneath his breath before he cast a quick glance in her direction. He returned his eyes to the road before he answered her. "'Twas not my intention to worry you so."

"And you think not speaking to me about an important issue that has put a wedge in our relationship is not a matter that should immediately be discussed?" She swore her anger was about to get the better of her, but now was not the time with the children overhearing every word.

"'Tis a matter of grave import, Bridgette, but one I hoped to discuss once we were settled at Dunster," he said but still did not look upon her.

PROMISES MADE AT MIDNIGHT

"Tonight then?" she asked.

"Aye... this eve," Ulrick replied and flicked the reins to keep the horses moving.

They did not have to ride far, and Bridgette saw the stone walls surrounding her new home. Soon they passed through the main gatehouse entering the inner ward or bailey of the castle. The four story keep rose majestically and she saw only one turret, along with what she assumed was a chimney for the fireplaces inside. The large iron door opened and out came a middle-aged woman along with Ulrick's brother and sister. They were younger than Bridgette expected. The girl appeared as though she was around sixteen, the boy maybe two years older.

Ulrick's mother waved her hand in welcome and, as the team of horses came to a stop, a lad ran from the stables and took the reins. Ulrick helped Bridgette from the cart, along with the children, before asking her to wait and leaving her to head toward the keep. Ulrick gave his brother and sister each a fierce hug before turning toward his mother. He knelt before her, bowing his head, until she placed her hands upon his hair as though giving her blessing on his return. He rose and kissed both her cheeks. They began to have a brief conversation and his mother's appearance quickly changed. She now seemed upset while she turned hostile eyes in Bridgette's direction.

The last thing Bridgette expected was for Ulrick's mother to dislike her. She could only wonder what further angst was now going to surround their lives, especially when they all lived under one roof!

CHAPTER 37

U lrick barely concealed the rage he felt at the woman who gave him life whilst she reprimanded him for taking a wife without her knowledge... as if she actually had a say about who he could or could not wed!

"How could you do this to me, Ulrick. Marry some woman who brings nothing to fill your coffers. And who are these children? From what you just told me, you have not been married long enough to sire them yourself," his mother screeched.

"Lower your voice, madam, for you do my wife and family an injustice with your words," Ulrick warned, in a low tone.

"You place this woman above me and your brother and sister? How can you be so cruel to Rowan and Seraphina?" Her eyes flashed in anger before she continued her tirade. "'Tis because I remarried after your father died, even though my second husband is also long gone from this world. You wish to usurp the children's connection to Dunster. Is this not so?"

"Mother!" Rowan and Seraphina called out in unison. Shock

etched quickly across their features whilst they looked between each other and Ulrick.

Ulrick held up his hand to his brother and sister, knowing they did not agree with their mother's words. "She is my wife. They are my children," he reiterated with another warning his mother apparently had no intention of heeding. "You are all a part of my family, and no one is above another in my heart. Dunster has always belonged to me after Lief's passing, but this does not mean my brother and sister do not have a place in my household. This also includes you, madam."

She cursed beneath her breath. "Your father must surely be distressed in the heavens above for you to treat me thusly," she said, crossing herself.

"This is not about you, mother. Be civil whilst I introduce you to my family," Ulrick said, before raising his hand and flicking his fingers for his wife and the children to come forward. He watched Bridgette's brow rise at his unspoken command and hoped for once his willful wife would just obey him instead of asserting her own sense of independence. Now was not the time for her to voice how her own life was led.

Bridgette placed an arm around each of the children and they moved forward until Ulrick took her hand to bring her to his side. "Bridgette... may I present my mother, Lady Helena," he said, whilst his wife curtsied.

"My lady," Bridgette said before rising. "'Tis a pleasure to meet you."

Ulrick was about to berate his mother once more, since she silently stood there inspecting Bridgette as if she were a peasant invading her home. But apparently 'twas not necessary.

"Lady Bridgette," Helena finally said, although Ulrick could see 'twas done reluctantly. "Welcome to Dunster Castle."

Ulrick then introduced his brother and sister. "And these are Rowan and Seraphina."

Seraphina stepped forward to give Bridgette a hug. "I am so excited to have you here, Lady Bridgette. I have always wanted to have a sister!" she rejoiced, her excitement brightening her entire visage.

"I am certain we will become good friends," Bridgette exclaimed before turning to Rowan. "'Tis also a pleasure to meet you."

"My Lady Bridgette. The pleasure is mine," he said, with a roguish smirk, and Ulrick gave a warning look to his sibling, who only laughed.

Rowan threw up his hands as though backing down from a foreseeable argument. "Nothing to fear here, brother. You have done well with your bride. She is exquisite."

Bridgette gave a brief nod before turning a bright smile toward the children next to her. "And these are our children, Eustace and Eva." Eustace gave a short nod of his head, clearly uncomfortable in the presence of new people. Eva only stuck her thumb in her mouth and grabbed hold of the edges of Bridgette's gown.

Helena turned from the group and headed toward the door. "You must be tired after your long journey. Come inside and I shall see the rooms I ordered for you have been prepared," she said over her shoulder, before proceeding inside.

Ulrick took Bridgette's hand to his lips. "All will be well, *ma cherie*," he whispered when he felt her fingers tremble.

"Will it? I am not so sure, Ulrick. I feel like we have just walked into a hornets nest," Bridgette answered as they followed his mother inside the keep.

"'Twill not be so bad," he answered, hoping that his words of reassurance would come to pass. "Let us see to getting everyone settled and then I can show you about the keep if you feel up to it. We can save the rest of the estate and village for another day."

His wife gripped his elbow tightly and he could tell she was nervous. How could he blame her? His long-awaited arrival at Dunster had not been a very welcoming one. He could only ponder what his mother would do next in order to bring further strife into his life.

He did not have long to wait for his answer when his mother showed him to his old bedchamber and not the one belonging to the lord of the keep. She began making excuses even whilst he demanded her belongings be removed to one of the lesser chambers. He then ordered fresh linen for the bed and a thorough cleansing of the room. He would not begin his time at Dunster as a doormat for his mother. The sooner she realized her right to run the estate as she saw fit was over, then the better. He was now home.

CHAPTER 38

B ridgette sat upon their bed with her legs crossed beneath her waiting for Ulrick to join her. The day had been…interesting for lack of a better word. She had seen Helena's attempt to control her son from the moment they were shown to a room, but this didn't only extend to where they would sleep. She continued to assert her dominance while showing them the keep, but luckily Ulrick put an end to her assertions. He had actually gone so far as to tell his mother that if she didn't like the fact that he was now home and Dunster was under his control, then he would have her moved to her dower house. She sputtered an angry reply before she finally told him that wouldn't be necessary.

Bridgette wasn't completely convinced that their life from this point forward would be full of unicorns and rainbows. Ulrick's brother and sister were a delight… his mother was another matter, and she could see that day-to-day living with the woman was going to try Bridgette's patience.

All Bridgette wanted at this moment was for Ulrick to return to their chamber after he finished whatever business he was still concluding for the day. Her children had been settled down two chambers away and they knew where to find their parents if they needed them. Bridgette needed her husband to come and lay down beside her and make everything right in the world. She didn't care about the past argument from the event at Bamburgh. She wanted to put that all behind her so they could look forward to their new life together. That wasn't too much to ask or was it?

The man of her musings opened their door as though she had magically conjured him up because he knew she needed him. "Ulrick," she cried out before leaving the bed in a rush and launching herself into his arms.

She heard him chuckle while he held her lovingly in his embrace. "Have you missed me, wife?" he asked, before tipping up her chin from his chest so he could gaze upon her. He gave her a wicked wink with one of his hypnotic blue-grey eyes before she returned her head to the placement on his chest and again grasped him firmly around his waist.

"You couldn't tell?" she asked in a breathy whisper.

"Aye. I suppose I can, but I was not far if you had need of me. The lord's solar is but down the passageway past the children's room. Is there anything wrong?" he asked, as he put the bolt in place. He picked her up and her arms wound around his neck to play with his hair. Kissing her upon her lips, he carried her to their bed to lay her down upon the pillows. She moved them against her back so she could prop herself up and watch him undress.

"No. Nothing is wrong other than being in a place I'm not

familiar with. It's been a long day." She watched him carefully and he gave her a nod.

He took the belt off around his waist and placed the scabbard holding his sword against the wall near where he would sleep. He then sat down on the edge of the bed and his boots dropped to the floor with a thud as he took them off. She couldn't help herself from going to him and molding her body against his back.

"Gosh, how I've missed you, Ulrick."

He took her hands and again brought them to his lips. "I have missed you as well, Bridgette, and the closeness we shared at Berwyck," he began, before pulling off his tunic.

She sighed in pleasure to now feel his warm skin beneath her hands. Her fingertips traced over his broad shoulder blades and his muscles flexed at her touch. "We can have what we shared again here, my love," she replied quietly waiting for his response.

"You wished to talk about Bamburgh and the turret." His flat tone almost broke her heart.

She shook her head in denial, although this had been true earlier in the day. "I don't care about any of that now, only that you believe me when I tell you I never meant to leave you. Not then... not ever."

"Your words give me strength after I was too stubborn to listen to you prior to us sailing. I must needs admit, when you told me you had been dreaming the whole thing, I reacted poorly," he confessed as he stood to remove the rest of his clothing.

Bridgette took off her robe and climbed over the bed before turning down the coverlet so Ulrick could join her. "I really didn't understand why," she said, reminding herself how heartbroken she had been at the time.

Ulrick joined her and pulled her into his embrace. Her head rested on his chest with the steady beat of his heart beneath her ear. "Now that I have had time to ponder the matter, I think perchance 'twas the magic of Bamburgh itself. You see, Katherine and Riorden de Deveraux shared a special gift."

Bridgette traced the hair on her husband's chest. "And what was that?"

"They shared and saw each other in their dreams... visions in Riorden's case, but Katherine had been dreaming of Riorden for most of her life, or so she told me."

Bridgette looked up into Ulrick's face with wide eyes. "Really?"

"Aye, I am not jesting. I suppose when you mentioned you had been dreaming of leaving, it reminded me of their situation. To be honest, I was frightened to the point of being unreasonable. I am most sorry if I broke your heart, *mon amour*. 'Twas never my intention."

"If you broke my heart then, you have now healed it. I don't ever want to fight again. Deal?" she asked with a warm smile and she giggled when Ulrick rolled her over to lay on top of her.

"I make a vow to you that if I ever get cross with you, and I am certain I will since you, too, can be most stubborn, then I will ensure we talk about the problem so it does not cause issues to grow between us." He kissed her, thoroughly, and she ran her fingers up and down his bare back before giving his buttocks a squeeze. She watched his brow rise and another smirk appear at the corners of his mouth.

"Did you just call me stubborn?" she teased before squeezing a little harder this time.

"I am certain I can make it up to you," he replied and his

eyes began to smolder with desire. It had been too long since they had last made love.

"I believe, my dearest husband, you have just determined how we shall end any arguments we may have in our future," she laughed.

His joy was reflected in his face as he ran his hand through her hair and down her cheek. His serious look, however, transformed into a devilish grin before he began to tickle her as tears of happiness ran down her cheeks with her pleas for him to stop. "We may never leave our bedchamber!"

"I'm okay with that," she replied, before any further conversation they might have had left them. Ulrick's kiss took possession of her mouth and all thought left her.

Far into the evening, Ulrick showed her in all ways possible how much he loved her and, as their bodies became one, Bridgette swore she was standing on the edge of heaven itself. Their life here at Dunster had begun.

CHAPTER 39

Nigh unto a se'nnight had passed since Ulrick's return to the place of his birth. His mother and steward Hadrian had seemingly taken good care of the land and its people in his absence. Ulrick could not complain about its upkeep, only that his mother continued to act as though he was still abroad. The condition of the fields and serfs who tilled the land were thriving and all appeared well at Dunster... at least on the surface. But an accounting of the monies that should be in his coffers did not match what was on Hadrian's ledgers. Something was obviously amiss.

Ulrick walked along the path leading from the village with Bridgette at his side. They had taken the children on their little family excursion so he might show them the marketplace along with the seaside. He had bought them fruit and cheese for their outing, a wooden sword for Eustace, along with ribbons for his ladies. Thanks to the castle's proximity to the ocean and river, Dunster was a thriving port providing merchandise to be

SHERRY EWING

bought, sold, and transported into the interior of England. 'Twas no small wonder the king wished for Ulrick to protect the keep in his name.

'Twas good to be home but, as he saw the keep rising up from the hill in the distance, happenings at his estate continued to trouble him. He wanted his wife's thoughts on the matter, but he did not wish to be overheard by servants who may be loyal to his mother or his steward. Hence, today's trip to the village.

The children walked up ahead but still close enough they could keep an eye on them, especially since Eva walked on short wobbly legs. He was proud of the young lad, for Eustace was as protective of the young girl as Ulrick and Bridgette had become. With enough distance between them and the children, he felt comfortable enough to bring up some possible unpleasantries to his wife.

"May I speak my mind, Bridgette?" he asked, whilst he slowed down their pace to keep the conversation between themselves.

"Always. What's the matter?" She lifted her head and he could see for himself the worry suddenly reflected in her green eyes.

"Nothing between us, *mon amour*." He bent forward to place a kiss on the top of her head and he heard her sigh of apparent relief.

"Then tell me your thoughts and let's work out the problem together," she replied, giving his arm a gentle squeeze. The tingling sensations that raced up his limb at her touch were a reminder of that wonderful connection *Time* had blessed them with. He prayed it never went away.

"I have not spoken these thoughts aloud but now I fear that I must. We must remain vigilant for happenings that may cause us harm," he began, before taking his free hand and raking his fingers through his hair.

Bridgette yanked on his arm to stop their progress. "Now you're scaring me." Her eyes were wide with alarm. He pulled her closer before they continued their stroll. "Tell me everything."

"As I mention to you, my father's passing was years ago, robbed and killed on the road for the small amount of coinage in his purse. I was but a lad of sixteen summers, the same age as Seraphina is now, and made to return where I had been fostering in Lancashire for his funeral."

"Yes, you told me that, and I'm so sorry for your loss. You squired with Fletcher's father. Fletcher was one of Dristan's personal guardsmen, right?" she asked, as they continued to walk the path before them.

"Aye, that is the right of it. But that is not all. After the incident, my mother quickly married again, giving birth to my new brother and sister, whilst my brother Lief began to run Dunster and its lands."

"That doesn't seem strange, Ulrick. She would have still been young and would look to marry again to ensure an alliance with someone who would bring money into the estate for more income."

"Aye. Such arrangements are common and my brother was too busy learning the workings of Dunster to worry about finding a wife. I had runners occasionally arriving from Dunster whilst Lief kept me informed that all was well for many a year. Time passed, as it often does, and one such missive somehow found me in France whilst I was attending a tourney. My mother's second husband had been killed aboard a ship. Apparently, a scuffle broke out amongst the men and he happened to be caught in the middle of the fight. He was buried at sea."

Bridgette nodded. "Again… I suppose something like this could be common and a risk you take in these times."

"I suppose you are correct, my dear, but I find it odd that my brother Lief was also killed in a riding accident whilst attending the outskirts of our land several years ago. By the time a runner had arrived at Berwyck, he was long since buried and my mother said there was no need to come home."

Bridgette frowned. "Not come home? But you are now the Earl of Somerset since both your father and brother were deceased. Why wouldn't you come home to run the estates?"

"Mayhap I was too full of myself thinking Dristan needed me. I should have returned sooner. And then when I thought my return was long overdue, a certain young woman fell into my lap by a well. As much as I was needed here at Dunster, I could not leave you nor burden you with the happenings here when I myself had not been home in many a year."

Bridgette once more halted their steps and she began holding out her fingers as she spoke. "Let's recap this situation. Your father is killed, your step-father is killed, Lief is killed, and that obviously leaves you as the successor to the title and lands, not that your step-father would have inherited the place. What else are you not telling me?"

"Monies are missing from Dunster's coffers. I asked for the ledgers from my steward, and the records do not match," he replied, in concern.

"How long has Hadrian been Dunster's steward?" she asked, as they began to walk again.

"Many a year, since the time prior to my father's demise."

"Well, we either have a lot of unfortunate accidents that are plaguing your family or we have a murderer in our midst who is picking off Dunster's heirs, one by one," Bridgette surmised, before she shivered. Ulrick brought her into his arms.

"I will not allow anything to happen to you and the children, my lady," Ulrick reassured her before placing a kiss upon her lips.

"I believe I'm more concerned with your own life, Ulrick. You may be targeted next." She grasped his waist tighter, as if she was the one who would protect him.

"We must keep alert to anything that possibly appears unnatural."

Bridgette once more shuddered. "That's easier said than done, my love. There are many ways to kill someone. How would we know if our food or wine wasn't poisoned?"

"Poison is a woman's ploy," Ulrick muttered in a low growl. "I cannot believe my mother would stoop so low. She is grasping to remain in control of Dunster, I know, but to kill off her own family?"

"Then that only leaves your steward. He is in charge of keeping an accounting of your books, Ulrick, and ledgers can be altered sufficiently if a person knows how to hide the income. He appears as the likely suspect."

"They both must needs be watched. Although in my heart I cannot imagine my mother would arrange such horrendous deeds, I have not been in her presence to know the true depths to which she may have fallen."

"She has a lot of hatred in her demeanor," Bridgette exclaimed, "which could account for her disposition upon your arrival with a ready-made family. But this could also be explained by the fact the poor woman has lost much in her life. To lose two husbands and a son? That's a lot of pain that could cause anyone to become very bitter. No parent should ever outlive their own children."

"Aye. Mayhap this explains much of the woman who barely resembles the lady of my youth. But enough of all this for now. Let us catch up with the children and try to make the most of the rest of our day. I wish such unpleasant conversations did not need to take place, but I needed you to be aware of what I have learned since we have returned home."

Ulrick leaned forward to kiss her lips again whilst his wife snuggled into his side. Arriving back inside the barriers of Dunster's stone outer walls, he swore he caught a brief glimpse of his mother watching their arrival. Aye... she needed to be watched in case she was the culprit behind everything.

CHAPTER 40

B ridgette finally managed to get dressed after another horrible morning that had been anything but pleasant. She had thought she might be pregnant prior to leaving Berwyck over a month ago. Her stomach seemed to agree with her diagnosis. She continued to get ill after trying to eat her morning meal each and every day. Ugh! Morning sickness in the twelfth century was going to be disgusting, because she really didn't wish to run down the passageway to hang her head into the smelly garderobe to throw up the contents of her stomach however long this would plague her!

Luckily, Ulrick was one to rise early, sometimes even before the light of day touched the horizon. She had succeeded in hiding a deep enough bowl she kept under the bed and, with the assistance of a servant who managed to bring her a light meal, Bridgette had been able to keep her secret from her husband... at least for now. Knowing how easily it was to have a miscarriage early on in a pregnancy, Bridgette didn't want to give Ulrick false hope in the event she lost the child.

But soon time wouldn't be on her side, since she couldn't hide her pregnancy forever. She could already detect the subtle changes in her body and, considering how in tune Ulrick was to every aspect of her, he, too, would notice eventually. Already, she had observed his gaze lingering on her from time to time. Somehow, Bridgette had the notion he already guessed her condition but had remained silent until she decided to tell him her news.

Four rapid knocks at the bedchamber door had her rushing to see what was so urgent. Opening the door, she witnessed Lady Helena's worried expression.

"You must hurry," she urged, grabbing hold or Bridgette's arm and rushing her down the passageway.

"What is the matter?" Bridgette asked, trying to keep up with the woman who was all but running toward the turret stairs.

"'Tis Eva. She somehow got away from her nursemaid and fell. She may have broken her leg, the poor little lamb," Helena said frantically.

A startled gasp left Bridgette. "Take me to her!"

Helena looked over her shoulder before she scowled. "What do you think I am doing?"

Her abrupt answer left Bridgette wondering what was wrong with the woman but she dismissed her nasty attitude and instead decided she was only concerned for the welfare of the child.

They made their way outside and Bridgette moved her hand to her forehead to block the glaring sun from her eyes. The bailey was relatively quiet for this time of the morning but this, too, Bridgette dismissed. Helena's next words, however, startled her.

"You are to have his child," she snapped with a furrowed brow. Helena swiftly continued through the courtyard.

"How did you know?"

A short laugh escaped her lips. "The servants are loyal to me. Did you really think I would not know what is going on in my own castle?"

Bridgette halted her progress, now leery of the woman's motives. "This is also now my home, or did you forget that I am now Ulrick's wife?"

"I have forgotten nothing." Her eyes narrowed, giving Bridgette a brief glimpse of this woman's true character. The disdain the woman showed her was a grim reminder this lady had run the estate for far too long since Ulrick's absence. She wanted to be in charge and nothing was going to stand in her way.

"Where's Eva?" Bridgette demanded, concerned for the girl's safety.

"This way. She's in the stable," Helena answered before rushing forward once more.

"What the devil is she doing in the stable?"

Helena didn't give her an answer and Bridgette had no choice but to keep up with the woman, who may hold the child's life in her hands.

They entered the dimly lit barn. Dust motes danced through the cracks in the ceiling. Several horses munched on their hay or neighed at the intrusion of the women. Helena stopped in the middle of the room and motioned to the last stall near a rear entrance.

"She is there," she said, pointing in the direction she now wished Bridgette to go.

"Eva," Bridgette called out, rushing forward only to see for herself what her gut had been trying to tell her. Her daughter wasn't there. She was just about to turn around when she was struck in the back of the head. Her cry rang out as she fell forward into the soft straw in the stall.

Through blurry vision, she saw Helena stand over her with a wicked grin. "You will not take Dunster from me. Not now, not ever. This place in *mine!*" she hissed, before looking over her shoulder.

Bridgette raised her hand to the man who came into view. "Help me. Please," she whispered, until his laugh made her realize that help wasn't coming from Dunster's steward.

Hadrian kneeled down and a rag was shoved inside Bridgette's mouth, preventing her from calling for aid. Her head spun and she tried to fight him off, but her strength was lessening while she attempted to remain conscious. Rope was tied around her wrists and ankles and a feeling of helplessness consumed her. He then threw a coarse woolen blanket over her before lifting her up into his arms. Bridgette groaned when she was all but tossed into what she assumed was a cart.

The two laughed. Helena's voice held nothing but malice. "Have your man get her as far away from here as possible. I never want her to set foot on my land again."

The cart began to move. Bridgette struggled against the ropes binding her before her eyes rolled back and she knew no more.

CHAPTER 41

U lrick frowned, staring at the ledger before him, praying that he had been mistaken, but 'twas no use after a second accounting. The figures did not add up and he now knew for certain that Dunster's steward had been stealing from the coffers. There was no other way around what was before Ulrick's very eyes. And he had help... he was certain his own damn mother was behind the man's every move. He had known she was ambitious in her determination to remain in charge, but this was going too far! A growl of outrage left his lips, and he raised his head to stare at the brothers who had remained at Dunster, delaying their return home to Berwyck until they were certain all was well with Ulrick.

"I suppose you have your answer," Turquine stated, "and 'tis apparent you do not care for the results."

Ulrick swiped his hand across the back of his neck, rubbing away the pain from being bent over the ledger for what seemed like hours. "Aye. 'Tis my steward and my mother."

Taegan scowled. "Bad luck that. For your own mother to dishonor you so..." his words trailed off before Ulrick slammed his fist on the table.

"I should have known she would be up to no good but I never thought she would go so far as to steal from the estate," he growled out, before rubbing his eyes as if this would clear the mess before him.

Turquine came over and patted him on the back. "If she has gone this far, *mon ami*, how much further would she go to gain all she feels she is entitled to?"

Ulrick raised his head to stare at his longtime friend. "What do you mean?"

The brother's shared a silent look before Turquine continued pointing to the ledger. "She and your steward have been taking monies from the coffers, it appears for years. Your own father, brother, and step-father all died from accidents that could be coincidental, but what if their deaths were planned?"

Taegan nodded. "And this is only the beginning of what should now worry you."

"Aye," Turquine agreed before continuing. "You now return not only with a wife but—"

"—two children you have taken in as your own," Taegan finished with a shrug. "You have a brother and sister who would inherit upon your demise as long as they live. How safe are any of them with a woman who cares nothing about family and is looking out for her own self-interest?"

"She would not dare harm my family!" Ulrick bellowed.

"She would not?" the brothers chimed in unison.

"*Bloody Hell!*" Ulrick swore, before pushing back his hair that had fallen over his forehead.

Taegan began to pace the room. "Which brings up the matter

of exactly how much did your mother truly know about your father's, brother's, and step-father's demise? Mayhap this, too, was arranged by your mother."

Turquine nodded. "A woman who would go to such lengths might not stop at killing off a husband or two."

"She would not..." Ulrick could not finish his thoughts, knowing his two friends were most likely correct in their assumptions. "We must protect Bridgette and my family. One of you go to my brother and sister, for I know in my heart they are not involved with any of this. The other, please go find my children and ensure they are safe. I will go to my wife."

They all but ran to the door, but when they pulled the portal open, there stood Eustace. Tears of grief ran down his face as he threw himself at Ulrick.

"She's gone! Someone took her, father," he sobbed.

Ulrick quickly realized his worse fears were coming to fruition. He hugged the boy to him. "Who was taken, son?"

"Mother!" he cried out. "I followed yer mother and milady tae the stable but I hid so they did not see me. The steward threw her in a cart that left Dunster just a short while ago. Ye will bring her back, will ye not?"

"Aye, of course I will, Eustace." Ulrick vowed before turning to the brothers. "Take the boy and find Eva and my brother and sister. I am going after my wife and then will deal with the traitors beneath my own roof!"

Ulrick wasted no time making his way to the stable. With a bridle in place, he did not worry about a saddle but quickly put Herman into motion. They could not have gone far and he had the notion the villain who had taken his wife may head to the harbor. God help him if they boarded a ship before he could reach his wife.

CHAPTER 42

Bridgette moaned as she regained consciousness when the swaying motion of the cart beneath her hit a rut in the road. Her thoughts fuzzy, she tried to unscramble the scene that had put her in her present predicament. It certainly didn't take a rocket scientist to come to the realization that Ulrick's mother and steward would go to any lengths to keep Dunster to themselves. A pity... Bridgette had held such high hopes that she would get along with the woman upon their arrival. Obviously, some families were dysfunctional, not that she would lay the blame of this mess on her husband.

With no idea of how long she had been out, Bridgette shifted in her makeshift prison, while attempting to rub her hands together to bring back the circulation. She could use the fact that they were bound in front of her as an advantage. Hadrian and Helena weren't as smart as they thought, or maybe they just hadn't thought their plan out far enough. Bridgette could feel the ropes loosening as she attempted to wiggle free without rustling the straw beneath her to give her away. She had to get free in order to save herself from whatever they had planned for her. Better to die trying to live than to let them get away with their plans.

Bridgette inhaled, bringing the saltiness of the sea to the forefront of her mind. The harbor! God forbid if she were put on a ship sailing for parts unknown. She'd never find her way back to Ulrick and the children if that were to happen. To hell with remaining silent. She needed to escape her captor now!

The driver cursed and the cart came to a jerking halt when he pulled mercilessly on the reins. She could tell he had left the conveyance when the wagon rocked from side to side. He pulled off the blanket and Bridgette stared into the face of a stranger.

"Stop yer fussing, ye damn wench!" he bellowed. "I 'ave a job ta do and only git paid upon finishing it."

He crawled up into the cart and began checking the ropes. Bridgette in turn began kicking her feet as best she could; She didn't want him to undo any progress she might have made. Luckily for her, he was so focused on what he was doing that he didn't see a well-aimed kick that caused him to double over. Another push with her boots, and he was tumbling from the back end of the wagon.

"Ye bloody bitch!" he screamed out in agony. "Ye got me in me jewels."

Bridgette was now sitting up, wiggling the ropes digging into her wrists before she lifted her hands and was able to free the cloth holding the rag into place at her mouth. She spit it out gasping for air before using her teeth to free herself.

"Come at me again and you'll receive the same damn treatment, you friggin cur!" she taunted before going to work on the ropes at her ankles. Though her captor was writhing on the ground still, Bridgette knew she didn't have long before he recovered enough to come after her again.

The sound of a horse in the distance caused Bridgette to move faster, not knowing if the rider would be friend or foe. She had just finished with the last knot when a sight to behold filled her vision and she cried out to her hero, coming to her rescue.

"Ulrick!"

Like a knight in shining armor in a romance novel, Ulrick rode his horse as though the hounds of hell were licking at his heels. He jumped from Herman and, with a determined stride, he neared the wagon. His blue-grey eyes roamed over her body to assess her condition before he took hold of the man's tunic, bringing him to his feet. He gave him a might shake.

"It appears you have taken someone I hold very dear to my heart. You were a fool to think you would get away so easily," Ulrick roared, giving him a shake.

The man's eyes widened in fear. "I was just following orders for a bit of coin. I did her no 'arm—"

"—other than take her from those she loves," Ulrick hissed, before raising his fist to send the villain sailing through the air when it connected with his face. The man moaned in agony while Bridgette, now free of her restraints, threw herself into Ulrick's arms.

"You came for me!" she cried out, hugging her husband with all her might.

A chuckle escaped him. "You had so little faith in me, *mon amour?*"

She shook her head before cupping her hands to his cheeks. "No... I knew you'd come to save me."

A grunt of disbelief erupted from his mouth. "'Twas hardly any effort on my part, my sweet. 'Twas apparent on my arrival that you rescued yourself or at least were in the process of doing so."

Bridgette continued gazing into her husband's face, not knowing how she would ever be able to tell him who was behind her abduction. "Ulrick... I must let you know—"

He leaned downed, placing his forehead to her own. She heard his heavy sigh. "There is no need, wife. I am well aware my mother and steward were behind the whole thing."

She kissed his lips. "I'm so sorry, Ulrick."

"As am I. However, you are safe and no harm has befallen you."

"The children! What about the children?" she asked, frightened something may have also happened to them.

"Eustace and Eva are just fine, as are my brother and sister. How I will tell them their mother was behind all this is still a mystery."

"What will become of them?" she inquired. Bridgette could see the grief that was affecting him with whatever decision he must make.

"What I would like is to see their heads on a pike outside my gates for attempting to take you away from me!" he shouted.

Bridgette shuddered knowing that, while a common practice in this century, she just couldn't imagine actually having such a horror outside of her home. "You can't do that to your own mother, Ulrick."

"I do not see why not. 'Twill serve as a reminder to anyone else who feels they can take what is mine away from me."

"Ulrick... she is still your mother."

"She is *not* my mother. At least not anymore, but I will deal with her and Hadrian upon our return to Dunster. For now, I see your abductor is attempting to gain his feet. Hand me those ropes and he can learn how you felt when you were tied up and left defenseless."

Bridgette did as he requested and before long she was riding in the saddle with her husband. Her abductor was tied with a rope and was forced to walk behind Ulrick's horse and the one that had pulled the wagon. The cart, they left behind. They would make arrangements for its return once they were back at Dunster.

She snuggled into the warmth of her husband, knowing she was safe. Life in the twelfth century was sometimes brutal and she would need to learn that this included the punishments for those who did their liege lord wrong. She only prayed she could survive the aftermath of what had been done to her today.

CHAPTER 43

U lrick entered his bedchamber hoping to find his wife resting after her ordeal. He should have known such would not be the case, as he found her pacing the room. The moment he opened the door, she halted her steps and then flung herself into his arms. He barely had time to clasp his own arms around her waist before she was demanding answers from him.

"Well?" she demanded. "What have you done with them?" Her tone more than told him he should answer her directly so there would be no doubt that he was in charge of disciplining his people according to the offenses they committed.

"Mayhap you could tell me good eve before you launch into your demands?" he teased, brushing her hair back to clearly see her face. "A kiss might also smooth my mighty temper a bit, too."

She laughed. "Just one kiss? Somehow, I think this is a ploy on your part to distract me from what I want to know. I live here, too, or did you forget?"

"I have forgotten nothing, *ma cherie*, other than I wish to spare you such unpleasantries." He gave her a quick kiss and made his way to a table to pour them both a chalice of wine. He handed her a cup before motioning to a chair for her to sit.

"Tell me," she said in a firm voice before settling herself in her chair. She took a sip of wine waiting for him to go on.

"As much as I would like to have all three of their heads sitting on a pike outside our gates—"

"Ulrick..." she dragged out his name until he held up his hand so he might continue.

"—I will not go to such lengths," he finished. "As you mentioned, I do not wish such a ghastly reminder to be so visible any time one of the children, you, or my brother or sister leave the estate," he began before also taking a long deep sip of wine. "Instead, the three are currently sitting in a nice damp cell beneath this very castle to await their fate."

"What of the money stolen by your mother and Hadrian all these years?" she asked leaning forward resting her forearms on her thighs.

"Mother would not confess, although I was able to search her rooms. I found a small cache of jewels that can be sold to return back to our coffers to help with the running of Dunster. Hadrian babbled like an old fool and surprisingly enough he handed over what he, too, had hidden away in his rooms with little difficulty. I believe he thought by doing so, he might keep his head."

"You can't keep them forever in the dungeon, Ulrick."

"Mayhap I can..." he stated before he chuckled seeing Bridgette's frown. "I only tease you, my love. Nay... I have a better plan. They will be taken from here as little more than slaves to be sold into service. They may keep their heads but I have ensured they shall never set foot upon English soil again."

"Slavery... that's almost as horrible as death in some cases. Are you sure you wish to go to such extremes?"

Ulrick stood and began to pace the chamber much as his wife had been doing not long ago. "They will live and perchance even this is more than they deserve. Better for them to continue to remain on this earth in servitude in some distant land so they may contemplate what they have done. In either case, we shall never see them again and I will be glad once they are all gone from our lands."

"I'm so sorry it has come to this, Ulrick, especially with your mother." Bridgette rose and went to stand before him. She reached out and took his hand. "I know how hard this must be for you to lose part of your family."

He bent forward to kiss her lips and he felt most of the tension of the day leave him now that his wife was in his arms. "You are my family now. You, the children, and my brother and sister. 'Tis all I need in life to have you all by my side."

A strange smile lit his wife's lips. "This is all you need? Are you sure?"

"Aye," he whispered before he began running his hands along her body. She suddenly stopped him by grabbing one and placed it on her belly.

"Then be prepared for another addition to the family in or around another six months, my lord," she said, while her entire visage brightened with her news.

"What?' he asked in disbelief.

"You're going to be a father, Ulrick," she whispered.

"A boy or a girl?"

She laughed and the sound echoed in the chamber. "Of course, silly. I certainly don't hope we're having twins, although they would be a double blessing."

Ulrick's world began to spin at her news. Several minutes later he awoke, finding himself on the floor, his head in his wife's lap as she placed a cool cloth upon his brow.

"What happened?" he asked wondering what had struck him down.

"I believe, my dearest love, that my news of your impending fatherhood was a bit too much for my mighty warrior and you passed out cold," she said lovingly.

"Surely you jest?" he said, aghast at what had befallen him.

"How else do you explain your current position on the floor, my darling?"

He groaned. "Please do not tell Turquine and Taegan that I was so easily taken down. I would never live long enough to hear the end of their jesting."

"Your secret is safe with me, Ulrick. You are pleased about the baby?"

He began to sit up so he might take in the beauty of his wife. He placed his hand on her stomach again. "Pleased? You have made me a very happy man, wife."

Bridgette stood, holding out her hand for him to take. She pulled him over to their bed. "Show me," she whispered, with a husky tone that caused parts of Ulrick to stir to life.

"We will not harm the babe?" he asked, reluctantly.

She unbuckled his belt, letting his sword fall to the floor with a loud clank. She quickly began working on the strings holding his clothing in place. "The baby is very safe, my love, but your wife desires your attention."

"I am yours to command for always, *ma cherie.*"

Far into the evening Ulrick did everything in his power to ensure his wife was fully satisfied. She was his heart and had crossed time to be with him. Never had he thought he would find a woman to love like Bridgette. A woman who came from across the stars and decided to stay with a twelfth century knight. His life with Bridgette and his children was indeed blessed.

EPILOGUE

Dunster Castle, Winter
Seven Months Later…

Bridgette entered Ulrick's solar cuddling her one-month-old baby in her arms. She took in the domestic scene of Eustace sitting at a table while Ulrick leaned over his shoulder as he helped their son with his letters. Eva sat on the floor near the hearth with Seraphina while the two played with cloth dolls. Her daughter's giggles brought a smile to Bridgette's face. Her love for their family blossomed like a fresh spring rose as each day moved into the next. A kind of normal routine settled around Ulrick, Bridgette, and the children and she was thankful for the happiness that surrounded them.

A woman rose from her seat and rushed over to Bridgette holding out her hands to take the precious bundle from her arms. "Let me take the baby," Lady Jade Kincade declared. "It seems like ages since I held a little one."

Her husband Thomas called out from across the room. "Please indulge my wife, Bridgette, else our trip here from Scotland will be all for naught!"

A rumble of laughter coursed through the room while Bridgette stared at the woman she had met over a year ago in their friend Zoe's apartment in another place in time. "We've certainly come a long way to find our happily-ever-afters," Bridgette whispered as she placed the baby in Jade's waiting arms.

"But wasn't it worth the trip?" Jade asked, looking over her shoulder at the man for whom she, too, had fallen through *Time*.

"Most definitely," Bridgette replied while her gaze met Ulrick's from across the room. Heat flooded her body and she prayed such a feeling never went away.

"Do you suppose we'll ever see Zoe and Megan again?" Jade asked, rocking from side to side to calm the infant she held.

"Considering what the two of us have been through to find our true loves, I have no doubt we may cross paths again," Bridgette declared and watched her friend take the child so Thomas could also coo over the babe.

Ulrick nodded to Rowan who came over to Eustace to continue his lessons. Ulrick must have felt her need to be by his side for he then strode over to take her hand, leading her to a window seat set into the wall. He pulled her into his lap to keep her warm, since there was a chill in the air.

"You are well, *ma cherie*?" The husky tone of his voice as he spoke the French endearment had Bridgette wishing they were alone instead of in a room full of people.

"I swear I'm living in a fairy tale. Our story is the stuff dreams are made of when I'm asleep," she said, running her hand up the front of his tunic.

"Then I pray we never awaken," Ulrick replied before placing a kiss on her cheek.

Bridgette placed her arm around his neck. "I have never been so happy and it's all because of you. Falling in love with you makes me feel as if I am soaring through the heavens."

"You have made me a very happy man, *mon amour*, with the birth of the child," Ulrick murmured in her ear.

She raised her free hand to caress his cheek. "You're not upset that the baby isn't a son?"

His brow rose at her question before he nodded to Eustace sitting at his desk. "I have a son, wife. What more can one man ask for?"

She nodded, while watching his face for any signs of regret. There was, of course, none, and her husband seemed more than content as he gazed around his solar at friends and family.

She leaned down to whisper in his ear. "Have I ever thanked you for keeping your promise you made at midnight?"

His arm tightened around her waist. "Have I ever thanked you for making a wish at that fountain in your future life?"

"Don't you mean past life?" she asked, kissing his cheek.

A low rumble of laughter met her ears. "Aye, I suppose I do. Who would have ever thought I would find myself married to one of those future girls showing up at Dristan's gates?"

Bridgette joined in with a light laugh of her own. "Well, I did fall through *Time* and land on you, if you recall."

"And I am glad you did, *mon amour*. I will not have *Time* taking you from me now that we are together. Life with you will continue to be an adventure as long as you remain by my side."

She stroked his cheek feeling the stubble beneath her fingertips. "There is no place on this earth that I'd rather be than right here in your arms."

Ulrick pulled her down to receive her kiss as though there was no one else in the room. For several minutes, Bridgette was woven into the spell he created for them until an untimely cough brought them back to reality. She looked up at those around them with a sheepish grin, although she would never apologize for any public display of affection her husband gave her.

But Ulrick's words rang true and Bridgette looked forward to the years ahead as their life together unfolded. She had fallen through *Time* to find the one man who brought joy to her very soul and even though she had to find him eight hundred years in the past, she, too, had no regrets. She was indeed thankful to the ghostly vision of Amiria's grandmother who gave her a magical coin to toss in a fountain designed in the very image of the breathing knight who had wed her. She'd do it all over again in order to be with him. Life with Ulrick was going to be worth every sacrifice she had made in her past life far into the future in the twenty-first century. She was happy. She was blessed. She was very content.

THE END

Sherry Ewing needs your help!
Book reviews help readers to find books, and authors to find readers. Please consider writing a review for *Promises Made At Midnight*, even a couple of sentences telling people what you liked about the story. Reviews can be posted on BookBub, Goodreads, and on most eRetailer websites. For links to this

book on those sites, see my website at https://sherryewing.
com/books/promises-made-at-midnight/

I really appreciate the time you take to write your reviews and,
yes, I read them all! Thank you for purchasing a copy of *Promises
Made At Midnight.* I hope you've enjoyed Ulrick and Bridgette's
journey to finding love!

AUTHOR NOTES & ACKNOWLEDGEMENTS

Dearest Readers:

Thank you so much for purchasing a copy of *Promises Made At Midnight*. I hope you enjoyed Ulrick and Bridgette's story and felt it was worth the wait! I do so love a good time travel, don't you?

How about a little history for the times?

Early on in this book, you caught a glimpse of Ulrick's confusion when Bridgette mentioned she was one of the Queen's ladies in waiting. While she was thinking of the fair she had been attending and the Tudor Queen, Ulrick's natural assumption was that of Queen Eleanor of Aquitaine. To get the full picture we need to go back a few years to the spring of 1173 when Henry II's son by the same name was upset with his lack of power and encouraged to do something about it by his father's enemies. The younger Henry then launched the Revolt of 1173-1174. He fled to Paris, devising evil against his father from every angle at the advice of the French King. He then secretly went into Aquitaine where his two brothers, Richard and Geoffrey, were currently living with their mother. He incited them to join him in his quest for power. Some say the queen may have sent her younger sons to France "to join with him against their father the king."

Between the end of March and the beginning of May, Eleanor left Poitiers, but was arrested and sent to the king at Rouen. Her arrest wasn't announced publicly. On July 8, 1174, Henry and Eleanor took a ship for England from Barfleur and as soon as they disembarked at Southampton, Eleanor was taken either to Winchester Castle or Sarum Castle and held there. For the next sixteen years she was imprisoned at various locations in England.

Jumping ahead to the year 1183 and we find young King Henry tried again to force his father to hand over some of his patrimony. In debt and refused control of Normandy, he tried to ambush his father at Limoges. He was joined by troops sent by his brother Geoffrey and Philip II of France. But Henry II's troops besieged the town, forcing his son to flee. After wandering aimlessly through Aquitaine, Henry the Younger caught dysentery. On Saturday, June 11, 1183, the young king realized he was dying and was overcome with remorse for his sins. When his father's ring was sent to him, he begged his father to show mercy to his mother, and all his companions would plead with Henry to set her free.

I thought it would be interesting to add this little bit of history into the story and having Dristan and his men being sent to France. Of course, I must admit, any time I can bring my characters back to Bamburgh Castle is always a joy to my heart. I do have a fondness for the place and can only hope that one day I may actually be able to stand in its shadows or walk its grounds!

And thinking of my modern heroine and what story she might tell a child from twelfth century England had me researching the legendary King Arthur. I had to ensure this would have been something a child from this time period would have heard about. The historical basis for this king has been debated but I learned that an actual person had been talked about since the late 5th and 6th centuries. Legend or a real person... I always found this story fascinating and hope you enjoyed this tiny glimpse of it.

As for Dunster Castle that became Ulrick's home, I can't begin to tell you why I chose this location. Let's just saw that Google Earth is this author's best friend! The castle was a former motte and bailey castle, now a country house, located in the village of Dunster, Somerset, England. The castle lies on the top of a steep hill called the Tor, and has been fortified since the late Anglo-Saxon period. After the Norman conquest of England in the 11th century, William de Mohun constructed a timber castle on the site as part of the pacification of Somerset. A stone shell keep was built on the motte by the start of the 12th century, and the castle survived a siege during the early years of the Anarchy. At the end of the 14th century the de Mohun's sold the castle to the Luttrell family, who continued to occupy the property until the late 20th century. During the early medieval period the sea reached the base of the hill, close to the mouth of the River Avill, offering a natural defense and making the village an inland port.

Kudos to Mary Nicholson Willard, reader extraordinaire, for noting in one of my *Work In Progress Wednesday* posts in my street team that I had Ulrick's name as Mohan instead of Mohun who was the actual owner of Dunster. And of course, since this is how I published his name in *Love Will Find You*, I had to change the spelling accordingly. Thank you for your eagle eyes, Mary!

Special thanks to Caroline Warfield and Jude Knight for beta reading my story. Your insight to what needed to be fixed is always helpful and appreciated.

Jude Knight has also once again taken time out of her own busy life and writing schedule to edit *Promises Made At Midnight*. I have no idea what I would do without her expertise in all matters concerning line and content edits. I am especially grateful for her knowledge of travel by horse, carriage, or boats. This woman is truly a marvel. Thank you, again, Jude!

My family always has my undying gratitude for all their continued support over the years.

Promises Made At Midnight is a nod to my Michigan upbringing and the reason for dedicating this story to my friends from elementary school. I went back to Michigan several years ago for our 40th reunion and was amazed that no matter how many years passed us by, we were all still friends that I cherish to this very day.

It was on such a trip that I did indeed head to Lafayette Coney Island to have one of their famous hotdogs. Thirty plus years later and they still tasted just as good as I remembered. And I was surprised to see a large parking structure where there used to be just a dirt lot where we used to park after the Tiger games. If fans still head to Lafayette after games, I honestly don't know but again... this was the case when I used to go many years ago. We always had so much fun!

To my readers... I cannot begin to convey how much I appreciate your support by purchasing and reviewing my work, especially when my muse up and leaves me for parts unknown. I know I've kind of been in a drought lately. Life sometimes can throw you a curve ball and it certainly has thrown a few my way over the past couple of years. I promise I will be working on Aiden's story soon as you've been kept waiting for years.

Before I get to writing Aiden's story, however, I'll give you a glimpse of stories to come. I am currently working on a new medieval three or four book series: *The Knights of the Anarchy*. The second book is in progress and I plan to pitch the series to Dragonblade Publishing. It will take place prior to the years of when my debut novel, *If My Heart Could See You*, took place. I think you may get the idea of where I'm going with this. I'll also be working on a novella (or possibly another series again for Dragonblade) in their Lyon's Den world. I'm super excited for this Regency story. And, of course, there are always my novellas I publish with the Bluestocking Belles. These ladies keep me motivated to keep writing those Regency era stories and I'm so very proud to continue working with them.

Until the next time, thank you again for all that you do on my behalf. I hope you enjoy these little notes at the end of my stories. You continue to be the reason I write. As long as you enjoy reading them, I'll be around to give you hours of reading pleasure. You can blame me for your next book hangover!

All my love,
Sherry

OTHER BOOKS BY SHERRY EWING

Medieval & Time Travel Series

To Love A Scottish Laird: De Wolfe Pack Connected World

Sometimes you really can fall in love at first sight…

To Love An English Knight: De Wolfe Pack

Connected World

Can a chance encounter lead to love?

If My Heart Could See You: The MacLarens, A Medieval Romance
(Book One)

When you're enemies, does love have a fighting chance?

For All of Ever: The Knights of Berwyck, A Quest Through Time
(Book One)

Sometimes to find your future, you must look to the past…

Only For You: The Knights of Berwyck, A Quest Through Time
(Book Two)

Sometimes it's hard to remember that true love conquers all, only after
the battle is over…

Hearts Across Time: The Knights of Berwyck (Books One & Two)

Sometimes all you need is to just believe… Hearts Across Time is a
special edition box set that combines Katherine and Riorden's stories
together from *For All of Ever* and *Only For You.*

A Knight To Call My Own: The MacLarens, A Medieval Romance (Book Two)

When your heart is broken, is love still worth the risk?

To Follow My Heart: The Knights of Berwyck, A Quest Through Time (Book Three)

Love is a leap. Sometimes you need to jump…

The Piper's Lady: The MacLarens, A Medieval Romance (Book Three)

True love binds them. Deceit divides them. Will they choose love?

Love Will Find You: The Knights of Berwyck, A Quest Through Time (Book Four)

Sometimes a moment is all we have…

One Last Kiss: The Knights of Berwyck, A Quest Through Time (Book Five)

Sometimes it takes a miracle to find your heart's desire…

Promises Made At Midnight: The Knights of Berwyck, A Quest Through Time (Book Six)

Make a wish…

Regency

A Kiss For Charity: A de Courtenay Novella (Book One)

Love heals all wounds but will their pride keep them apart?

The Earl Takes A Wife: A de Courtenay Novella (Book Two)

It began with a memory, etched in the heart.

Before I Found You: A de Courtenay Novella (Book Three)

A quest for a title. An encounter with a stranger. Will she choose love?

Nothing But Time: A Family of Worth (Book One)

They will risk everything for their forbidden love…

One Moment In Time: A Family of Worth (Book Two)

One moment in time may be enough, if it lasts forever…

Under the Mistletoe

A new suitor seeks her hand. An old flame holds her heart. Which one will she meet under the kissing bough?

A Second Chance At Love

Can the bittersweet frost of lost love be rekindled into a burning flame?

A Countess to Remember in *Desperate Daughters: A Bluestocking Belles with Friends Collection*

You can find out more about Sherry's work on her website at www. SherryEwing.com and at online retailers.

SOCIAL MEDIA

Website: www.SherryEwing.com
Email: Sherry@SherryEwing.com
Bluestocking Belles: www.bluestockingbelles.net/
Amazon Author Page: http://amzn.to/1TrWtoy
Bookbub: www.bookbub.com/authors/sherry-ewing
Facebook: www.Facebook.com/SherryEwingAuthor
Goodreads: www.Goodreads.com/author/show/
8382315.Sherry_Ewing
Instagram: https://instagram.com/sherry.ewing
Pinterest: www.Pinterest.com/SherryLEwing
TikTok: https://www.tiktok.com/@sherryewingauthor
Tumblr: https://sherryewing.tumblr.com
Twitter: www.Twitter.com/Sherry_Ewing
YouTube: http://www.youtube.com/SherryEwingauthor

Sign Me Up!

Newsletter: http://bit.ly/2vGrqQM
Facebook Street Team:
www.facebook.com/groups/799623313455472/
Facebook Official Fan page: https://www.facebook.com/
groups/356905935241836/

ABOUT SHERRY EWING

Sherry Ewing picked up her first historical romance when she was a teenager and has been hooked ever since. A bestselling author, she writes historical and time travel romances to awaken the soul one heart at a time. When not writing, she can be found in the San Francisco area at her day job as an Information Technology Specialist. You can learn more about Sherry on her website where a new adventure awaits you on every page.

Learn more about Sherry at:
Website: www.SherryEwing.com
Email: Sherry@SherryEwing.com
Newsletter: http://bit.ly/2vGrqQM